There's Gold In Them Hills! Gold!

by Gertrude Tupala

There's Gold In Them Hills! Gold!

Copyright 1987
ISBN# 0-932212-55-7
Library of Congress Catalog Card No.88-70036

Avery Color Studios
Au Train, MI 49806

Written by Gertrude Tupala

Historical Prospectus by C. Fred Rydholm

Published by Avery Color Studios
Au Train, Michigan 49806

First Edition - February 1988

HISTORICAL PROSPECTUS

Gertude Tupala (1922-1981) was born and raised in Ishpeming. She served as an administrative assistant at Northern Michigan University and was listed in the eleventh edition of "Who's Who of American Women". She was also a charter member of the Dead River Camp and Sports Association. This book, "There's Gold in Them Hills! Gold!" is being published posthumously.

This is a fictional story placed in the 1864-65 period when the Holyoke Mine was being worked but, so as not to be misconstrued by the reader we should attempt to shed some light on what the country and this specific area was like during this period since the author had made no attempt to keep the story within the historical setting as is usually the case in historical novels, though several local place names are used.

Our first thoughts were to place the story thirty years later but this might further confuse the issue. Another possibility was to rewrite the story so that it would fit into the historical period of the opening of the Holyoke Mine on the Dead River north of Ishpeming, but to do so would change so much of the author's original manuscript that it no longer could be called hers. So to keep this delightful story intact we have chosen to give the reader these historical prospectives separately as a guide to refer to for historical significance.

To begin with, in 1864 and 65 the nation was caught up in the Civil War, probably the bloodiest in our history and there is no mention made of it. It was a period of great turmoil with the southern states having seceded from the Union. There was great emphasis on the production of iron because of the war and though the mining of silver was incidental to the cause, the Marquette County Board did see fit to appropriate funds to build a road from Forestville on up to Silver Lake which later became known as the Holyoke Trail.

Then that Fall of 1864 there was the presidential election in which Abraham Lincoln was seeking his second term in office. Having been elected over challenger George B. McClellan in November of 1864. His inaugural took place in March of 1865 and he was assassinated a month later in April, all events which would have been of great concern even in communities as isolated as those in Michigan's Upper Peninsula, but again they are not a part of the story.

The Holyoke was a silver and lead mine which was located by some men in the employ of people from Holyoke, Massachusetts while they were building the road along the north side of the Dead River, long before there was a basin there, from Forestville to Silver Lake. It was while building this road that they recognized silver ore. Several gold mines were opened in the region much later, the largest, of course, being the Ropes in 1883 and the closest to the Holyoke was the Fire Centre Mine later still. At the time travel was from Marquette, to the Powder Mill Location, Collinsville, Forestville and on to the Holyoke. Ironically in January of 1864, Du Bois and Williams, analytical chemists of Philadephia, in assaying specimens of quartz from the Holyoke mine, were surprised to find gold, the quartz assaying at a rate of several hundred dollars a ton in this metal. They reported their finding back to representatives of the Holyoke company, but no attention was paid to it, as there was no thought that gold existed in that section.

Then many years later the Fire Centre Gold Mining Company did some work near that location. They took several thousand dollars worth of gold from a prospecting shaft sunk in the granite, in which there were many small stringers of quartz, and holding gold in small amounts at other places on the property of the company. These places were not sunk upon or given any practical tests to determine their real extent or value.

Julius Ropes was the first to pursue gold mining in the area when he discovered gold-bearing rock in 1881. Since that date nearly a dozen gold mining operations were opened in the region north of Ishpeming.

The Homestead Act of 1862 did not affect the Upper Peninsula for at least ten or fifteen years and even then there were no homesteaders in that region. It was 1900 before there were any homesteads within miles of there.

The story speaks of people coming from Chicago by train. Again the first connection with the local railroads to Chicago was in 1872 when the Chicago and North-western extended its tracks to Negaunee and Ishpeming. Travel to this part of Upper Michigan was by stagecoach or water in 1864.

The population of the region was French, Indian, German, Scotch, Irish and Colonials. The Swedes started coming to the area in the 1870's and 80's followed by the Finns and Italians in the 1890's. There certainly were no Finns here in 1864.

Prospectors to this region invariably came from the east. In the story the prospector came from Colorado which was not a state until 1876.

Old Ish was not in downtown Ishpeming until 1884 and an open winter road from Ishpeming to the Yellowdog River or even the Dead was unheard of in that day.

Then there is some confusion about wrestling in the story. It speaks of Greco-Roman wrestling which was used in southern Europe for centuries. They were using this style of wrestling in Germany at that time. Catch-as-catch-can developed in America in the 1850's and 60's and was completely unknown in Europe.

The style of wrestling that became popular in the copper and iron districts of Upper Michigan was Cornish "rassling" introduced here by the Cornishmen after the Civil War and the only style where the "traditional canvas jacket" as mentioned in the story, was used. There were a few matches after 1890 when both Cornish and Catch-as-catch-can rules were used in the same match. This was after Catch-as-catch-can style became popular.

Cornish "rassling" disappeared from the area by World War II and Catch-as-catch-can, while still around, is so brutal, that it is shamelessly faked in wrestling shows across the country. Greco-Roman wrestling is still an event in the modern Olympics but all wrestling done today in high schools and colleges is Intercollegiate style. A German from Europe would not have known Catch-as-catch-can wrestling in 1865 nor would a Finn from America know Greco-Roman wrestling. The canvas jacket wasn't used in either of these styles.

There was, however, a German wrestler from the area who became a World's Champion, but the title match was in Boston in 1929. He was Gus Sonnenberg of Marquette.

There are still a few more historical discrepancies in the story that the reader may come across but it should not be read with a critical eye. It is an interesting, entertaining, and sometimes exciting tale set in the backwoods of Northern Michigan. It delves into the problems of early day mining operations, the excitement and hopes of great riches and the all too often failures. There is the intrigue of murder, romance and a world-class wrestling match interwoven into times when there was no electricity or automobiles.

It is felt that this short explanation is necessary, especially for local readers, so that they will not become alarmed when something doesn't seem to fit in with some of the facts they know about in our local history.

The story is strictly a work of fiction and Miss Tupala was sincere when she wrote in the opening pages: "All of the characters, places, incidents and situations in this book are fictitious, and any resemblance to actual persons, living or dead, is purely coincidental.

C. Fred Rydholm
Local Historian
December 7, 1987

CHARACTERS   TIME: Spring, 1864

Jed Carter

Kelso family:
  Pa Kelso
  Petra Kelso - daughter
  Eric and Timo Kelso - sons

Egbert E. Austin - Lawyer

Henry R. Manson - President, Holyoke

Sydney E. Crawford - Secy. and Treas., Holyoke

Stanley R. Eland - Director, Holyoke and
  Proprietor of Land Office

Ed Morley - Editor of the POST

Holyoke crew:
  Jim Wills (married)
  Alex Wills (married)
  Ikey (single)
  Pete (single)
  Dan (single)
  Mikko (single - wrestler)
  John (married)
  Curt (married)
  Jallu (single)
  Nels (married)
  Charlie (cook)
  Clem Copley (Holyoke engineer)
  Bill Worthington (Holyoke engineer)
  Andrew Sommers (Holyoke mine captain)

Bart Fauquier - Owner South Arm Lumber Co.

Spud - Fauquier's foreman

Stig Nilssen - Bachelor neighbor of Kelsos

Blanche

Florence Neeley - school teacher

Dr. Von Muller - Quack optician
Rev. Culbertson
Mrs. Hildegard Anderson
Doc Billington
Mr. Slocum - School Commissioner
Jake - owner of livery
Nick - saloon keeper
Thor Blumstrom - store owner
Judge Horace Tittlebaum
Jorn Holmstrom
Marshall Tony Malaroni

CHAPTER 1
The Glitter of Gold

Jed Carter's pulse was gaining momentum.

He tore more moss from its rootings, scraped damp mold from the exposed granite with the blade of his knife. More veins, more numerous and closer spaced, traversed in every direction, forming an unsymmetric web over most of the surface. He reached for his hammer and began chipping on a vein carrying a significant amount of the yellow metal. There was something in the glitter that caused his heart to thump harder with each pounding stroke and he was unaware of goosepimples raised on his arms.

Gramp's voice echoed in his ears — 'there's gold in them hills, Jed! Gold! But the earth isn't going to push it up like a crop of huckleberries! Those who want it must probe the hills. And unearth it!'

He stopped chipping, to exchange the hammer for a hand lens, to examine the largest fragment. It read plenty strong. He hacked out a few more specimens. With unsteady hands he picked out the most yellow and dropped them into a small leather pouch.

It had been a long day, fatiguing. But a good day. Cautious with each descending move, testing each hand hold, checking each foothold before trusting full weight, he lowered himself from the cliff to the valley below. Ignoring a stinging cut on his arm, trickling blood, he

11

zigzagged the few remaining pockets of snow back to where he'd left Blaze.

He pushed his hat to the back of his head. From a weathered saddle bag removed a water canteen, upended it to gulp down the last of its contents, drawing a torn sleeve over his moist lips from force of habit. He unsnapped the scope from his belt, the hammer, and placed them in the saddle bag. Tremors of excitement tingled his spine as he unknotted the leather pouch from his belt and loosened the drawstring, to feast his eyes on the specimens, to graze his fingertips over them. He wondered. How could this precious metal remain undiscovered for so long? Could it be. That it was not meant that all precious holdings of the earth be released to mankind?

He slumped to a sitting position resting his back against a huge pine and loosened the rawhides on his boots. Once more Gramp's voice echoed in his ears — 'prospecting can be simple and enchanting, or rough and disheartening.' He rolled a cigarette and drew smoke slowly.

Nothing so stirs the blood of man as gold, and he was no exception. But a few years back, a gangling lad back home in Cripple Creek, Colorado, how his eyes glowed each time Gramp told of his adventure in this district, repeating time and again 'you got to see it for yourself, Jed. There's no place like it - it's God's country!' He recalled the quivering in his body when Gramp relinquished to him for permanent keeping the torn, salvaged part of his prospecting map! With printing legible - Upper Peninsula, State of Michigan.

How he had counted the months till he would be old enough to leave home and independently course the rich life of prospecting which Gramp so vividly colored, only to find that his mother took exception to the trend of public thinking, that education wasn't all that important. Educate him she did. Culminating in

12

restless years spent behind books while his physical being cried out for free action.

Jed Carter jostled his thoughts to the present. It was only yesterday he first toed the sandy soil of the district. He smilingly remembered grubbing up a bit of the soil, fisting it. There was that rotted log with the hole underneath, where he bellied himself on the ground and reached deep, cursing lightly the dozen ants that crept into his collar. Withdrawing small stones containing specks of alaskite, greenstone. Reaching deeper in, to pry loose granite showing gash veins of galena.

Hours had been consumed, zigzagging the rugged gulleys, breaking boulders. Sifting through his fingers material clinging to roots of overturned trees. He had found gash veins of galena in granite broken, and chalcopyrite in wide evidence. Not uncommon in gold bearing country.

*　　*　　*　　*　　*　　*

A ribbon of smoke — rising lazily beyond a cluster of spruce across the stream caused a frown to crook his brow. A sign of human habitation! He got to his feet and toed the tobacco into the ground. From the saddle bag he sought out the scope, removed the leather protecting caps and steadied it to one eye. The lens was adjusted for clearer focus, now he stood still. His frown faded and a thin smile moved his lips.

The circular picture framed in the lens presented him with an unexpected treat. Pretty, she was, fully matured. Stooping at intervals, she'd pick something from the ground. A breeze was lifting her fair hair. Her lips seemed to move, was someone accompanying her out of view, or was she singing to herself.

From what he saw, she was a product of nature's beauty. Yep...human beauty.

The scope was collapsed. The eyes of the young prospector became magnetized on the darkening countryside, upon the tumbling hills smothered with virgin timber, upon the uplifts of granite looming skyward. Suddenly he became aware of a special fragrance around him, the scent of arbutus. Was it the untamed flower she was picking?

He untied Blaze, talked to her and patted her affectionately on the neck, then led her through dried weeds and brush to where the stream eddied into a quiet dark pool. Blaze drank long and deep.

The long drawn howl of a wolf was heard in the distance.

Jed Carter removed his hat and stuck it in the crotch of a tree. His lips moved in whisper,".....as you said, Gramp. God's country."

CHAPTER 2
Backing Money

Jed Carter rolled over on his bed of balsam and opened his eyes to the brightness of the morning sun. He had bedded down as was the custom of the outdoorsman - head due north, feet south, so the mysterious currents of the earth would flow freely through his body and remove all impurities. His sleep had been sound, dreamless, but as he opened his eyes to see the sun already an hour high the thought of gold infiltrated his mind.

He propped himself up on his elbows and cast a glance to where Blaze was tied.

Embers from the night's fire which had combated the chilly night air still glowed red, and the blackened coffee pot setting close to the coals was still warm to the touch. He stretched an arm out to unhook a tin cup dangling from a branch and proceeded to fill it with the sludgy black liquid in the pot, almost void of aroma. The tin was hot on his mouth and he set the cup on the ground. Events of the preceeding day began passing rapidly through his mind, those good hours of yesterday. Thoughts began to forge ahead to the next matter of importance - getting backing money, some hard cash. The cuttings were rich. They'd shake up any man with a wad of greenbacks.

His hand encircled the cup, he downed the black liquid with one swallow and refilled the cup to the brim. Yep.

15

He'd head right back to town and hunt up Gramp's lawyer friend. More coffee was drained. He stood up, inhaled deep the pure, bracing air, then flexed his shoulders. The sludge in the bottom of the coffee pot was splashed over the embers and the smoking black coals smothered with a heavy coating of sand.

He saw to it that the canvas sack containing the specimens was safely tucked away in one of the saddle bags and the straps pulled tight. He turned his head to once more focus his gaze across the stream, where that pretty gal had been roaming. A rising white smoke ribbon signaled breakfast. Oh well, girls on the frontier were married as soon as they were old enough.

He laid a hand on his mare's neck and vaulted into the saddle and nudged her into motion. Through stands of virgin timber, around lakes, up and down hills. Blaze was proving herself a real good critter, she had powerful haunches, stamina, true horse sense. It was pure luck how he came about to possess her. Arriving in the area just last week, it had been his intent to buy a good mare at a horse auction. But temporarily sidetracked he found himself slapping down cards in a poker game played in one of the saloons in Iron Bay. In the first game a participant staked, and lost his new leather boots, though later Jed had cheerfully returned them. It was good cards more than skill that resulted in his departure from the saloon premises the owner of a horse.

Couldn't be much of a horse, he had mulled over, when a man stakes it in a card game. But he had proved himself wrong.

Closer to town, now, were blazed trails, blazed no doubt by settlers who took precautions to mark the trees to guide them back to where they entered the dense woods. At the edge of town he heeded a small cemetery, he reined Blaze to a walk.

The settlement lay in a valley surrounded by hills on which maple and birch thrived. Ishpeming - the very name of this place was intriguing. Legend told at the hotel was that an Indian in years not long past wounded a deer. Following the bloody trail to the crest of one of the higher elevations he found himself in a setting of haunting beauty. Seven lakes were in view. "Ish-peming", he uttered, meaning "Heaven" in his Chippewa tongue.

It was country where winters came early and hung on late. Sustaining a hard breed of men of mixed nationalities, mostly bearded or moustached, their faces roughened from the weather. Men characterized by a quality of individualism, who matured early, who were not affected by winters of isolation. Their clothing varied but little, summer or winter, mostly heavy wool shirts worn unbuttoned at the neck, or half-buttoned, revealing heavy underwear which hinted of being put on in the fall and not coming off until spring. Most wore plaid mackinaws, britches hung up by wide suspenders, big boots or shoe pacs large enough to insure the wearer room enough to put on two or three pairs of heavy wool stockings. Those who owned no mackinaws wore more shirts.

Past a slaughter house he rode, with a huge advertisement painted broadside - "Beck's Hunting Smoking Tobacco". He skirted a small lake sparkling blue in the sunlight. Virginia, the hotel owner's daughter, had mentioned this particular lake - how the local Chippewas believed that it was bewitched and refused to camp near it, and believing that the adjacent bluff likewise was an evil omen.

He paralleled a row of roughly hewn log houses, chinked with white mortar. In view were scattered outhouses and sheds constructed of newly milled lumber and slab edgings.

A creek had overflowed its banks and the principle thoroughfare designated Main, reading a hand painted sign on a post, was soupy. Jed Carter dismounted Blaze and walked slowly, working the saddle stiffness from his legs while reddish muck sucked at his feet. Narrow roads, branching off Main, wound sinuously in all directions. As Virginia had told him, ending in locations of hastily built houses in the hillsides, houses separated by stumps.

It was a town built entirely of lumber, few of the buildings having ever been touched with paint. He noted a set of rails, linking the town to the rest of the country. On one side of the street was a bank, barber shop, pool hall, general store, a few saloons. A sign in a lower corner of the store window indicated that the post office was also housed there. On the opposite side of the street he noted a land office, blacksmith shop, carriage dealer.

Plank walks, set on posts sunk into the swampy ground, paralleled the shop fronts to provide safe footing for pedestrians. Short planks had been nailed across the thresholds of some of the businesses to divert the excess flow of creek water. Jed Carter braced a foot on the trough broadside the general store while Blaze nosed the cool water. He observed a small group of loggers standing on the plank walk, smoking, talking as much with their hands as their tongues, giving full appreciation to a female who passed by. A wagon rolled by, carrying a family and apparently all their possessions. His eyes absorbed much, and as a stranger with a clean face his presence was not overlooked.

A gaunt youth, younger than himself but taller, passed by, burdened with the weight of a packsack. Two unattended cows roved down the middle of the road. Another lad, showing an inheritance of Indian blood, carrying heavy traps and with a mink pelt hung on one shoulder, paused to admire Blaze. Virginia's words came to mind - plenty of fresh streams and lakes in the vicinity which abounded with beaver and muskrat, which exploded with trout. Excitement of hunting deer at night by boat and lantern. And that wolves could be heard howling during the night very close to the settlement.

The tempo of this place was beginning to please Jed Carter.

He was oblivious of passersby as he led Blaze down the middle of the road, concentrating on signs indicating places of business. Mixed surprise and elation glowed on his face when black lettering stood out on an upstairs window of the blank building --*E.E. Austin, Lawyer.* He broke his pace to let two ladies pass, one of whom gave him a pleasant side glance. He tipped his hat in acknowledgment, again looked up to the lettered window. Egbert Austin, a reputable lawyer whom Gramp had come to know in earlier days and whom Gramp spoke most highly of.

*   *   *   *   *

He hitched Blaze to a post on the side of the bank building, retrieved the leather pouch containing the specimens and lashed it onto his belt. He climbed the enclosed flight of stairs attached to the side of the bank which led to the second story. The walls of the musty corridor were broken with doors, lettered on the nearest, slightly ajar - *E.E. Austin, Law Office.*

Jed rapped lightly before making his entry.

The office was small and dingy, unimpressive. It was furnished with a rolled top desk evidencing better days, two straight back chairs, a filled bookcase topped with pamphlets and junk. A cabinet set in a corner contained matching volumes of books. Standing by an open window, sharpening a pencil with a clasp knife was a stocky man, presumably in his early fifties. His complexion showed windburn, his face was friendly. He had lost most of his hair, save for a fringe which ran from his ears around the back of his head.

Jed pushed his broad brimmed hat back from his forehead. He extended a hand. "Morning, sir. Jed

Carter. Home town - Buffalo Hill, Colorado."

The lawyer snapped the knife to a close and crossed the bare floor to meet his client halfway. He raised a hand to lock it with the outstretched hand of his visitor. "Carter...Carter...Buffalo Hill....?" The lawyer's handgrip tightened as his eyes met the face of the young stranger. "Now, you wouldn't happen to be a kin of Clint Carter...?"

Jed's face showed a wide smile. He nodded affirmatively and his words flowed with unrestrained pride. "He's my grandfather."

"Well I declare! Another Carter!" The lawyer's face came alive, there was new light in his expression as he drew up a chair and motioned his guest to sit down. "I had the pleasure of knowing Clint. He's well, I hope?"

Jed briefly told of Gramp's health and activities.

"He's a man with big aims," added Austin, going on to tell of some of Gramp's exploits Jed had never heard of, all the while studying Jed's face. "You certainly have inherited the Carter features."

Jed cocked his head sidewise and chuckled lightly. Yep. He couldn't deny it. His features were much like Gramp's, everybody remarked on the similarity -- steady blue eyes, high cheekbones on a lean face, a mouth that formed a near smile. A rugged, outdoor look was borne by both men. Whereas Gramp's hair once had been brown, Jed had been cropped with fair hair, like his mother's. Hair that appeared windswept, regardless of how it was combed or cut. Gramp grew a moustache, whereas Jed's extra facial growth was limited to trimmed sideburns. Characteristic of Gramp, Jed was toughened, yet showing of culture.

"So, what business has lured you way up to this north country anyway?" inquired Austin. "Furs, maybe?"

Jed shook his head sidewise, his voice held matter of fact. "Gold." There was utter conviction in his tone of voice. He rose to his feet, and with faked calmness unknotted the leather pouch dangling from his hip. He moved to Austin's desk, loosened the rawhide drawstring and spilled out the contents. His eyes met Austin's. "It's gold!"

The fragments on the desk were magnets to Austin's eyes. He stood for a moment, motionless, then unconsciously dropped into the chair behind him. He picked up one of the richer specimens and rolled it over in his fingertips. He looked up, his eyes narrowed.

"You didn't find these around here.."

A look of smugness stamped itself on the face of the young prospector. "You're not guesssing right." He dragged a chair from behind him and sat down, pocketing his hands and stretching his long legs out before him. "North of town, if you'd really like to know."

"Out North?" Austin's eyes remained intent, not a muscle in his face moved.

"As the crow flies no great distance. For a good horse and good saddleman, could be a span of eight miles."

Austin grazed his fingers over the specimens before him, turning them over, one by one. He tugged on a warped desk drawer, took a magnifying lens from a rubber case and squinted at the chips. He methodically reached in his pants pocket for his knife and proceeded to nick some of the yellow. A cloud covered his face, momentarily. It faded. Then again, that uncertain look showed itself. It just couldn't be... gold... in this region! It was known that certain men in the district were probing the red soil for other minerals.

Egbert Austin felt in his coat pocket, located a cigar and with an unsteady hand put a light to it. He puffed hard, thinking deep, saying nothing. There was well known treachery in rich, but small mineral veins... but... if this was a "big" lode! A find! It could explode this whole countryside into a boom place overnight! It could mean... The lawyer's mind was full of crowded thoughts. thoughts.

After prolonged silence and half filling the room with smoke he threw the cigar butt through the open window and heaved himself out of his chair. His eyes again glued fast on the fragments. Again his fingers needed to touch them. Jed looked on, with burning curiosity, biting the inside of his lip. Difficult it was to comprehend the meaning of this professional man's reticence. A frown creased Jed's brow, he squinted through the smoke. When he spoke, his voice was with emotion.

"Man! Don't you realize what you're looking at? If a find like this was made anywhere else things would be in an uproar. You stand here scanning rich specimens and don't grasp their value?" Jed Carter cut his speech. He stared into the face of the man on the other side of the desk. His lips moved as if he were to utter something more, but no words came. Crossing the floor to stare out of the open window. He wondered. Are people here so backward they don't know the meaning of gold?

There was the approaching sound of heavy boots clumping down the outer hallway and the banter of male voices. In burst three men, obviously dressed for the woods. All older than himself, yet their quick movements and peppery pratter reflected no loss of youthful energy. The brims and bands of their shapeless hats were splattered with colorful fishing flies, their shoulders supported canvas creels. One was gripping a fishing pole with a price tag still dangling on it. Their smiles reflected no concerns for the hour.

"Top of the day!" ejaculated one of the men, slapping Austin hard on the shoulder.

"Hell. You're all wet. It's already the middle of the morning," chorckled Austin. "What's brewing, anyhow? You look like you're going someplace in a doggone hurry."

"We are. And we'll even let you share our good company. Hang your 'out to lunch' sign and saddle your old colt. Word leaked out at the poker game last night

22

that the trout in Deer Creek are pul-lenty hungry."

"Yeah," piped another. "It's a real strong rumor."

The youngest of the trio was examining a black gnat on the brim of his hat. "They'll strike this one!"

"I'll put my wager on red. Loser buys the beer tonight."

"Hold on, men. Hold on." The potential rabble of the fishermen was interrupted by Austin. "I want you to meet this young fella here. Jed Carter." He turned to Jed. "Meet some fishing maniacs."

The eldest appearing of the three, an intelligent looking man, possibly in his forties, broad shouldered, slightly graying at the temples, was the first to grip Jed's hand. "Manson's the name. Hank Manson. Operating shipping facilities out of Iron Bay. Hank Manson's hand grip fell limp as he took a double look at Jed's countenance. "Haven't we met somewhere before? Seems like I should know you."

Jed's smile came quick. "Sure. We met just last week. And you ended up minus a horse."

"That's it! I'll be a son-of-a-gun! For a stranger you sure get around."

Stan Eland extended his hand. He was the youngest of the three, tall and muscular, skin bronzed by sun and wind. His countenance reflected a happy-go-lucky way of life. Syd Crawford, looking around the thirty year mark, was introduced. Broad faced with alert features and appearing to be a secure man with his feet on the ground.

"Jed's been doing some prospecting north of town. He's brought in some gold."

"Gold! Do I hear right? Gold? In this part of the country?" Manson's words were more than inquiring.

Austin motioned toward the desk. "There's a few mighty rich looking rocks."

A look of stunned curiosity now showed on the faces of the men. Syd Crawford set his new rod against a wall.

23

Jed stood back while the fishermen hovered over the desk, turning over the veined samples with great interest. Their silence was offset by the glow in their eyes, their questioning features. They rubbed the richer pieces, responding with affirmative nods. There was little doubt what was going on in their minds. Manson's undivided attention was now on a rich sample. He had learned to distinguish gold bearing quartz and knew this to be gold as soon as he saw it. He turned to Jed, and it was obvious that his curiosity was becoming insatiable.

A smile deepened itself on one corner of Jed's mouth. "Pretty diggings, aren't they?"

Manson wet his lips, there was a swift glance toward his cronies. His eyes once more came to rest on the face of the young prospector. "You certainly got our curiosity roused, young fella. Think you could find this site again? A gunny sack full of this stuff could get you some backing."

Jed smiled quietly, saying nothing. Four pairs of eyes watched him, as he reached for the empty sack and with forced nonchalance dragged his hand across the desk, scooping up the specimens in one big hand and letting them fall back into the pouch, very slowly. All but the biggest which revealed numerous chunks of gold embedded in white granite, which he handed to Austin. "You might use this as a conversation piece."

He knotted the sack with care, again his steady eyes met the eyes of the fishermen. "Okay. So you're interested. You might meet me at the livery tomorrow morning. Eight sharp. Take along some gunny sacks to bring the goods home in." He reached for the fishing rod against the wall and tested the spring. "You better fill those creels today, because after tomorrow I wager you won't have much time for the sport."

Footsteps again sounded heavy in the hallway. Now standing at the threshold was a heavy set, red-faced woman in her middle years, breathing hard from

24

elevating her huge body up the long stairway. Mrs. Hildegard Anderson herself, smiled the lawyer to himself, not surprised at all with her appearance. She paused to mop her perspiring forehead with a handkerchief, then proceeded straight ahead to Austin's desk, thumping down on it her large overstuffed purse. She seemed immune to the presence of others in the room besides the lawyer himself.

"Mister Lawyer, Mister Lawyer." Her head was shaking perturbly, her voice carried a tone of disgust.

Egbert Austin set himself to once more listen to another of Mrs. Anderson's problems, which averaged about one every week. She was no stranger to him, nor to anybody in town. She was one who presented herself, and made known her presence, at all public meetings. Surely her discourse always followed one particular pattern. She stated facts as she saw them.

"I honest taxpayer in dis town and I need lawyer's talk. I don't know vat dis place coming to. Dem cows! Dey roam up and down my road all day long, dangling dem bells, lifting their tails in my garden, breaking my fence. And dis morning I vake up and find vun sitting on my porch. Vat you think bout dat, Lawyer man? Don't ve get notting for paying our three dollar tax?"

The lawyer cleared his throat, when he spoke his words were soft and easy. "It's getting to be a problem, Mrs. Anderson. We can't deny it. Let me tell you, though, that Marshall Malaroni has been real busy lately. Chasing down law-breaking animals. And if I know Tony, his efforts won't slacken. I'll look him up and tell him exactly what your feelings are. I assure you that as a tax paying citizen your concerns will not be overlooked."

Mrs. Anderson wasn't so easily convinced. "You not gif me vat dey say 'run around'?"

Egbert Austin smiled reassuringly. "No, Mrs. Anderson. No run around. Honest to goodness straight

25

talk."

She deliberated silently, wiping the corners of her mouth with her handkerchief, then slipped her hamlike arm under the handle of her purse. "Vell, Lawyer Man. You see me next veek agen if dem cows don't move off my porch." She took her departure, then made an unexpected return. After searching through the contents of her bulging purse she withdrew a printed card and presented it to Mr. Austin. "A pledge card, ve are looking to buy a church bell vat vill ring evry day in dis town." That said and done, she again took departure.

Jed Carter fitted his hat on his head, shook the men's hands and said he'd see them in the morning. He started for the door, stood there a moment, then glanced back. "I'll wager that red takes the most trout."

He bounded the stairs into the sunlight with the leather pouch still clenched in his hand. Business had perked up. Wagons were moving in diverse directions, there were people on foot. From the blacksmith shop emanated the sound of hammers striking on iron. He paced a few steps, then stopped to scan posters nailed to a light post. They described wanted men, advertised a medicine show, a wrestling match. Suddenly appeared a runaway horse attached to a wagon, wooden crates in the street marking the path taken. Right before his eyes the wagon turned over, the remaining crates were spilled out but the horse kept running.

Hell's Town. Such reference had been made to this place, passing through the neighboring towns of Iron Bay and Coyuta. Hell's Town? There were saloons and gambling joints patterned like those back home. Virginia had mentioned the principal shows being burlesques, of questionable quality. There was Lil's place, a port of iniquity, but he couldn't think of a town he'd passed through that didn't shadow one.

At the Y in the road he lingered. To ponder over a statue of an Indian cast in iron. "Old Ish" the townsfolk

26

called him and already there was beginning to grow civic pride in the statue. He was a cast image of the warrior, they maintained, who had given the town its name. The warrior was cast with his left foot resting on a boulder, armed with bow in his left hand and arrow in his right. A headdress fell down his back, a buckled strap crossed his naked chest. His garb consisted of a blanket partially covering his right shoulder, and buckskin trousers. The Indian's gaze was riveted eastward toward the hills, bent on game or enemy.

Stories told at the hotel on how the iron sentry got set here were many and conflicting. Some knew it to be part of a barter, honoring the Chippewas who swapped some land, while one inhabitant positively asserted that it was the doings of a wealthy old pioneer, infected with superstitions of all sorts, who placed it there to guard over the town and his riches. The iron Indian, so magnificently cast, held Jed Carter with puzzling fascination. He pondered the truth. Why a frontier town in this rugged northern wilderness, struggling for mere existence, should have been so beautifully remembered.

He registered mild surprise when he felt a touch to his shoulder. He turned halfway, and found himself looking once more at Lawyer Austin. Bareheaded and without his coat, he wore a dead serious expression on his face.

"Just wanted to let you know. You're damn lucky to have bumped into that guy Hank Manson. He's an important person around this part of the country and he's got plenty of money. And those other two fellas - they're good men!" Jed listened without adding words of his own. Austin continued. "Just wanted to make sure about tomorrow."

The words were good to hear yet Jed kept a straight face. "I'll be on time."

The muscles in Lawyer Austin's face relaxed and he patted Jed on the shoulder. "Good. Just wanted to be sure." He turned, and headed back toward his office.

Crossing the road, now, was a stocky, swarthy-skinned man, clad in an ill-fitting jacket trimmed with brass bottons, baggy britches and high top boots. The black bushy moustache he sported almost covered the portion of his face below his nose. A lawman's badge was displayed on his jacket and he wore a large revolver in a holster on his right hip. He wore a look of importance on his face. Marshall Malaroni, mused Jed. He'd heard of him.

Tucked under the Marshall's arm were some billings. The officer neared, and passed, and the smell of garlic penetrated the air. Crooks in this town would never get caught, thought Jed. From afar that odor would crease anybody's nose.

The Marshall stopped by the front of the bank. He set the billings upright on the plank walk, leaning them against the wall of the bank. He removed the uppermost one and nailed it to the building using more nails than seemed necessary. Jed noted with curiosity. The officer's left hand was covered with a heavy black leather glove. The officer backed up a bit to smugly survey the important task just performed, then pocketed his hammer and picked up the remaining billings. Jed stood with folded arms and read the black print.

NOTICE

Word reaches this town that quack Dr. Otto Von Muller is reported coming back from Iron Bay. He is the quack who wants to sell you glasses or treat your eyes. He is a fraud. Let not your two eyes be ruined by him as your stock of eyes is not large. Warn everybody that he is an imposter and to give him the toe end of a boot. Stay clear of him.

By order of the Common Council

Jed Carter inhaled deep of the clean spring air. Von Muller or no Von Muller. It was a beautiful day!

* * * * *

A beam of early morning light was striking through the corner window of his room on the second floor of the Chippewa Hotel. Jed rose from his bed, rolled up by hand the broken green shade and stuck his head through the open window. The road was puddled from a night rain, but the morning sun was breaking out and a south breeze was carrying new freshness. All in all it held the makings of a good day to come.

He washed lightly in the crockery basin, dressed, and ran a comb through his hair. He skipped his shave, and made but one stop, at the coffee table downstairs where he ate heartily of hot oatmeal washed down with black coffee, all prepared by Virginia. He moved on foot toward the livery, whistling softly to himself.

His three new acquaintances of the previous day were already there, checking their horses, stowing last minute needs in stuffed saddle bags. They hailed him like an old friend when he approached.

"Morning, gentlemen," smiled Jed. "Since you're right on time I might assume that the true stuff you saw yesterday is bothering you a bit."

"Glad to see you!" Manson's face was sparked with excitement. "Were kind of 'fraid you might change your mind about sharing information."

Jed met the issue head on. "Truth is, I need backing. He paced the runway between two rows of stalls, untied Blaze from her stall and led her out into the light. Egbert Austin was approaching on foot at near distance. Jed glanced at Syd Crawford who was pulling the straps of his saddle bags tight in the buckles. "Got a good map?"

Stan Eland spat spent tobacco to the ground and responded for Syd. "Yep. And everything else we'll be needing. Compasses, surveying instruments, drill.

Powder and fuses, hammers. Lawyer Austin, clad in a dress suit and top hat and obviously unable to make the trek but desiring to see the men off, butted in. "They even remembered grub and tobacco."

Jed grinned with full satisfaction. "That should do it very nicely, Mr. Lawyer Man." He mounted Blaze, shifted his weight in the saddle and looked to see that everybody was ready. He flipped open his pocket watch to note the exact time and signaled a departing wave to Lawyer Austin. "Be seeing ya, Mr. Lawyer man!" Then he whacked the rump of Blaze.

They jogged at half-trot. They had covered no more than a mile, leaving the last of the log houses behind them, when a funeral procession was overtaken. Wagons bearing black clad mourners wound slowly ahead. They saw that one wagon supported but a driver and pine box. In respect to the deceased they walked their horses behind. But a short distance on, the procession would leave the main road and follow a short wagon trail into the graveyard.

Jim, the deceased, had been a popular man with the townsfolk. The thoughts of the horsemen paralleled one another. Too bad that lung inflammation snuffed out Jim, leaving a young wife, little ones...The Lord giveth and the Lord taketh.

Suddenly without warning a sharp piercing whinny erupted, and Stan's mare was on her hind legs, tossing her head, frightened by something unknown. Stan pulled hard on the reins. Another lifting scream from the mare! She was rearing, uncontrollably. Four hooves touched the soil, again she was only on hind legs...now veering toward the wagons.

"Easy girl! Easy!" Stan pulled furiously at the mouthpiece. His eyes took a frightened look. There was screaming from women in the wagons ahead.

"Easy girl!" Stan couldn't check her and there was a paralyzing look on his face. Hard again on her

30

mouthpiece he pulled, he fought to stay mounted. More shouts, alarmed cries. A splintering thud and the horse came down on a wagon. Stan lay on the ground, motionless. Men leaped down from their vehicles. There were hysterical shrieks. One grieving woman swooned while others sat petrified.

"It's Stan Eland!"

"Is he dead?"

"Get Reverend Culbertson back here right quick."

"Check to see if he's got a pulse."

"We need one of the wagons. Got to get him to Doc Billington fast!"

*   *   *   *   *

Doc Billington was at home in his surgical quarters, methodically patching up a foreigner who had several bloody knife wounds in his arms and torso, ignoring the man's cussing words to hurry up so he could get back to the saloon to square off with the trapper who slashed him.

The last gap was stitched and Doc accepted from his patient a hearty handshake which was meant to be token of payment. It was close to ten o'clock in the morning when Doc motioned to bring Stan Eland to an inner room.

Jed circled the parlor floor, in silence, burning up one cigarette after another. Twice did he stop to put his eye to the open crack of the door leading to the inner room where Doc was bent over Stan, but the most he could make out was Doc stirring salve and applying it on his patient. Hank Manson and Syd Crawford were slouched low in overstuffed chairs and saying little. The ticking of the clock in the corner seemed to grow louder, seemingly ticking off something more than time. Finally the door connecting the inner room was fully opened. Doc Billington came out, easing the door shut behind him. Jed butted his cigarette while Doc put a light to one of his

31

own. Crawford and Manson got to their feet. Crawford's voice shook. "How bad, Doc?"

The doctor exhaled smoke, then peered over the top of his steelrimmed glasses. "Not half as bad as it looked when you brought him in. He's suffered a concussion. Cleaned him up good and all I could find was cuts and bruises and a fractured bone in his right foot. He's comfortable now, suffering no great pain. Says to tell you guys to get on with your work."

*   *   *   *   *

It was close to the noon hour. The three horsemen heeled their horses to make time, riding hard, trying to rid their bodies of the strange feeling that events of the day had imbedded in them. Eland's horse was known to be a trained thoroughbred, a fine horse. What caused her to rear was unexplainable. Miles were covered without a spoken word. Only the beat of the horses hooves, the creak of saddle gear or an occasional snort broke the silence. Their minds were in accord. Was it so intended, that for man's earthly gain there should be sacrifice?

They ate up the miles to their destination, drawing near, their eyes were alert to indications in the vicinity which gave hints of great value.

Good hours of the day were already spent. They had saddle stiffness. Yet there were enough hours of daylight to do some searching. The horses were secured. Equipped with hammers and compasses, pistols should protection be necessary, they were soon out of sight.

Hours of daylight passed much faster than hoped for. When the sun began dropping low on the horizon, Manson and Crawford emerged from a heavily wooded area, disheveled and shaken, clutching small weighty bags. Awed by locating a lode Jed had marked on the map which was traced 200 feet without showing signs of exhausting. They had already seen enough to convince them.

32

Jed was squatting beside the banks of the Yellow Dog, washing the dirt from a jagged cut on his hand. A large brown trout broke water close by, and left an ever widening circle before their eyes.

"Forget him," quipped Crawford. "We'll hook him when he's a couple of pounds heavier." Hank Manson didn't react. For the first time in his life he cared less about trout. His thoughts were swirling in rapid motion, his gaze was on the fast running waters of the Yellow Dog. He dropped to a knee to reach out and grab a handful of gravel from the river bed where the water ran shallow. Examination revealed nothing of particular interest. He washed the wet aggregate from his hand and grubbed, deeper. Another cupped hand of gravel was stirred about in the palm of his hand. His eyes caught fire. "Sure looks like gold!" A water worn yellow nugget, heart shaped showed bright in his hand. He picked it apart from the gravel. Rising to his feet, he slipped the nugget into the pocket of Jed's sheepskin vest. "You should be the one to have it."

They bedded down early on pine boughs, under the wide open skies, to be ready to rise with the crack of dawn. To follow grass root veins discovered.

They slept deep, while the night breezes stirred cool air around their heads, and the huge pine logs burned to low embers.

A rosy dawn offered a hint of good things to come. With continued fervid, unsuppressed drive they worked the areas Jed pinpointed, tracing the bright materials with narrow veinlets in some places pinching out in barren rock. Following connected systems of veins, some branching off to intersect larger lodes. Drilling holes in the lode which showed the best with rich content, tamping powder and firing the charge. And with the lifting of smoke their minds near delerium. Before them, a vein of gold quartz six feet thick, bearing into the bowels of the cliff. They staggered over the broken rock, unbelieving.

"Would take a good many years of prospecting to catch up with the looks of this place!" ejected Syd, "if such luck were to be had!"

"The Yellow Dog...powerful enough a stream to furnish drive for machinery..." Hank Manson's eyes were far reaching, to the continuity of hills completely coated with timber. "Wood galore for building and mining. The terrain offered no nature created obstacles to getting supplies in." His eyes touched upon the low valleys, "even pastures for the horses."

Jed was bent over an open map, marking the finds, coding the x's at the bottom and writing details on a note pad. He spat on the ground, folded up the map and sprung to his feet. "Now, to register our claim."

On the brink of darkness they rode into town, and gold fever was singing their minds.

CHAPTER 3
The Birth of the Holyoke

Thirty days passed. News of the discovery of gold had burned the country like wildfire and the pulse of the town was beating with gold fever. Nothing rouses people more quickly than a report that gold has been found close by. There was gold talk everywhere, in the saloons, the shops, street gatherings.

Long before the hour of the meeting the town hall was jammed with people, most of them seated on wooden planks placed over kegs. Townsfolk, mostly, but there were some complete strangers. Sheer excitement was vibrating the air. Men who had fisted one another in the saloons shook hands and surprisingly all were sober and serious.

For Jed Carter it was a big night, long and anxiously waited for. He kept looking toward the door each time it was opened, awaiting the arrival of Hank Manson. Manson's presence at this meeting was vital. Hank carried power. Influential power throughout the district. Lawyer Austin was already on the scene, having arrived early to open the door, since the key to the building had been placed in his charge. Again he humbly apologized to Jed, for any apprehensions about samples first viewed in his office, the issue now being clarified with the assays of chemists of known worth and standing.

Stan Eland, supported by crutches, but still none too steady, was examining some papers on a table in the front of the room. Mrs. Anderson, fingering pledge cards for the church bell, was scanning faces of those present hoping to spot potential donors who had not yet been solicited. Present was the editor of the POST, big lumbering Ed Morley, who stood six feet four inches in stocking feet. Big Ed, ever sporting a pompadour haircut, who footed it up and down Main Street every day seeking news for his paper. Big Ed, with shirt sleeves rolled back, a pointed pencil stuck on an ear and writing pad locked under an arm, ready to write what was to be talked about. Knowing it would be the hottest news since the press was set up. Yet being beset by the presence of Mrs. Anderson, who was never afraid of speaking up wherever and whenever she presented herself, and who was now deluging him with questions about the gold field to which he certainly yet had no answers.

A half dozen more men entered the building and found themselves seats, then Hank Manson, his effervescent self. He talked briefly about the rotten condition of the road from Iron Bay and of his hope that plank roads connecting the towns would soon be laid. Hank Manson worked his way to the front of the room to lend assistance with the meeting, should the need be. Lawyer Austin read his watch, seven minutes after seven. He faced the babbling room full of people filling all seats and standing against the walls. He raised his hands for attention, but only those near him silenced.

"Quiet! Quiet everybody!" He fluttered his hands for complete attention and the prattle miraculously abated. Austin's face was radiant, his broad smile infecting his audience.

"Friends and neighbors." The tension of the important moment caused his voice to crack and he cleared his throat. "It is with pleasure that I welcome you this evening to this first and all important meeting of persons who are interested in developing the newly discovered gold fields in the staked district north of town.

"Before I proceed further you should know that this meeting would not have been existent were it not for a young man, a recent arrival in town, who made the initial gold discovery." Austin looked to where Jed sat and extended an arm. "Jed Carter!...stand up, Jed. Let everybody see what a real prospector looks like!"

Jed rose to his feet, his face taking a tinge of color. There was an outbreak of applause, yea's. He rolled the brim of his hat. "Thanks, folks. Sure, we're going to do a lot of digging. But it's the fact that I like wilderness living, just like everybody here, is why I'm staying." And with that he sat down. Faces of the people reflected that they liked what he said, and when the encore of approval subsided, Lawyer Austin proceeded.

"There are two more men who have given much time to this prospective development who I'd like to introduce.. Hank Manson, from Iron Bay, and a local man who I'm sure most of you know, Syd Crawford." Austin turned to his two colleagues who enthusiastically got to their feet and nodded warmly.

Austin's words became freer flowing. "As most of you already know, last month Mr. Manson, Mr. Crawford, Mr, Carter and myself staked a claim on property where gold veins are running wild. Several veins were extensively followed up with trenching and blasting. The staked ground gives every indication of holding a powerful gold deposit. Specimens sent to laboratories in New York and Philadelphia have been returned along with assay sheets and are on the table before me. The assay sheets are intensely gratifying! To the point, that it is the intent of the claimholders to incorporate with round figures of $500,000, and set up a mining operation. It is safe to predict, that the ceaseless din of the stamp mill will be heard in the not distant future around the lakes of this region.

"Analyses have been made by distinguished chemists and geologists who express themselves in the highest terms of the permanency of these veins, and agree. That the quality contained therein is more than sufficient to pay the expenses of mining.

"No venture of this dimension can be set up without capital. And town unity. That's the reason we're here tonight. To enlighten everybody about our plans..to give each man and woman who so desire an opportunity to purchase stock in this undertaking and personally benefit from rich dividends.

"We should elect officers who will proceed in the drafting of legal documents. I shall be most happy to guide anybody along these lines."

The subsequent hours were rapidly consumed with everybody listening intently to each voice of thought, the claimholders being interrupted at close intervals. At times the meeting turned into a noisy affair, everybody touched with the spirit of the meeting at once. Excitement reached high pitch when minds became saturated with the fact that they would soon possess a gold mine. They agreed, that Articles of Association should be submitted to the state for approval.

Hank Manson took the floor, he talked on, impressively, and the meeting shifted back to a semblance of order.

"...I thank you for the faith and trust shown by electing me President of this newly formed company, which soon will make its name in gold mining in this Upper Peninsula of Michigan. I promise to direct this company with my fullest ability and sincere efforts and to promote to the fullest extent the interests of all stockholders.

"I am most pleased with your discreet decision in electing Syd Crawford as secretary and treasurer, knowing that under his direction funds will be dispersed in the proper direction.

"While the capital sum needed may appear considerable to many of you, I assure you it is not even close to the sums being placed in enterprises at other points in this country. With hard work and the cooperation of each interested party, I carry no doubt that this enterprise will erupt with resounding success. Prospects for a dividend paying mine are certainly of unusual brightness. I will be asking the officers to initially meet each week for the purpose of making operating decisions."

The issue of naming the mine had arisen earlier in the evening and again the name loomed of importance.

Some liked "Sunset Mine"...others favored "Yellow Dog" after the stream. Mrs. Anderson insisted it be "Carter Mine".

On the issue Hank Manson had a bit to add. "It is my intent to ask of our officers, that we contact the Holyoke Mining Company in Minnesota. Comprised of knowledgable and experienced people in this field of work. Asking if they will handle our operation. If it would be our fortune to obtain their services, we would be under guidance of the highest technical skills."

"If plans proceed and the reply received is affirmative, I move that the mine be named the "Holyoke".

"Holyoke?" "The Holyoke!" Low murmurs throughout the room repeated the name. Few men ever challenged Hank Manson's thinking with his knack for making money, and that his statements always were within the limits of truth. Now a giant of a man, a logger, stood up in the middle of the room, his thumbs stuck in his wide suspenders. His voice boomed loud and clear. "That's good fitting name, Manson. Can't think of none better." Rippling murmurs of assent transformed to loud voices of approval. Curious expressions changed to smiling faces as the name sounded better each time it was said.

"Yea. That's good name as any!"

"I'll swallow that one!"

"That's a durn puurty name... yeah..."

So it was with a sweeping vote agreed upon, to be named the "Holyoke".

Reverend Culbertson led the clapping that closed the meeting, and not to be overshadowed, Mrs. Anderson rose to her feet and called for a standing ovation to the newly elected officers.

All the while Ed Morley's ink stained fingers were rapidly writing on a note pad propped on a knee. Everything said was the makings of front page news. Hank Manson faced Ed with a directive. "First thing in the morning, Ed. Bear down on the job of setting up plates for printing stock certificates. And fast as you possibly can, hustle out a good amount of booklets like we talked about here tonight and get them into circulation. Stay with the job, even if it means losing sleep." Hank Manson looked askance at Stan Eland. "Might be a good idea to keep specimens on display in your office."

*   *   *   *   *

Time was not long passing, before the decisions made at the meeting broke into reality. Situated diagonally across from the Black Bear saloon, the Holyoke headquarters were established in a building occupied by one other agent. Two rooms, yet scantily furnished, with the one larger room furnished with two chairs and a table, a cabinet, coat rack, brass cuspidor and calendar. The smaller adjoining room holding but a small iron safe in one corner and a single chair. Syd had seen to it that the Articles of Association had been filed with the county clerk. Now he was enacting duties entrusted his care, counting and recording numbers of the stock certificates which Ed Morley had delivered this very day. Printing of the certificates had taken more time than hoped for, no reason given from the printer in Chicago. Hank Manson had made his presence this day to sign the certificates and see that they were properly countersigned and under seal of the company. They were impressive

40

looking - a crossed pick and shovel formed a neat design near the top, while jagged pieces of rocks were pictured at the bottom. Print stated that the certificates held a value of twenty-five dollars.

Syd pushed aside the shiny new black leather covered ledger, and reached over for the last issue of the POST. Once more his eyes skimmed the large advertisement set in heavy black type.

> May 28, 1864
> HOLYOKE MINING COMPANY -
> 20,000 shares, Sec. 2 Town, 48, North
> of Range 27 West. Henry R. Manson,
> Pres., of Iron Bay, Jed Carter, Vice
> Pres., of Buffalo Hill, Colorado,
> Sydney E. Crawford, Sec'y. and
> Treasurer, of Ishpeming, Directors
> Stanley R. Eland, of Ishpeming, Paul
> Witter, Henry R. Manson, Mark B.
> Chilton, and C. Curt Landers of Iron
> Bay, Chester M. Muller of New York,
> and Gordon Trombley, of Phila-
> delphia, Andrew Sommers, Agent.
> Office in Jamison Building,
> Ishpeming, Michigan
> April 14

Syd Crawford stood up to loosen his limbs, he removed the eyeglasses he used for close work and set them on his work table. At random he picked up a stack of printed booklets which Ed also had delivered, booklets describing the property, containing assay findings and letters from geologists and chemists. Syd's eyes covered the room, coming to rest on the black lettering on the window - **HOLYOKE OFFICE**, reaching beyond outside, to 'Old Ish'. An expression of complete satisfaction smothered his face.

The Holyoke was born!

CHAPTER 4

Early Operations

News traveled fast around the district. Everybody knew there was dissension between Bart Fauquier, operating the South Arm Lumber Company up on the Mulligan Creek north of the Holyoke, and the men who worked for him. Just last week gunfire had taken place in the sprawling pine camp when Bart had short-houred a good man. Some later said it was Ikey who dueled Bart, though Ikey never admitted to it. Young Ikey, limping slowly along the bank of the Yellow Dog, whose arrival at the Holyoke Captain Sommers watched from a distance.

Ikey slipped the battered knapsack off his back, he flexed his shoulders a few times to loosen bound muscles. The sound of axes, marking trees to be felled, struck a pleasant tone in his ears. Shortly, Captain Sommers found himself looking at a rugged young chap, about twenty-one years of age. His dark uncombed hair hung long beneath a tattered cap, curling over his ears and growing far down the nape of his neck. His clothes were threadbare beyond repair. He was lean and sinewy, but gave the quick impression of being able to handle himself, pound for pound, against anyone his size or maybe bigger.

Another French-Canadian, figured Captain Sommers. Who ended up in the area from involvement in fur trading, whose possessions were all in his knapsack.

Ikey's dark eyes held fast on Captain Sommers.

"Who's bossin' 'round here?"

Captain Sommers rolled a chew of tobacco over in his cheek. "You're talking to the mining captain.. the boss. Sommers the name."

"Rumor is yer gonna blast some real gold outa them hills."

"Yep. That's exactly what we're here for."

The young logger's eyes covered the timbered site with a sweeping glance. "If yer needin' a good man to clear heavy timber yer lookin' at one. An if ya wanna crew jest say so."

"You been up working the South Arm I calculate?"

Ikey nodded affirmatively.

"Troubles?" Sommers feigned ignorance of Bart Fauquier's slippery maneuvers, though he'd heard plenty of stories.

Ikey didn't answer right away, not knowing how hard to knock Bart. But he'd speak the truth. "Rotten deal fer any man. Nobody would stick it out if he didn't have'ta. Watery soup 'n oatmeal at every meal, non't nohow fill a man's belly. Bunkhouses stinkin' lousy. No guards on them saws. That Bart is a son-of-a-gun 'bout payin'. On paydays no cash jest hands out hunks of paper with 'ritin 'bout payin' later. No man thinkin' 'bout takin' a wife kin go on like that."

Captain Sommers was studying Ikey outwardly, from his shaggy head to his bandaged foot, bound in dirty burlap. Inwardly, sensing the youth had guts and perseverance which would be needed for a long time at the Holyoke.

"Know anything about chopping down trees?"

"Enuf."

Sommers picked up an axe, crossed a thumb over its honed edge and gestured toward a pine, which like

43

hundreds around needed to be felled.

"That one," said Sommers. "Lay it south."

Ikey sized up the tall timber. A chew of tobacco was spat to the ground in preparation for the work at hand. He took the axe and slid his rough hands along the handle, gauged its weight. He bared his head and took a stance beside the pine.

A notch was cut low, soon broad wedges of wood flew from the deepening gash. Captain Sommers eyes were quick to detect the skill of this logger. How he held his hands on the handle to guide the swing and for power.

In less time than anticipated the timber swayed precariously, yielded to the broadening gash and severed its long hold on nature. Ikey let the axe drop. Whereas Captain Sommers immediately picked it up and set it aside. Ikey waited. Hands on hips. His eyes were questioning Captain Sommers.

"Your foot? Why you carrying it around in a gunny sack?"

A bashful smile crept on the youth's face. He shrugged his shoulders with indifference. "Hell. Ain't no chopper in the country who's followed the business long who kin boast 'bout havin' a full set of toes."

Sommers had long worked on pioneer fronts, and it had been something long realized, not to depend on unmarried men. It had been generally conceded, that to keep a skilled, or even ordinary workman for any length of time, he must be married. Yet in the short moments of their acquaintance, Sommers sized up Ikey to be an all right guy. What he saw in the man satisfied him.

"Soon as that foot is mended you can start dropping the marked timber. After that there'll be plenty of work if you choose to stay on. Round up a dozen of your cronies. Will put them on for a couple of weeks to see what they're made of. Every man who proves himself will have work for a long time. With pay and grub."

Ikey lifted his battered knapsack from the ground and

slung it over a shoulder. He extended his free hand. "It's been a good day, man. A real good day."

*   *   *   *   *

The sound of axes, saws, and falling trees filled the woods around the site of the Holyoke. One large cabin was built, a combination dining room and cookhouse which was equipped with a cook stove and lumber camp outfit purchased in town. Shacks sprung up for use by the work crew until permanent bunkhouses could be built. Some shacks were windowless, or with raggedy pieces of burlap nailed over proposed window openings. The tiny insides held bunks that were never made, enhanced by straw stuffed burlap sacks serving as head rests. Clothes were hung on spikes driven into the walls. Sacks hanging from spikes contained meager personal possessions.

The yarn swapping woodsmen were a happy crew. They were in large majority single men, the families of the married men dwelling in log houses in town. Every man accepted tobacco and whiskey as part of his living.

When the day's work was ended some sought rest in their bunks. Others sat around outside, drinking and smoking. Stories of their past were swapped, some carrying unadulterated truth, many fringed with exaggeration or outright fabrication. Frequent mention was of Lil's place in town, about bosomy Lil herself.

Good company was found in Jallu. A single man, though not by choice. Jallu, who possessed a wild imagination. Who kept everybody laughing, with him and at him. As sure as day follows day, when the sun was at its highest and hottest and work was ceased for wolfing down mid-day victuals, usually hunks of dark bread and salt pork and plenty of black coffee, Jallu would gaze up at the trees and rant on.

"Should ferget the bloody gold! 'Fore our eyes is beverage. Ready fer the takin'. Yep. Ready fer the takin'. Standin' right fore our eyes... timber... ground to

45

sawdust makes good booze. Yeah! Fine booze. Plain old sawdust and my secret treatment. No bloody expensive machinery needed. Jest bucksaw an' a lil' sweat."

There was Charlie, who had worked in lumber camps for several seasons, qualifying him for the job of camp cook. Short in stature he was, and paunchy as were most men of his trade. His professional mark was a printed flour sack bound around his waist to serve as an apron. There was Dan, unmarried, who carried a harmonica in the buttoned pocket of his shirt. Not seldom was it that in the quiet of the evening tingly melodies played by ear could be heard coming from the direction of Dan's shack.

On the payroll there were Nels, John, Jim and Alex, all married with wives and offspring in town. Bachelors Mikko and Pete. Mighty Mikko Rymponen, who was admired by every man in the countryside. A cheerful chap in his mid twenties, who carried a body of bulging biceps, Mikko had an enviable reputation among local people as a catch-as-catch-can wrestler, having won over 200 matches, a good number against opponents well spoken of. Mikko carried but one blemish on his canvas record, losing a fall in his first official match against his own cousin back in the old country. From which time on he had made headlines in five foreign countries and in America by putting nationally known wrestlers on their backs. Mikko's most recent matches last month in Coyuta, during a three day tournament, brought him a silver cup and $50.00 top money. Injuring his final opponent so badly he was unable to finish the match. Mikko was known never to have evaded a booking. Despite all his big wins, the title of world champ was currently resting on Big Hans Schimmler over in Germany.

Pete was a good fella, yet sort of different a man. Who frequently and for lengthy periods of time remained in complete isolation with his thoughts. It was a general way of thinking, that since Pete's divorce he had failed to firmly plant his feet on the ground. Yet Pete had a head crammed with knowledge, mystifying to everybody where it was acquired.

This very evening, walking alone in the moonlit dark, Jed Carter found himself standing at Pete's threshold. A shack with quarters for only one man, it was Pete's choice of habitation. A smudge pail smoldered outside the doorway. Inside the shanty a sooted lantern burning low on a shelf flickered a feeble light.

Jed entered, ungreeted, and took rest on an empty box. Pete was propped in his bunk doing some serious writing. Crumpled scraps of brown paper lay on the rough floor. Pete wrote in silence, words flowing from the stub of a pencil gripped in his thick fingers onto a paper sack. Pete frowned, fisted his writing into a ball and tossed it across the floor. It was obvious there was to be no discourse. Jed picked up the crumpled scrap at his feet and smoothed it out.

> Sharp wedge of steel, in woodsman's hands
> > slicing the bark
> > through the pith
> till thunderous crash rends total severance
> > from earth's hold.
> By the hearth he sits, the woodsman
> > by the warmth of burning birch
> > in the twilight hours of day.
> Now setting the empty maple victual bowl
> > upon warm hearth stones
> > a pine match flames his briar pipe
> > he leans back in his oaken chair, and smokes
> Till heavy eyelids cause him to climb
> > the ash ladder attached to pine wall
> > to seek sleep in his popple bed.
> Tomorrow his son will sow seedlings
> > while sharp wedge of steel slices the bark
> > through the pith.

Jed Carter tucked the paper into a shirt pocket, decided that Pete didn't need company and left. Outside the doorway he lingered with no special thoughts in mind.

The quiet peace over the entire camp, now bathed in moonlight, was broken by the call of a whippoorwill. He set his back against a pine and his eyes rested on the glimmering ripples of the Yellow Dog.

He looked up at the clear sky, and his lips moved.

*   *   *   *   *

What had been a rabbit trail through the gulches a month ago was cleared of timber and a wagon road blazed. It proved to be no small job. Elevations up which a loaded supply wagon couldn't be hauled by a team of horses had to be avoided, likewise deep gulleys and swampland. The lead crew went ahead locating and blocking, with a second crew finishing the rugged miles for the supply wagons.

The townsfolk referred to the wagon road as the Holyoke Trail, and the name stuck fast. It was a rough road to travel all the way, getting stuck was a common thing on low terrain after heavy rains, when wheels sunk deep in mud and deep holes. In many a place hanging branches came as low as the horses heads, necessitating the drivers to vacate their seats and rein the horses from alongside the wagons. Despite the rough travel, wagons heaped high with supplies pulled away from the general store each day, squeaking on to the mine site hours later. Barrels of flour, sacks of sugar and beans, lard, bacon, were stacked in two sheds adjacent the cookhouse by anybody nearby with free hands. With whiskey kegs being most delicately handled. Thor Blumstrom, the store owner, smiled over his luck, in that he had made the good decision of setting up his business in Ishpeming instead of Coyuta.

It was this bright sunshiny day that Captain Sommers

chose the shade of the cookhouse over the heat of his office shack for updating his daily logbook. There was a glint in his eye as he observed Jallu and John in the process of unloading one of the wagons. All the while bickering over the best method of stalking a deer. The keg of dried fish that had slipped their hand hold moments earlier had caused Charlie exiting the kitchen to leap like a bullfrog. Bouncing off stumps on the hillside, the barrel was caught in the churning current of the Yellow Dog, then bobbled out of sight.

The faces of Jallu and John reflected looks of unconcern. Jallu merely shrugging his shoulders, his protruding lower lip mumbling ”...dried fish..”

“yeah... dried fish, back where they naturally belong,” responded John, in complete harmony with his partner over this particular loss. Abruptly his thoughts shifted. “But don't think you kin stalk an old buck with dried fish...”

Captain Sommers closed the covers of the log book. Both men were agile enough. A loose barrel of whiskey would never have reached the edge of the stream.

*　　　*　　　*　　　*　　　*

Whisps of white smoke... rising above the tree tops across the Yellow Dog were in evidence every day. The Holyoke crew quickly discovered they alone did not breathe the pure air of the district. On surrounding forties of land homesteaders had rooted themselves, some fencing in portions of their property with split wooden rails. There were the Dolan's, the Kelso's, the large Holmstrom family. Stig Nilssen, who batched. They were respectable people, open hearted and religious. All had left foreign soil for America in search of a better life. The Dolan's and Holmstrom's had arrived together and had purchased forties of land adjacent the Yellow Dog. Stig Nilssen's property, and Kelso's, adjoined Holmstrom's, though not touching the

49

stream. It pleased Captain Sommers that the homesteaders could supply Charlie's larder with dairy products, and garden produce, and the homesteaders were eager to sell for ready cash.

Most intrigued were the homesteaders, and thoroughly pleased, when they stood on the sandy shore of the stream one warm evening. Observing the smooth operation of Jed's latest engineering feat. Transportation across the Yellow Dog without a boat! What a wonderful contraption! This smart young prospector was full of good ideas! He's all right, they were beginning to think. How useful it would be, when so often the fast current would push their light crafts far off course. Simply constructed it was. A combination of pulleys and a cable, suspended across the water, from which suspension hung a board seat to hold one passenger. By working the cable with alternating hand movements one could easily transport himself across the water.

Eric Kelso, his golden curls clinging tight to his tanned face, was swaying in the seat, dangling his legs over the shallow water. His face reflected the thrill of his first crossing. "It works good!" he hollered to everybody watching from shore. "It's really fun!" Looking at his sister he shouted, "Petra! C'mon try it!"

Petra's face lit up. Unhesitatingly she left Stig's side, fast walked the short distance to the water's edge and gracefully slipped her slim body onto the seat. She tucked in excess material of her full skirt, looked back, her eyes glistening with excitement. "Here I go!" And with that smoothly pulleyed herself to the opposite shore.

Smiling and happy. All but Stig Nilssen, looking on unmoved. Watching coolly and without comment, himself not in the least impressed.

Jed's eyes were glued on Petra's back. Petra! The fair haired girl he had caught in his scope lens when he first searched the hills. His eyes lingered on her form, and he

50

knew it was not all gold that glistened.

She was delicate featured, of average height, willowy.

He steadied the cable while she alit from the seat. She was quite sunbrowned for so early in the summer. Her natural blond hair was gathered at the base of her neck by a clasp, her wide spread blue eyes shone with a light of contentment. Her clothing, washed so often in home made soap that the colors failed to hold true, fitted her symmetrically. She stood barefoot, and in harmony with the rest of her body, her bronzed feet showed of beauty.

Jed took note. Her hands were without rings.

*   *   *   *   *

It was to the Kelso homestead, inhabited by people of Finnish descent, that Jed's trips for eggs and butter increased. Pa Kelso, a widower left with two small sons and a daughter, always welcomed him with warmth. He was a small, wiry man of bubbling spirit, whose physical endurance at hard work measured that of bigger men. He spoke Finn-English heavily accented. His working attire consisted of overalls, much too large, pulled in at the waist by a belt. A shirt buttoned right tight at the neck. His feet shod with heavy cowhide shoes. He walked with a slight sort of swagger. Pa Kelso was proud of the two story log house he had built and the sauna serving bath needs for his family and neighbors. He was proud of his children, his two horses and jersey cow Daisy.

Jed Carter diagnosed Pa Kelso as a gem in the rough. He was the homesteaders' doctor, curing their various ailments with his home boiled concoctions of herbs and roots and various barks. Occasionally the only therapy he recommended for an ailment was a long session in the sauna. Pa was a fair fiddler, and a story teller with his dry humor kindling his narratives.

Pa had one most prized possession. A black steel ball, weighing over 200 pounds, so Pa claimed, which rested by the side of the wood shed. How it ended up on Pa's land was a secret Pa hadn't revealed. Many men tried, but found they could raise the ball off the ground only slightly. All the brawn of Mikko Rymponen could but raise it two feet and at that just for a matter of seconds. Nobody but Pa Kelso himself could conquer the weight, and Pa had the power to raise it chest high. Never was he more in his glory, when amongst men guests at his home, he alone could raise the ponderous weight to any appreciable height. He'd steady it, at chest height, and smugly look into the eyes of those who failed to perform the feat.

"I say, an not change mind," Kelso had said to Jed, which same words had been previously iterated to other men. "No man theenk 'bout marry Petra vat no can leeft ball high as me... No leeft ball high - no marry my Petra, I say."

Yet Jed Carter soon found out. Something important and exciting was scheduled to take place at the Kelso homestead. The opening of a school for the first time in the district. Pa Kelso had propositioned the School Commissioner with the idea that school be held in his home, and the school board liked the idea. Pa Kelso had but a few years of schooling back in the old country, though he learned to read and write. Notwithstanding he was a strong believer in education and felt that all children should be schooled at least an average amount. And that the children in the district should be no exception. Schooled properly, with books and pencils and writing paper. It was the largest room upstairs of his log home he offered for the purpose. This very day, lanky Mr. Slocum, the commissioner, had rode out with preliminary information. Mr. Slocum was an important man who carried the responsibility of managing school finances and hiring of teachers.

"Mr. Kelso. I'm most happy to inform you that nine children will be attending school here this fall, ten if Jorn Holmstrom changes his mind. At sixteen, Jorn thinks he's too big to be schooling himself alongside little ones. We have contracted the services of a young lady, Florence Neeley, to teach the winter term. She had considerable talent and will train obedience and motivate minds. She'll be a great influence in molding character, and seeing that in each child there will be an acquisition of knowledge."

The full meaning of the commissioner's words passed over Pa Kelso's head, yet he understood them to mean well. "Dat's goot," he replied with a twinkle in his eyes. "Ve be ready ven you say. No vorry, Mr. Schoolman. Ve lock them kids upstairs and nobuty come down till he read goot."

*　　*　　*　　*　　*

If there was no need to go to the Kelso homestead, Jed Carter began making a need, hoping he could get to know Petra better. Timo and Eric warmed up fast. Petra - such not the case. Her lukewarmness toward him held steadfast. Jed wondered. Was it that she just chose to hold her distance with strangers?

When she spoke to him her accented words were friendly but few.

She kept a shiny clean house. Often during hours of leisure she would seat herself at mother's small loom still set up in the living room and continue her weaving on the colorful wool wall hanging. Not an ordinary weave, she made clear to Jed when he fingered the partially finished product, but a Finnish traditional weave which her skilled mother had taught her. Resulting in a designed double reversible fabric.

Jed lingered, one evening, watching her hands move in coordination with her feet working four pedals, seeing Petra's original design slowly evolve. His heart telling him to edge over and sneak his arms around her.

He had loved others, not so many that he couldn't remember them all. Yet Petra, delightfully sweet a girl. Nineteen years of age, Timo had revealed.

The wild thought struck that someday he just might marry her. Yep, he mused. A man could have the pick of the female crop around him and never be obsessed with a haunting charm like Petra's.

*   *   *   *   *

Though a disturbing certainty was in evidence. Stig Nilssen presented himself quite often at the home, in the capacity of being more than just a good neighbor. That Stig's heart was set on Petra became clearer to Jed every day. Stig was hauling rock almost daily, for a foundation of a new dwelling situated but a stone's throw from his present above.

The handwriting was on the wall, but Jed tried hard not to read it.

Jed's unexpected presence one afternoon at the homestead had almost interrupted Stig and Petra in the midst of tender embrace but he managed to leave unnoticed. Today again Stig was a visitor. Comfortably slouched on a bench by the kitchen doorway, his hands tucked in his overall pockets, his feet outright. His possessive eyes on Petra, at the cookstove, boiling fat to make soap. Jed casually studied the strapping, ruddy cheeked neighbor, whose straight hair fell from beneath a beaten cap pushed backward. His attempted discourse with Stig, touching on what kind of house plan he had in mind fizzled to naught, Stig's reserve letting it be known he chose not to talk about anything personal.

Despite how things seemed to be, beginning with Jed Carter's first appearance when he waited for eggs by the doorway, and throughout the weeks that followed, Petra found her thoughts becoming tangled.

She always awaited Stig's visits. But lately more so those of the prospector! She thought. How foolish of me! He's a stranger. Am I losing my mind?

Outstretched on an upper bench in the hot sauna, her bare arms over her head, Petra meditated amid clouds of moist steam.

Stig. Kind and sincere. Nothing about him she disliked. Problems were nothing at all when Stig made an appearance. Time and again, Pa mentioned their good fortune in having Stig as a neighbor.

She remembered that day last summer. Stig came upon the boys trying to burn out a wasp nest beneath a window ledge in back of the house, using a fiery kerosene soaked rag tied on the end of a stick, and the window ledge already smoking and blackened. Stig helped father break in a horse. He showed the boys how to take trout from the creek which cut through his field. Dear Stig! Last Christmas he had bought her a pair of ice skates and when the ice on the Yellow Dog became thick and clear he had taught her how to skate.

She closed her eyes.

But this gold prospector. He was excitingly different! He had a clear thinking mind. Never complaining, everything always good. At ease with new friends. He said please, and thank you. He thoroughly enjoyed every minute of living. She liked his perpetual reckless smile.

Last week as she was climbing the ridge to put some wild flowers on mother's grave, she liked the pleasantness of his voice calling her name, the sight of his straight form running across the field to catch up with her.

"Petra! Are you still alive in there? Pa said I should come check on you!"

She opened her eyes. It was Eric hollering to her from outside. She sat up, interpreting her heartbeat - Jed Carter was kindling her inside with new love.

"Petra....!"

She opened the window of the steam room and stuck her head outside. "I'm alive!"

*   *   *   *   *

A long week passed. A dreadfully long week in Petra's life before Jed came by, this time to have a butter crock

55

filled. Again, one of those uneasy situations came into existence, when she found herself entirely alone in the house with him. Pa had gone into town, to make applicatioin for citizenship papers, taking Timo and Eric with him. She endured an uncomfortable moment when he took the crock from her hands and his fingers overlapped hers, and her heartbeat gained erratic momentum. She turned aside, headed straight for the cookstove and though no need began poking at the fire. Without lifting his eyes off her sunkissed hair he methodically set the crock down on the table. A few quiet steps, and he stood behind her, and his strong arms encircled her slim body. He kissed her softly, lingeringly, on the back of the neck. She slid the stove lid into place, rent herself loose of his grip, plainly disturbed. She reeled to face him, simultaneously a flushed look of annoyance worked over her face.

"You'd better git yerself to the doctor 'cause yer arms ain't in place."

Jed grinned sheepishly. "Ever give thought I could change your life?"

"I have a good life."

And Jed Carter sensed, that it was with effort that her voice took firmness, that her words were not from her heart. He mused to himself. "Lil Finn gal. Haven't come close to reading you yet." He reached for the crock and tucked it in the crook of his arm, then pushed the door wide open and squinted into the sunlight. He pulled down the brim of his hat till it touched his eyebrows, then looked back and regarded her for a moment.

"I expect to kiss you again."

He waited, but she answered not a word.

*   *   *   *   *

Just as Captain Sommers had promised, the pay at the workings was ready cash on the right days. At mealtime second and third helpings of good victuals were devoured, and the loggers stayed on.

Best of all they liked working for Captain Sommers. He was a big man, a steady man, who knew from hour to hour how operations were going. He issued orders clear and firm, but was particular how a job was done. He was slow to anger, he was patient and kindhearted. He asked no more of a man than he was willing to give himself. Every evening, after the supper meal was consumed he joined his men in the cookhouse for a snort of pure whiskey.

The weeks passed with smooth progress. The hot summer sun beat down on the land, slowing the movements of the men, still work was moving at a pace better than hoped for. Captain Sommers was plenty satisfied with the clearing of timber. Vegetation around the site was burned off to keep chance fires from creating devastation. Two large bunkhouses were half completed. Clem Copley and Bill Worthington, professional mining engineers from Minnesota, were mapping the adit, in complete accord with Captain Sommers, that the terrain was most favorable for a horizontal tunnel which would ultimately connect with shafts, and that a tunnel likewise would eliminate any problems of surface water.

After sunset of each day, Captain Sommers took care that facts and figures were carefully recorded in the log books.

It was the first Monday in June when the restlessness of the crew in getting after the ore began to reach the point of appeasement. With the breaking of dawn they rose to another day's labor, to bear down on the work of stripping the earth from the side of the cliff where the adit was marked.

Come sundown, a meeting of the engineers was imminent.

The cleaned wall was traversed in every direction with veins of quartz, making it difficult to determine what dip predominated.

The original plan held firm, the adit would be driven on the vein at the foot of the cliff.

In the days that followed, a grimy faced crew put full strength on the hand drills. Boring holes deep into the rock, struggling to free the drills. Rotating men when strength sapped to maintain progress. It was slow work, work comprised of intervals of exhausting physical labor and intervals of rest. Every man worked for all that was in him, Clem Copley and Bill Worthington taking no exception of themselves and availing themselves to jobs of common labor when needed.

With each passing day the sun became decidedly hotter. Sand flies attacked their bodies where flesh showed, puffing their ears, welting the tender skin about their eyes causing more than one eye to go near shut. But it wasn't all bad. After Charlie's supper meal they would soak their welts in the sauna and for hours later enjoyed swigs of whiskey from the keg. Scattered around on rough plank benches in the cookhouse they drank, inevitably the harder work hours of the day came into discourse.

On this particular day it would have been Jed's preference not to leave the workings at all, holes were being charged for blasting, but Charlie's urgent plea for a tankful of milk could no way be overlooked. Charlie, who had reservations about the merits of the cable operation, who doubted its safety, and found one reason after another for not trying it out.

At the Kelso homestead Petra was busy cleaning out the hen house. Jed waited while Pa Kelso finished setting gopher traps by the roothouse. On the return trip the filled milk tank hooked beneath the board seat swayed freely with each tug on the cable.

Midway across the stream there was a thump in the earth, another thump, another. A gigantic upshooting of rock and dirt, then smoke blackened the air over the workings. Jed winced. His sweaty hands eased their grip on the cable. The first blast!

At the water's edge he took a stand beside Clem Copley who was wiping dirt from the corners of his eyes.

"All the charges go off?" inquired Jed.

Copley blew clear his nose into a wrinkled bandana. "Enough for a goddam good blast. Near perfect adit far as we can make out right now. Pretty close to our calculations." Clem paused, looking self pleased, packed a chew of tobacco in his cheek. "Soon's the smoke settles down we'll move that loose rock and jest keep agoing with the powder. Hell can't stop us now."

For days on end. Days that quickly blended into weeks, the crew taxed every muscle and bone in their bodies. Getting up at the crack of dawn they labored the daylight hours away. Clawing into the bluff till almost sundown, drilling holes and packing them with black powder. Touching fuses with candle power till they spit to life. Then skeltering to high ground and blocking their ears when the blasts went off. Tramming the broken rock with wheelbarrows.

Earth and loose rock stripped from the wall had been hauled to the shore of the Yellow Dog specifically to serve as a base for the stockpile. Smiles were growing bigger and every man looking self pleased with construction of wooden rails spanning the distance from the face of the workings to the landing. During which days Worthington and Copley concentrated their efforts on getting fresh air pumped into the adit. Their experiences in other mines were put into good practice. A large blower operated by hand was firmly secured to the ground outside the adit.

*   *   *   *   *

Tram cars began rolling, carrying jagged ore chunks and fine dirt to the stock site. Sporadically now, Jed Carter found himself musing on matters other than gold,

59

his attention to important work being frequently diverted by the whisp of smoke, rising from the vicinity of the Kelso homestead. Oh well, he mused. Every occupation has its ramifications.

Blasts echoing through the valley stirred the curiosity of the homesteaders. By rowboat, by cable, they crossed the Yellow Dog, whole families, or singly. Mining was something new, and they stood as near the workings as Captain Sommers permitted them. They wandered over the stockpile, turning over chunks of ore to catch their first glimpse of gold. With Captain Sommers approval they carried to their small craft chunks of rejected quartz for building fireplaces in their homes.

But Petra was never among them.

CHAPTER 5
A Night In Town

It was the middle of June. Close to noon hour of the day, with work moving routinely in the tunnel. The thirty foot mark had been logged. A crew of ten grimy faced men, clad in wool shirts, canvas pants and slouch caps was scraping up broken ore by flickering candle light. Shoveling it into a wooden tram which would set another day's record. One more load, and they would knock off for noon victuals.

The tram was heaped, the men drew back and gestured to let it roll. Dan at the controls released the brakes, the wheels began to turn. Briefly light that infiltrated the excavation was cut off when the tram passed through the entrance.

The diggers flung their tools aside and stumbled out between the rails, their footsteps slipping in oozy muck. A few, with long swinging gaits stepped on the sills where the track was laid. Once outside they blinked to the brightness of daylight. Captain Sommers was waiting for them, resting against a wheelless tram pulled off to one side, rubbing his stubbled jaw with the edge of his thumb. Sighting his men he stood erect resting his open hands on his hips. His face showed definite smugness.

"Got one helluva good report on the trial run sent out last week!" Mouths dropped open and eyes fired up. The diggers drew near Sommers knowing he never minced words. Captain Sommers reached into the breast pocket of his shirt for a folded paper. He opened it and proceeded to read aloud.

"Sixty-six tons of rock tested. Total in bullion $453.19, of which $443.67 is gold, the balance silver, the gold being 69.7 fine. Total loss as shown on the tailings is $2.16 per ton of which 12¢ is silver. The quartz also shows the presence of copper, lead and galena in spectromatic traces."

He creased the paper on its original folds and put it back into his pocket. "That gold reading certainly means something! And the silver reading damn surprising. Lab tests from Philadelphia last month didn't show much silver. I'll break it nice and gentle. Holyoke stock is gonna be one of the hottest selling stocks in the country!"

Ikey responded. In his usual matter-of-fact tone of voice. "So that means better go fire up the sauna..."

"Eh...?" Though Captain Sommers kind of knew what Ikey was driving at.

"Man!" added Ikey. "It's a helluva good day to celebrate. Gotta scrub up and go to the Black Bear to give Nick some business."

"Yea, yea, a helluva good day!" one of the diggers hollered out. Then the chant began. "Yea, yea, a helluva good day! Yea, yea..."

And with that they clamored up the hill toward the cookhouse to seek mid-day bread and salt pork, giving Captain Sommers no opportunity for rebuttal.

Jed Carter stood in the adit of the tunnel gazing into the dark opening. If Gramp were here.... he would write him first chance. Tell him how well things were going!

*   *   *   *   *

The sun was lowering in the West like a red ball of fire when their wagons rolled into town. Main Street was

62

swarming with activity, jammed with vehicles and people. At close quarters wagon wheels snubbed against wagon wheels as wended the road, churning up the red dust of the soil.

"Hey Pa! Pa!" Nels kids were calling to him. He spotted his wife holding their youngest, and leaped down from the wagon to join her. The wagons paralleled the Holyoke office, where the rest of the diggers jumped down from the wagons leaving Ikey and Mikko at the reins. Syd was still working, when he recognized the gang he hustled to the open doorway to holler out his hulloa. At the livery the horses were reined in. Jake was busy shoveling horse droppings, and the heavy scent of his work permeated the unmoving air. The drivers leaped down from their seats.

Mik raised his voice. "Hulloa, Jake! What say you take care of a couple of horses and wagons tonight?"

Jake lazily set aside his shovel. Hands in his baggy hip pockets, he turned a chew of tobacco over in his cheek. Not a muscle in his face moved when he spoke. "Yer outa luck, digger. Askin' too much."

Mik sent a hard slap to Jake's shoulder. "Aw, come on now you liniment stinking horse keeper. That's no way to make talk to a friend."

"You should know on parade nights the wagon shed gets jammed full. Set 'em over by the tracks. Won't cost ya nothin'."

Mik spat on the ground. "Not these horses and wagons. Not by a long shot! Last time over there some nut swiped the wagon and ran the wind out of the horse. Almost killed her."

Ikey reached under his wagon seat for a hidden bottle of whiskey. He stuck it in Jake's hand. "It's all yours, Jake. Jest keep an eye on the horses and wagons."

Jake's face showed life at last. His eyes moved upon sight of spirits and he grinned, a toothless grin. He looked at the label on the bottle, pulled the cork and took

63

a swig. "I'll roll some wagons outa the barn and put yers in."

As they trooped back toward Main Street the siren on top of the town hall began whining out the eight o'clock hour. It sounded every evening at eight, giving notification of the closing of shops. Now from the direction of the hotel could be heard the steady beating of drums. Mik and Ikey elbowed their way into the crowds standing by the bank, brushing shoulders with all the other parade viewers. They caught sight of Jim and Alex who had made contact with their families.

The parade had already started moving while they had been dickering with Jake, and the air was thickening with red dust. A brass band passed by, neatly uniformed, but frightful in performance. Another brass group clad in plain street clothes paraded stiffly by. Members of the Scandinavian Society marched in dignity, as did other groups - the Pedestrian Club, the Sons of this and Sons of that, their leaders proudly carrying colorful banners before them with insignia of their organizations pinned on their shirts. The tail end of the parade was comprised of bicycles, rigged in contorted shapes by wire frameworks. Fitted with lanterns illuminating the early darkness. There were Japanese lanterns, railroad lanterns, plain candle lit lanterns. One bicycle rigged up with a dozen lanterns took fire when a tossed match found its target.

The parade ended and the hundreds of onlookers dispersed. Some heading straight for home with their kids, others choosing to remain in small groups to chat. Darkness was taking hold of the land, save where poles on some corners shone faint circles of light. Dan and Ike began walking in the direction of Lil's place. Bill Worthington and Clem Copley held their pace to scan a billing nailed on a lamp post, telling of the Paris Gaiety Girls who had just hit town. The billing gave the girls a big build-up - "a classy singing and dancing act. A good group and their specialties "out of sight". Coincidence or not, a pert young lass from nearby Coyuta with whom Mikko had been occasionally keeping company, who had formed the habit of showing up in town very frequently in hopes of crossing Mik's path, found luck with her tonight. She stood at Mik's side, smilingly holding his hand, then together they disappeared into the darkness.

Sam's barber shop adjacent the bank still showed light. Jed ran his fingers over his ragged sideburns, sauntered to the shop doorway where he greeted Ed Morley exiting the shop spruced up with a fresh pompadour. Jed entered, leaving behind the rest of the crew who took the beaten route to the Black Bear saloon. The Black Bear, where liquor was cheap. Built on the very spot where a Chippewa lad had come to an untimely death by the claws of a bleeding pain-frenzied bear.

In the barber shop Jed waited his turn in the chair, but time was not long. Patrons pressed him for news from the mine and a stockholder, recognizing him through the window came in to inquire how things were going. Sam neglected his lathered customer to gaze at length, at the specimens Jed held in his hand. Sam had the reputation of being the best conversationalist in town, and when Jed took his turn in the chair Sam's tongue reached an apex of discourse.

"...more families got off the morning train... sure hope the fellas find work.... Did'ja hear that some of the shops will be closing on Sundays from now on so's everybody can get in a little hunting and fishing. That poor widow Lindstrom over in the Salsburg location. She sure had tough luck last night. Some damn crook stole sixteen of her best chickens and left the heads in the coop... hard to believe that anybody could be so bloody mean. And jist listen to this... jist this afternoon Thor Blumstrom saw a man carrying a black suitcase, going house to house knocking on the doors, and he's dead sure it's Von Muller back in town...."

The removal of the fuzz on the sideburns took little time, but Sam showed no intent of releasing his special customer. When he turned his back to reach for a bottle of sweet smelling lotion Jed took the opportunity to whip the towel from his neck. He stepped down from the chair and flipped Sam a coin for his fees. "Been real nice talking to you, Sam, real nice..."

The sky was starless, the street dark. He stood on the edge of the walk, observing people entering a listing building directly across the street. All six windows on the face of the two story structure shone light. Music from within was escaping through the open doorway. He crossed the street, to read the handscrawled sign in one of the windows.

Big Dance Tonight   Promoted by
Sons of Sweden
Lunch   25¢   Surprises

The music within ceased. A medley of laughter and men's boisterous talk and women's shrill voices cluttered his ears. He put an eye to a knothole but could make out little inside.

Disinterested, more or less. He pocketed his hands and headed toward the Black Bear. But a hundred feet he paced, past two buildings recently destroyed by fire, as far as an adjoining lot filled with buggies and rigs. A loving couple brushed by, he glanced back as they entered the dance hall. Not giving himself any time to think, he retraced his steps and followed them in.

It was a lively place, reeking in smoke. Crowded with males and females obviously having the time of their lives. Flags of America and Sweden hung from the ceiling. On one side of the room was a plank table well stacked with grub. There was the "Watering Hole", tended by a shy skinny girl, her shiny golden hair flowing onto a shapeless body. Her attire was entirely Scandinavian. Busy she was, dipping a ladle into the

66

"water hole" to quench the thirst of dry throated dancers.

Jed Carter skirted the edge of the floor, acknowledging greetings from several acquaintances. In a corner stall sat a Madam Shavitsky, a clairvoyant, with a clear glass ball set before her. She managed to attract Jed's attention and her raspy voice called out. "Let me tell you your past, your present, your future, young man. Let me cure your corns and bunions or whatever ailments you have."

Jed responded with a grin. "No troubles, thank you."

"Let me tell you about the girl you will marry." Jed kept moving. Persistent, but then it was her livelihood.

A fiddler and banjo player situated on a platform took command. Jed leaned his back against a wall to watch the carefree, laughing couples swirling in the center of the floor. The mood of the place was beginning to catch, unconsciously his foot beat the rhythm.

A twosome, of very special interest swept by...Petra Kelso in the arms of Stig. There was bright sparkle in her eyes, she was smiling big, really enjoying herself, mused Jed. Stig was holding her close.. too close. Jed rolled a cigarette, he put a light to it and drew smoke slowly.

Now a big burly man, a character he'd never seen before, passed directly in front of him. He was supporting a wooden tub on a shoulder heaped with odd shaped packages tied up in store paper. The man moved to the musician's platform and eased the tub down. The music stopped. The burly fella looked over the crowd, he clapped his hands loudly to attract everybody's attention. He raised his square jaw.

"Attention! A-ten-shun, ev-ra-body!" His voice boomed to the far corners and the laughter and drone of voices transformed to a semi-quiet.

"Ev-ra-body clear the floor so's we kin git on with the s'prises we promised ya tonight. We're gonna have an auction, folks. A real, genuine auction. In this here tub are lots of s'prises. All carefully weighted up at one pound each. Yep. Egg-zactly one pound each package. Each package going to the highest bidder. Each s'prise must be opened for all to appreciate."

For a while the presence of Petra and Stig eluded Jed's mind. The auction was turning out to be more than amusing. One by one, the auctioneer held the packages high above his head, for all to see the shapes and sizes, shaking and rattling each package to promote interest and suspense. Bidding became furious, and when a package shaped much like a broom was held aloft two men well affected by intoxicants fisted one another for possession of it. The contents of the packages varied, some containing kindling wood, soup bones, nails. "Something for your garden!" the auctioneer called out, and Stig was high bidder. A pound of dirt!

The tub was emptied. "Now fer the grand s'prise of the evening. Every lady here is gonna be a winner. Every lady here now has the privilege of choosing the partner of her liking for the remainder of the night's dancing.

A wild flash jolted Jed's mind. Maybe Petra had noticed his presence. Though she seldom took her eyes off Stig for long. He bit his lip hopefully.

A light hand fell on his shoulder. He turned. She was auburn haired, a green eyed five two, curved in the right places. Her face was heavily powdered and tinted with artificial coloring but her efforts failed to conceal deep seated wrinkles on her forehead. The low cut neckline of her crisp cotton dress could not be overlooked. She had the appearance of being thirtyish in years.

Her soft manicured hand lingered on his shoulder. "Ain't seen you dancing, handsome." Her voice was coarse, as though touched with sandpaper. "Anyhow, honey. I'm gonna change that 'cause yer the partner of my choice."

Jed Carter removed his hat and set it atop the flat room of the "Watering Hole." He reached in a hip pocket for a bandana and wiped his forehead. Not long could he deliberate, for her outstretched arms were pulling him toward the center of the floor.

In his arms she was as light as a feather.

They whirled round and round, through the hazes of smoke. Brushing by Stig and Petra, whose faces showed surprise. Again around the floor, by the Watering Hole Petra's eyes met Jed's over Stig's shoulder and her lips formed a smile. Stig saw it too, and drew her closer.

Beads of perspiration matted his forehead and he was glad when the music stopped. The shapely creature clutching his arm began talking.

"Yer new in the territory, ain't cha? Though I seen ya around with those Holyoke guys. So... what's yer name?"

"Jed Carter."

"I'm Blanche." She set her green eyes on his windburned face, then drew a deep breath and smiled from one corner of her small mouth. "Woman's intuition tells me we could become good friends." She paused awaiting his response which failed to come. "Yer quiet. But I kinda like yer approach."

The smell of food reached their nostrils. "... hungry?" she asked.

He smiled politely, nodded negatively. He became aware of uneven streaks of color in her hair, the result of dye. She slipped an arm comfortably through his. "If you ain't got nothin' better to do, then we'll go to my flat for a drink. It ain't very far. Besides, a breath of fresh air will do us both good."

Once more he wiped sweat from his brow. His eyes searched out Petra, and Petra's eyes were on him. She winked. He thought. Was she playing games like the girls back home did? He took his hat from its resting place. "The idea of a drink suits me fine. Just fine."

They walked down the middle of the road, unsettling the dust, her hand tucked under his bent arm. Few words were exchanged. The clouds had separated and a half moon and scattered stars broke the darkness of the sky.

Her body nudged his, to follow a road branching off Main. They climbed the loosely attached stairway on the side of a shop which led to her flat. At the top of the flight she reached in her bosom for a key, unburied it. She fitted the key in the lock, lifted the latch and pushed the door open.

Jed Carter scratched a match on a thumbnail to break a light. A round table set in the middle of the room held a lamp, he raised the chimney and put a flame to the wick. Glow of the light overcame the darkness and his eyes absorbed the layout. None too fancy, for a woman, with no hint of freshness in the air.

Blanche flung her handbag on the table top. Quite routinely she moved to the one window in the room, opened it wide and pulled down the torn shade. Not talking, she crossed the wooden floor to the opposite side of the room and from a ricketty cupboard took two drinking glasses, from a curtained enclosure underneath the sink she retrieved a full bottle of brandy. A black cat appearing from nowhere curled its body around the back of her legs. She picked it up, talked to it affectionately, then shooed it outside.

Now she was standing near, very near, her fingertips resting on his shoulder blades. He swallowed deep, and suggested a drink.

*   *   *   *   *

The brandy had been potent. He didn't know what time it was when he looked around for his hat. Not that the time mattered much. At the doorway his arms encircled her warm body once more, he said he'd see her again. Simultaneously he pressed some greenbacks into the palm of her hand.

The stairway was shaky under his descending weight and he hung onto the side rail for support. Three

.70

oversized men passing the front of the shop observed his descent. One snorted his query, "did she entertain you good?"

"She never short-changes anybody," piped another. Jed answered not, but cut the street diagonally.

Time to be catching up with the diggers. Nevertheless he maintained a slow pace, drawing deep the night air. The street was deserted, save for a small group of men standing outside a saloon enjoying the fisticuffs of two inebriated patrons.

He passed the dance hall, now completely darkened... every lady a winner...

Outside the Black Bear a half dozen black clad Good Templars were stoically parading. Holding high on sticks their printed placards - 'Drink Not Once Lest You Thirst For More'. He was stopped in his path of travel by one of the marchers. She loosened the drawstring on her black beaded purse, took out a card and shoved it into his hand.

"Sign this, young man. For your own good. For the salvation of your soul."

"Might you tell me just what it is?" asked Jed.

"A pledge card. Promising that you will abstain from use of all intoxicating beverages for life or down to two years time."

Jed fingered the card, then slipped it into a shirt pocket. The Crusader didn't approve and became more determined. She released a scornful sniff and shook a finger under his nose.

"Put not off till tomorrow what should be attended to today!"

A second Crusader closed in to rally support to the cause. "My neighbor sold his wife's coat for spirits while she was on her death bed. Take warning, young man. Don't go in there and get full and foolish."

During the discourse Jallu and John, both a little

under the weather, had come out of the saloon seeking fresh air. They held ground close by, listening to the message of the Crusaders as best as they could.

"My brother shinged the pledge an' he never schmiled agen," mumbled John in a thickened tongue.

Jallu was having trouble holding his head straight. "Never told me ya had a sad brodder."

The Crusaders dropped to their knees and prayed that the sinners within the walls of the saloon be forgiven. Their mission complete, they picked up their signs and disappeared in the darkness. Jed walked through the open door of the saloon followed by John and Jallu.

The air was heavy with the odor of stale beer. A barmaid at the piano was plunking out some tinny music. Her eyes lit on Jed and followed him, when he seated himself amongst the Holyoke diggers she abandoned the extra curricular work of her trade. She stood by his side, then slid her voluptuous body onto his lap. Her white arm encircled his neck.

"Mister, I like your looks."

Jed looked at Dan and put on an arrogant grin.

"Yes sir! You're my type of guy - I knew you were the one the minute you walked in. Now Nick, the proprietor, was beckoning the barmaid back to her duties. She pinched Jed's cheek. "Don't you dare go away, handsome. Cuz I'm comin' back. I promise."

Some of the diggers emitted low moans of envy.

"You get 'em every time," drooled Dan.

"Lady killer Carter," quipped Bill Worthington. He was tilted on the back legs of his chair, with a large brown teddy bear resting on his lap.

Jed twisted his face upon sight of the stuffed bear. "Thought you guys went over to see the girly show. What in the hell is that?"

Bill Worthington directed his chew into the brass cuspidor. He reached in a vest pocket and tossed a ticket stub on the table top. "We hit the girly show, all right.

Enjoyed front row seats."

"Don't tell me that guys who been living in coyote country found girls not to your liking?" questioned Jed.

"Liked them? We loved them! They were putting on one helluva good show. Nobody would ever argue that. Whistles, hats waving. They were pretty babes! Had to grab Clem's suspenders a couple of times to keep him from leaping right up on stage. Yep. Everybody whistling. Hollering for more ..."

Jed was interested. "So.."

"So the lead gal comes out. Prancing! Shaking! Announces her next specialty. Then a crash like the building falling in. An axe shows through the side door and Malaroni and his men charge in. Right up on stage. Hustled the gals off to the lockup."

Jed nodded sympathetically. "And that teddy bear....?"

Bill Worthington almost fell from his tippy chair. "Cripes. It was the bloody door prize."

* * * * *

The barmaid was pounding the keys of the piano as though retaliating to Nick's reprimand, and noise of the patrons drowned out Dan's holler to Nick for more beer. Nick couldn't hear. Dan got up and went over to where Nick was wiping a beer stained table. Reaching out a browned, muscular arm, he snapped Nick's suspender.

"My friends are thirsty, Nick. I'll pay this round."

Nick was a short, stocky man in his middle years, always immaculately groomed, identified by a white apron tied around his paunchy mid-section. "Be right wid ya Danny boy," he responded, pouring the remains of a mug into a patron's glass. He disappeared briefly, then reappeared at the Holyoke table with pitchers of beer in each hand. He set them down, with a firm forefinger he tapped Dan's shoulder, his voice was taunting. "An how you pay for thees, ma boy? Wid da cash or da nugget?" He proceeded to wipe up the table.

"You reech gold deegers. You make da mon so queeck!"

Dan dug deep for some greenbacks and handed them over to Nick. "Cash tonight, cold cash." Nick rubbed the bills between his stubby fingers. "Beeg money. I go getta you change."

The beer flowed freely. Stories were told, all ending in guffaws of laughter. Ikey observed Jed, whose habitual fun making antics had gradually recessed to a mien of near silence. Ikey's fingers drummed the table top, sensing that all was not good.

"Yer not talkin' much, pard."

Jed reached for his beer and took a deep swallow. He set down the glass and wiped his mouth with the back of his hand. He spoke low.

"That pair of bums... on the far end of the bar... Bart Fauquier and that light-fingered foreman of his. They've been looking this way for quite a spell now... matter of fact, they're headed this way. Could be trouble. Bart's known to be tough as all hell."

"Full of rotten blood," mumbled Ikey, watching their approach from a corner of an eye. "Blew up a guy's sawmill last week and dynamited two beaver dams. Kin shoot good with either hand. Malaroni's even 'fraida talk to iim. Bart loses his temper easy."

"Speaking of Malaroni," interrupted Jed. "Why in the hell does he always wear a glove on his left hand?"

"He's branded!" knowingly responded Ikey to the query. "They say he was a prisoner back in his old country."

Their talk ceased when they became aware of Bart Fauquier and his foreman standing near. Bart was holding a black iron arrow, his fingers sliding over the length of it.

The diggers all knew. 'Old Ish' had been robbed!

Bart calmly raised a boot to a rung on Bill Worthington's chair. He scanned the contented faces around the table, and a sneery expression crept over his

74

own. Stretching a hairy arm across Worthington's face he helped himself to a cigar protruding from Copley's pocket, placed it carelessly in the corner of his mouth and took a long time lighting it. He blew smoke across the table, then extended an immense hairy hand to pour some beer. Drained the glass. Then jerked a head motion toward Spud, his appointed foreman and bodyguard.

"Jest help yerself, Spud. The diggers are buying tonight." Bart's hands continued to stroke the full length of the iron arrow, his newly acquired possession.

Spud obeyed like a trained dog.

Clem Copley was in no way amused with the activity taking place. "You're quenching your thirst at the wrong table."

Jed released his thoughts. "That arrow. There's only one place it belongs!"

A malicious smile curled Bart's lips. "Will make a very nice decoration in my quarters."

Bart was a big man of dark complexion. He had a muscled face, sharp piercing steel eyes. His cheeks were spotted with pock marks, and on one side of his neck was a shapeless birthmark. Unruly strands of oily hair kept falling over his forehead. He grew a trimmed moustache which followed the continuous sneer on his thick upper lip. His body was hard, his hands strong. He wore a gold ring studded with large diamonds.

Some men referred to Bart as a plain lunkhead who somewhere along the line had managed to acquire a little money by hook or crook. Mostly crook. Several men who had attempted business dealings with Bart maintained that he had a definite absence of intellect. When angered he invariably deviated from middle of the road language.

Bart stuck a hand inside his wide leather belt and his chest expanded.

"You diggers makin' big money should treat more

often. Ya know, me 'n Spud here been wonderin' how come the workings would hire a man who needs a teddy bear for comfort."

"Yer supposta remove your louse cage when addressing gentlemen," growled Ikey.

Dan shifted in his chair. "Bart, you're a loud-mouth bastard!"

Bart's face twisted. "That's a lousy remark." He looked at Bill Worthington. "Mother's darling... maybe teddy bear would look better without eyes." He held out the iron arrow for Spud to hold. With broken-nailed fingers Bart yanked out the glassy beads and with a slow deliberate aim dropped them, one by one, into the cuspidor at his feet. He spat into it. Spud looked on with approval.

Jed's eyes locked with Bart's. "I admire your brawn.."

Dan got to his feet. "You're rubbing my grain the wrong way."

Bart scowled, the cords in his neck began to swell. "What in the hell d'ya mean by that?"

Ikey was a man who liked action. He opened his mouth. "Ya ain't my boss anymore and ya ain't anyone special." He leaned over the table. He grabbed Bart by the collar and with his left hand smashed him between the eyes with a sudden right. Vulgar words left Bart's lips. Ikey's other fist made contact. Bart's head snapped back, his body bounced off the next table and he was down. Near motionless. With fists still clenched Ikey put his attention on Spud. "What in the hell you waitin' fer, small potato. The same?"

Spud didn't budge but held ground, knowing that his boss would any moment regain his feet. And Bart was up! His face was hardened. He struck a well aimed fist to Jed's jaw. "We'll tame you diggers!"

Jed threw up a protective arm too late and staggered back. Bart followed with a blow to the midriff. Jed was down, but picked himself up.

Fists flew, tables tipped over and glass clattered to the floor. Jed found his target and Bart slumped once more to the floor. He rolled over and groaned before going limp.

"Rest good, you lousy chisler!" roared Pete.

But the brawl was just beginning. Bart's men who needed job protection left their booze and came over swinging. The saloon door opened admitting Mikko who joined the fight without a bid. Fists thudded against flesh as the two gangs went to work on each other. Legs were severed from tables and chairs splintered to kindling wood. A spittoon was hurled past Jed's head. Stuffings from the brown teddy bear floated through the air. Nick was making a valiant effort to get near Dan, his hand outstretched with Dan's change. Tufts of the stuffings from the teddy bear were now resting on Nick's head and shoulder. Nick stood pleading. "Quit da fight, boys! Quit da fight! I no lika dis kine trouble!"

But the brawl continued, with an increasing number of participants, all muscular hard. Suddenly the door of the saloon burst open and a shrill whistle pierced the air. Malaroni and his men charged in and sized up the situation. There was mad scrambling toward the rear door and a loud crash. It was Bart's cronies who escaped through the much used exit, but the firm grips of Malaroni's men escorted the diggers outside. Leaving only Mikko behind, whom they well recognized and preferred not to touch. Nick followed his friends out, as did Mikko, who watched as the bruised and swollen faced, lip bleeding diggers were shoved into an enclosed wagon.

Dan's grinning face showed from the rear. "We fixed them good, Nick! Nobody licks the diggers!"

Now Ikey's head stuck out, a genuine smile on his swollen mouth. "Be seeing ya, Nick. We had a real nice time!"

A fist, gripping the black iron arrow, suddenly jutted

out from the wagon, and a voice hollered out...
"Tomorrow it'll be back where it belongs."

The back of Jed's head was throbbing and he held a hand to a bloodied nose. A disheveled and definitely drunk gentleman, slouched opposite him, was attempting to focus his half-closed eyes. "Do I looksh dishorderly. Drunk and dishorderly?" he mumbled. "Otto Von Muller never ish dishorderly. Not Dr. Otto Von Muller."

   *   *   *   *   *

It was pre-dawn at the Holyoke. Charlie rose in good spirits from a dead sleep on his makeshift bed in back of the cookhouse. He pulled on his pants, pulled up his suspenders over his underwear and laced his cowhide shoes. He took a minute to strike a match to kindling wood in the cookstove before hurriedly pacing the pathway to the outhouse. By intuition he paused to take a look in the horse shed. Empty stalls.

"Another bloody lost day," he muttered, finished his mission and went back to bed.

CHAPTER 6
Pay Dirt!

The going in the tunnel was markedly good. From the adit to a distance of thirty feet in, and the striking of a pocket of rich ore, production ran high. It took minimal time to push out the loaded cars and dump the ore on the leveled off base. The crew labored, from the depth of the face rock to the site of the infant stockpile, ten hours a day and six days a week, each man producing nearly a ton and a half each day. Only when a blast was ready to be fired did they rest outside with not much to do. Waiting for the powder smoke to evaporate, then striding back into the tunnel to muck and tram, to push the loaded cars out to the stockpile. Then to repeat the cycle all over. For days that melted into weeks they broke and shoveled ore, their muscles and bones uniting with their souls. With nobody discouraged, regardless of effort involved.

Following work orders issued by Captain Sommers, Jed Carter spent numerous days mapping the tunnel, checking the grade. Late each night in the office shack illuminated by lamplight, he pored over blueprints, sometimes listening to Captain Sommers, Clem Copley and Bill Worthington put facts and figures together.

It was Midsummer Day when Captain Sommers recorded in the log book that the one hundred ten foot mark had been reached. That the tunnel was beginning

79

to form a winding, twisting contour, that it was showing stronger than ever in rich rock. Indicating the fact that the walls consisted of hard granite with no loose rock and no timbering at this point being necessary. And of importance, that the entire distance was hollowed large enough for the men to work at an erect position and not jeopardize their physical health.

Captain Sommers itemized the negative facts. Almost a daily occurence that a loaded car or two would tip over on one of the curves. And that cars were leaving the tracks on one particular section of rails by reason of hastily laid sills causing rail joints to become separated.

*   *   *   *   *

Dusk was beginning to fall when Captain Sommers summoned Copley and Worthington to the shanty office, later to be joined by Jed, and it was nearing midnight when the lamps in the office were extinguished. Considerable discussion had taken place over the past month on more extensive development of the property, blueprints had been drawn and redrawn. Tonight all minds were in accord, there was no reason to hold back on expansion. Tomorrow ground would be broken at the staked out site beyond the bluff for the sinking of a vertical shaft. The North Beaver it was designated on the blueprints, acquiring the name from tiny Beaver Lake situated on the same forty, which shaft would ultimately intersect the ore in the tunnel.

Boss man Sommers stoked his pipe and meditated aloud. "Seen plenty of shafts sunk. Tricky work. Dangerous. Takes men with guts... ready for plenty of punishment. But Nels and Curt will hold up. Dan..John, too. Both always had shown a liking for danger.

*   *   *   *   *

The sun scorched the land and the heat in the daylight hours became almost unbearable. There wasn't enough moving air to waver the leaf of a popple. The surface crew labored in sweat wet clothing. The tunnel crew, wetter still, from continuing seepage of surface water. The shaft, six by eight in dimension was broke open, and deepened, to the ten foot mark, fifteen, the vein holding its width. Working space was afforded for only a team of two men, who alternated at holding the drill and striking it with the hammer. After the smoke of a blast had settled, men with fresh strength descended the rope ladder to hoist the broken ore in wooden buckets.

Dan emerged from the shaft, blinking to the brightness of daylight. Close by Clem Copley and Jed were kneeling, checking ore samplings, and two newly hired surface workers were wheelbarrowing waste rock aside. Not far off was John, pulling long timbers off a wagon.

Dan flung his hat to the ground and drew an arm over his dirt streaked face. He walked over for the water jug which was kept in the shade of a broken wagon and hoisted it to his parched mouth, rinsed out the dust spitting the spent water to the ground. Then swallowing a long thirst quenching guzzle. Captain Sommers appeared over a knoll with a box of powder on his shoulder which he set down near the shaft opening with care. For the shaft crew, days of late had been hard labor with but little gain in footage.

Dan's face showed concern when he addressed his boss. "The drills are struggling. The rock is a helluva lot harder than the tunnel rock. Ain't getting no tonnage even close to what's been calculated."

John let the last of the long timbers slam to the ground before taking time to adjust the bandana around his neck. His ears were swollen red from bites of mosquitoes and deer flies. He querried both Sommers and Copley. "Ya sure we gotta keep cribbin? Ask my opinion, I say that rock ain't gonna jiggle."

Clem Copley's response was instantaneous. "She'll be

cribbed, pard. All the way. Every damn foot or the Holyoke name will be mud. Can't say when, but we'll tie onto the tunnel..."

Jed butted in his opinion. "Don't anybody worry about production. When we start stoping, hell, we'll all have heavy money bags dangling on our hips."

Shouts of "hulloa's" were heard just beyond the crest. A rugged route of ascent for any man, but still preferred by most to the long roundabout wagon road winding up the side of the bluff. Syd Crawford was sighted. Game Syd, proving that men in the clerical profession weren't all weaklings.

Dan cupped his hands. "Want a rope, Syd?"

"Keep it to hang yourself," Syd hollered back. When he finally stood on the crest he was panting heavily but managed to holler out "good news!". He paused to rest for return of his wind, knowing he couldn't take it like he used to.

Syd's special trip was twofold in purpose. He had seen to it that a letter entrusted him by Thor Blumstrom addressed to Mik Rymponen was brought out. Now near the shaft opening, stumbling over crisscrossed timbers he spoke out the main reason for his unexpected presence. "The whim from Denver is in! It's spotted on the siding by the livery. One of the prettiest doggone pieces of machinery I've ever laid eyes on!"

It was word long waited.

Captain Sommers put a hand to the back of his neck and rubbed the tight cords. His eyes shifted to Dan. "Won't have to worry about tonnage. You're gonna see plenty of ore coming out of this hole pretty quick."

Had Mikko known that the letter Syd Crawford had personally delivered to the mine earlier in the day was from the manager of world wrestling champ Hans Schimmler, he would not have waited till after suppertime to read it.

"Dear Herr Rymponen," it read. "Hans Schimmler of Germany, heavyweight wrestling champion of the world, desires to match his skills with you on the canvas providing a purse of $500 is guaranteed.

If you choose to accept this challenge it is the hope of Hans Schimmler that the match be held in America. Terms: Graeco-Roman style, or catch-as-catch-can, which type can be agreed upon at a later date.

Please write of your interest in challenging the world heavyweight champion.

Yours truly,

Max Grubenstein, Manager

From the very hour on, exciting rumors rippled the area, fibers spread into town and the outside world, that the heavyweight wrestling champ of the world might be making an appearance in the district.

*　　　*　　　*　　　*　　　*

Less than a week had passed and Clem Copley and Bill Worthington had the new whim assembled and secured at the head of the shaft. It was a sound mechanism, lightweight, operated by horsepower. Its performance was flawless. The ore kept coming up, and the North Beaver deepened. Everybody in camp was cheery, above all, the shaft crew. In the evenings alongside the keg in the cookhouse, the merits of the new whim were thrashed over and over.

Dan was over sold on the new rigging. "Helluva lot easier raising them buckets by horse power than winding that bloody old hand rig."

Nor could John give it enough praise. "Pretty smart that guy who invented that friction band. Sure kin manage the bucket a lot better. Cripes, we don't need to worry about hoisting like we used to.

*　　　*　　　*　　　*　　　*

83

It was early in the evening, right after the supper meal. Captain Sommers entered the rough shanty office and sat down at the warped wooden table. For a while he studied the dates on the wall calendar, allowing a few moments of admiring appreciation to the calendar picture portraying in delicate colors a southern maiden, fittingly captioned "A Southern Rose".

He pushed aside litter from the center of the table and began writing his report for the forthcoming stockholders meeting. Briefly he wrote, then broke his train of thought to call outside to Dan passing by, about ordering more drills.

He continued his writing, when he finished he read to himself the report, half-aloud.

>According to your request I will give you my opinion concerning the result of the openings at the Holyoke property. I have examined carefully the appearance of the openings and the nature of the rock opposed. I can confidently say that I regard it as a most favorable and promising show. I do not hesitate to say, that the prospect is sufficient to warrant extensive mining operations. The shaft is sunk 15 feet, all the way through a rich vein. The vein is 7 feet wide, of which 4 feet on hanging-wall side is perfectly filled with silver-lead ore, intermixed with yellow sulphuret of copper, and appears to improve in quality as depth is obtained. Forty feet south of shaft is another vein or branch, 4 feet wide, which intersects main vein about 400 feet east of the shaft. Cross cut made at this point shows the vein to be 12 feet wide. The cross cut being obstructed with water, I could not examine the bottom, but saw good specimens lying alongside the cross cut. Seventy feet, west of the shaft, on the south branch, is another cross cut. The vein at this

point is 4 feet wide showing very rich in silver-lead ore from foot to hanging-wall. So far as I can judge from the richness of the openings for a distance of 200 feet, the many advantages which this location possesses for laying out and continuing permanent mining operations, it is almost certain that proper and judicious management will, in a comparatively short time, develop here a rich and profitable mine. Surface improvements are two log cabins, a blacksmith shop, a roothouse, and a shelter for the horses.

Yours truly,

Captain Andrew Sommers

He creased the report and slipped it inside a log book, his bronzed face looking self-pleased, brought on by a conception of work well carried through.

It had been a rough, strenuous month of heart and soul labor, testing the stamina of every man on the property. It was a slow, precarious operation. Digging with confidence into the dark bowels of the earth, penetrating deeper and deeper, unafraid, he knew, as did every man on the property, that headway could not be realized without brawn and sheer guts.

But a hundred yards away excited Mikko sat in Pete's shack, rubbing his hands together uneasily while Pete composed for him a letter of response to Hans Schimmler.

"Dear Mr. Schimmler,

Mikko Rymponen of the United States of America is ready and conditioned to accept your challenge to a wrestling match at a date to be selected by you and your manager. Either a straight or handicap match acceptable. Mr. Thorvald Blumstrom, of Ishpeming, Michigan, U.S.A., had personally backed the match with $500 cash which is in a sealed envelope in the local bank. The match will take place in a heated storage building behind the mercantile store in Ishpeming, which place allows room for a sizeable attendance of spectators.

Please mail contract paper as soon as it is drawn up.

Yours truly,

Mikko Rymponen

*   *   *   *   *

It was another routine day of cribbing the shaft and mining the tunnel. At mid-morning Captain Sommers drew Ikey aside.

"That spur, southwest of the shaft, one of those we trenched on last spring. Gonna blast it open today, Ikey. To satisfy our minds about what alls laying underneath. Get Jim and Jallu to give you a hand in loading some powder in a wagon."

Ikey shook his head sidewise. "Payday yesterday, they ain't back from town."

Sommers rubbed the wirey stubble on his chin and momentarily frowned. "Take Pete. Watch them cases, we don't want any premature blast with them sliding off. When you're loaded up, holler. I'll go up and show you exactly where."

Shortly after the noon meal was consumed, there was heard a thump in the earth beyond the North Beaver shaft. Ikey and Pete had carried out performance of their duties, all right, and none of the surface workers gave much further thought until Ikey and Pete broke through the dense woods. They sought out Captain Sommers and met him eyeball to eyeball. Their words spilled out in jagged spurts.

"A helluva blast!" gasped Pete. "You'll never believe..."

86

Ikey interrupted, his lips quivering. "She's...she's.. yellow! Ya kin scoop it up by the shovelful. Could... could be.. the mother rock..!"

Captain Sommers startled, his mouth dropped open and his eyes took fire. His heart began pounding like it was being hit with a sledge hammer. For weeks, along with Clem Copley and Bill Worthington, he had been concentrating on deepening the North Beaver shaft, notwithstanding the fact that strong evidence of pay diggings had been found a half-mile southwest of the workings. Where trenching was done last spring, undetected to the casual eye since an accumulation of decayed vegetation and heavy underbrush surrounded the site.

Captain Sommers cupped his hands to his mouth and managed to get the attention of Mikko who was tightening the wide belt on the saw. Mikko, whose occupation in the old country had been woodswork and let it be known upon his hiring of his preference for sawmill work since wrestling green timbers was a good form of physical conditioning.

"Get the men outa the tunnel!" Sommers hollered to Mik. "Got a good blast!"

Mikko dropped his wrench to the ground and shortly disappeared into the adit, running the length of the dark tunnel to the face of the workings. He shouted out Captain Sommers very words, his voice echoing in the hollow. Men digging in short branch tunnels were alerted.

The curvy footpath to the top of the bluff was scaled in new record time and a pathless way taken through wooded terrain, with Charlie in his white apron bringing up the rear of the single-file procession.

What the blast revealed made eyes bulge. Jagged chunks of yellow veined quartz were strewn all around, and at a seven foot depth the quartz was holding out in richness.

"Man! If I ever seen pay dirt...!" yelled Dan.

"Fill yer pockets! Fill yer pockets!" hollered Charlie.

"...the mother rock!"

"Wouldn't swap this for seven wimin..."

Nels stood by, his eyes drinking in the sight before him. Visibly shaken, he was, for the first time in his life. "Good blast," he uttered. "Can't ask for a more yellower hole."

Tons of pay dirt! Bill Worthington and Clem Copley stood near paralyzed with speechless disbelief. As magnificent a blast as they'd seen anywhere. A single blast - heaving out two tons of rich rock! A vein six feet in diameter! Captain Sommers continued to wipe sweat from his brow. Charlie fell to his knees. Holding up the corners of his apron, he began dropping choice pieces of ore into the folds. Jed Carter on bent knee was admiring a rich chunk. He'd box it and send it to Gramp.

Numb minds of some of the crew began churning thoughts. Each thinking. Maybe I won't always be poor. Captain Sommers was remembering what stock buyers were told - "a good dividend paying mine"

*   *   *   *   *

Jed departed the property immediately and rode hard toward town. Unlike his general self, he felt terribly shook up inside. He felt lightheaded, which feeling caused concern that maybe he was going loony with gold madness.

Time was not long from when he left the mine to when he reached the edge of town. He loped Blaze past the graveyard, past the lake so feared by the Chippewas, by the row of log houses. Two men he well knew were hammering on the roof of a newly constructed log house. They signaled their greetings, wondering why he rode on, not stopping to chat, which was habitual with him.

In front of the Holyoke office he reined in Blaze, bounded to the ground and threw the reins loosely around a post. Syd Crawford had witnessed his approach and stood in the open doorway ready to greet him. One look was enough, to know that something had happened at the mine.

Jed grabbed Syd by the shoulders, and Syd saw the fire in his eyes.

"We've struck it! Unburied it a few hours ago! Up to now we've been only nicking the edge of the real thing!"

Syd narrowed his eyes on Jed, who looked punch drunk from joy and excitement.

"Do you know what you're talking about? Or is it heat of the day that's touched you?"

Jed's entire face was alive. "It's for real, Syd! It's a big find! Pay dirt! Lock the safe. We gotta tell Austin!"

The news was too much, too sudden. Totally unexpected. Syd Crawford wasn't too sure about this, but he pulled the office door shut and raced after Jed, across the dusty red road, dodging horses and wagons. Up the stuffy stairway they sprinted to Austin's office. At the doorway they braked to avoid a collision with Mrs. Anderson who was standing in pensive thought, clutching her big purse in one hand and a brass cowbell in the other.

Egbert Austin was asleep. Slouched in a chair behind his desk, his stockinged feet propped up on the desktop. His hands, neatly folded on his stomach, were rising and falling with each breath of life. Crossing his vest was a cable chain from which dangled fragments of quartz showing pure gold. An edition of the POST lay on his desk, headlined "School To Be Opened In Yellow Dog District", and Austin's reading glasses rested thereon. But a few long strides and Jed was beside him, shaking him vigorously.

"Wake up you old buzzard!"

His voice penetrated Austin's subconscious mind and he woke with a start.

"How in tarnation can you sleep on such a day?" There

89

was fire in Jed's words.

Austin blinked once, twice. "What in the hell are you up to? What gives? Something wrong?"

"Wrong! Exactly the opposite! We've struck a 'big find'! Everything's coming up yellow!"

Jed raved on with Egbert Austin and Syd, wide-eyed, absorbing his each and every word. Austin's eyes now began to twitch with nervous excitement. Unbelievable! Was this true? Really true? A clammy feeling covered his body and he bit on his thumbnail. Momentarily he held his silence. Had riches found the way to his door? He was sure! Jed's face spelled it out. He became aware of a quivering throughout his body and he attempted to control himself. Men of means don't tremble like this. As a shareholder in the Holyoke he should keep his reserve even though riches were falling his way.

He heaved himself from the deep seat of his chair and grabbed his hat from a spike on the wall. "We've got to get the news to Hank. We'll pick up some fresh horses and hit the road to Iron Bay."

Jed shook his head negatively. "The day is near done. We'll ride with the crack of dawn."

*   *   *   *   *

The three men burst into Hank Manson's warehouse-office, ignoring the "Use Side Door" sign. The place was cluttered with crates, trunks, barrels, a few leaking. Hank was busy with a helper, explaining to him how to interpret shipping charges from a rate chart.

They were all talking at once, Egbert Austin and Syd Crawford repeating everything Jed said. Hank was quick to grasp the importance of their ride. He had Jed repeat, asking for no interruptions, detailed happenings of the previous day. Hank's mind was crowding with thoughts, and when Jed stopped with the expulsion of the last detail, he could no longer restrain himself.

"Do you know what this means? It's the best thing that

could happen to this area! A population boom! More tax dollars to work with. Prosperity... schools!" He turned to his helpers who had been listening and not working. "I'll be at the Holyoke all day."

By nightfall the town echoed with word of the big find.

It was morning, the next day, and the mine site was alive with dazed men, stumbling over jagged rock at the site of the blast, talking excitedly. Hank Manson had arrived on the scene early in the morning, as had Egbert Austin and Syd Crawford, with Directors Paul Witter and Chuck Landers arriving shortly after the sun read high noon. The entire Holyoke crew milled around the site, giving opinions on the opening in the ground. All the while Ed Morley was busy writing about what he saw, what he heard, quoting the diggers in their exact words.

When the air became pesky with sandflies and they could no longer be tolerated, the officers followed by some of the larger shareholders descended the bluff to enter the shanty office, to lay out plans. Unquestioningly work would be immediately started on sinking a second shaft. The "South Beaver" it would be named. Most surprising to all, the site hadn't even been indicated on the blueprints.

The new whim would be moved over to the South Beaver. Work to be held up in the North Beaver until another whim could be located to operate it efficiently. Order a stamp mill. Hire more men. Speed up completion of the "dry" building which would be used by the men in changing their mine clothes. Advertise stock for sale.

Clem Copley and Bill Worthington spent the remainder of the day discussing the special mill they wanted for the need at hand. They agreed on the fineness to which the quartz should be crushed, choosing to reject the type of mills being used in Minnesota, where the metal was caught in corse sieves but failing to perform properly. It would be logic to invest a larger sum of money, and order a mill where the quartz would be crushed by a rolling ball.

News of the good findings continued to twitch people's ears. In the weeks that were to follow, townsfolk, people from Coyuta and Iron Bay, came to inspect the property. Before long came strangers from afar, with booklets printed by Ed Morley protruding from their pockets. They rode in on horseback, in rigs, some clamoring into the small mine office to grab up what stock they could buy without looking at the property, only to be referred to the company office in town, to which place they hurriedly departed.

Syd burned the oil in the late hours of each night, recording the booming stock sales in the ledger and counting wads of cash. Money was flowing into the treasury. Ed Morley began making daily appearances at the mine to gather the latest news.

The Holyoke boom was carrying, loud and far.

CHAPTER 7
New Activities in the District

The air was heavy and humid this summer evening. Jed Carter sat in the doorway of his bunkhouse fatigued from a day of heavy labor, lazily rubbing bear grease into his leather boots, watching black ants scurrying over and into little mounds of sand. A smudge pail was smoldering near by to ward off the mosquitoes, yet frequently he swished the air with his hand to break up a swarm. He set the can of grease on the threshold and rested, watching a half dozen visitors roaming over the stockpile, querying Captain Sommers about the operation. He picked up a boot, shoved a hand inside and plied the soft leather. They were good boots, of quality leather, just nicely broken in. He dug his fingers into the grease and rubbed more on the uppers. Again he fanned the black air around his head. Now his eyes became fixed on the tranquil waters of the Yellow Dog. Nearing shore was a rowboat, slightly obscured by smoke from the sauna. Two people sat on separate seats. He narrowed his eyes to be more sure.

It was Pa Kelso, all right, rhythmically pulling on the oars... and Petra. The boot in his hand dropped unnoticed upon the sandy soil.

Dan came whistling up the pathway. He was grinning broadly as usual, his white teeth contrasting the tan of his face. His right hand held a green willow fork on which four brown trout were strung.

"Jest come up to inform ya, in case ya ain't yet noticed. There's a real puur-ty sight on the water, and I don't mean that setting red sun. Happens to be that lil Finn gal you're stuck on, down there in that boat pulling in." He waited for a reaction which failed to show, then held out the catch of trout. "Fishings good."

Jed was impressed with the fish but said nothing. He picked up his boots and set them on the end of the step. Again turned his attention to the small rowboat. In shallow water the bow wedged in soft sand. Captain Sommers was there, now, reaching out a long arm, pulling the boat halfway up on the shore. With one spry move Pa Kelso was out of the boat. Captain Sommers extended a hand to Petra. Pa Kelso pulled the boat up on shore further, and Petra wound a rope attached to it around a windfall. Pa Kelso must have said something funny, for all three broke into quick laughter.

Jed watched as they scaled the jagged stockpile, Petra's footing on the loose rocks shaky and unsure. On the flattened off top the three stood and talked, gazing around. Toward the adit they moved, then out of sight. Jed waited. Petra reappeared, her hair shining gold in the slanting rays of the sun. Around the stockpile she roved. Stooping occasionally to closely examine a chunk of ore. To the far side of the stockpile she moved, where he could see her no longer. Now on the flattened top, silhouetted against the sky was Pa, conversing with Ikey, emphasizing his feelings with elaborate hand motions. Jed waited, for the glint of yellow hair in the sunlight.

He reached for his boots and slipped them on, not bothering to lace them, got up and brushed loose sand from the seat of his pants. Quickly his long legs descended the pathway. Over to the stockpile. His greetings to Pa were warm, but short. His eyes flashed about. She was nowhere in sight. Chances were, that she had entered the tunnel. Wet and dirty, and hardly a place for a woman, she might have gone in a short distance as most people were tempted to do, to satisfy the desire of being in a tunnel, of experiencing the excitement of the cool excavation.

He paced a few steps into the adit and listened for any noise. He called her name, expecting to hear her voice in the near darkness. Silence. "Petra!" His voice was raised. Again he called out, without response. Only his voice echoed itself deep.

He returned to the top of the stockpile. Where had she gone? There was the path leading to the powder shack - well posted with danger signs. Captain Sommers had seen to that. Strangers around the mine had to be warned. His head bobbed in all directions. He scrambled down from the stockpile and took to the path leading to the powder shack.

He didn't get far before he stopped short. Radiant in her natural beauty, she was walking toward him, not seeing him right away, but looking upward at something making noise in a tree. When she saw him she smiled, a warm, tender smile. The kind he visualized when many nights he lay in his bunk thinking of her.

"Jed! Your mine! It's... so big! I never thought it to look anything like this! Stig didn't say it looked so... good."

A touch of anger flared within on hearing Stig's name. But mostly because she had endangered herself by her nearness to the powder shack. But her very presence quickly smothered his irk. It was real good seeing her again.

"We're moving right along. Everything's going just like we expect it to go. You can give boss Sommers most of the credit. That man sure knows everything there is to know about mining." He paused, his voice took firmness.

"But this isn't a healthy place for you to be roaming. There's a heap of powder in that shack behind you."

His abruptness of tone was unexpected. "I was just looking around, Jed. Not touching nothing. Just looking. Like you let other people do. Didn't think you would mind." Her voice carried a tone of irritated disgust.

"Sure, fine. Go ahead. Look around all you want. Anywhere but up here near the powder. All the signs say 'keep away'!"

For the first time since he'd known her the luster left her eyes. A shadow fell over her face. Her chin quivered and her lips tightened. There was unexpected silence between them.

Now a tear broke from beneath her long lashes and fell upon her bronzed face. She fumbled for a handkerchief from the sleeve of her gingham dress, turned her back, then broke into sobbing.

Jed stood motionless, perplexed, his eyes fixed on her back. What in this beautiful world had caused tears to erupt? He took a step toward her and laid his hands upon her shoulders. She flinched and pulled away from his touch. He took her hand but it was abruptly withdrawn. He gazed numbly. When he finally found words his voice was low. He touched her arm.

"Why are you carrying on like this? In case you don't know, you're talking to a man who truly loves you. So, what can be so bad as to bring tears?"

Minutes passed before her sobbing lessened, finally ceasing. She turned to face him once more, regaining self-possession, though tears were still embedded in the corners of her wet eyes. A trace of sadness revealed itself through her flushed features. Grasping his muscular arms in her hands she rested her head on his chest.

"Jed. I'm unhappy." Her words were choked. She released her breath in a sigh. "Unhappy because I love you too but I'm not worth you. What you should know...

will change your feelings for me." She released her hold on his arms and slowly lifted her face.

"You're book learned. Even learned in a college. You travel around, and me...? Raised out here in the sticks. Ain't never stepped foot in any schoolhouse. Never learned to read or write." Her eyes shifted to a sign posted on a near tree. "Can't make out a word."

Her voice became freer as she found inner strength. "Jest a backwoods girl, I am. Our bringing up ain't nohow the same. That's why I dared not like you too much from when we first met. It wouldn't work out that you and me..." Her words choked off.

Jed bit the inside of his lip but managed a thin smile. Illiterate. His eyes did not flick a lash while he considered her words. And he had no immediate answer.

He took her in his arms, their cheeks touched. They stirred only when voices close by were heard. He slipped his hands into hers and pressed her fingers. His voice was low. "What you've told me is nothing, nothing at all. Everything's just fine."

They walked to the edge of the water and stood there, the glow of the setting sun lingering upon their smiling faces.

Pa appeared. He descended the sandy embankment, paused to shake a slide of sand out of a boot before unwinding the rope from the windfall and loosening the bow from its sandy mooring. With one foot resting on the craft he looked to where his daughter stood. Jed pocketed his hands, he straightened his shoulders and together they sauntered the short span to where Pa waited.

"If you don't mind, I'd like to see Petra home tonight."

Pa stared down at a stationary, warty green frog which had concealed itself under the boat, then eased himself into the craft. "Not be late." He put an oar in the shallow water and pushed the boat out.

97

The air was soft, and a breeze which accompanied falling dusk blew the mosquitoes away. The road wound through moon drenched hills. Jed set the reins on the footboard, allowing Blaze to walk most of the way - up and down shadowed slopes, across the rattley bridge, through fields that sparkled with fireflies.

Their heads were close.

He heeded the advice of the carriage dealer in town -- take the longest road home when out riding with your best girl on a beautiful evening. It was a beautiful evening, and they both wished that the night might have been longer.

Burning the midnight oil the same night, Stig Nilssen finished drafting plans for what he figured would make Petra and himself a comfortable home.

*   *   *   *   *

The heat wave which had burned the countryside the whole summer long tapered off and now the flame of autumn burned through the green valleys. The hardwoods took on glows of red and gold amid the green of the pines. Stands of poplar blazed in yellow glory. The love between Petra and Jed deepened and they made no effort to conceal their affection for each other. Though Petra hadn't yet discussed the issue with Pa, he had it solidly fixed in his mind that Petra had fully given her heart to Jed. That she had put Stig in the background of her mind. She was continuously bubbling and laughing a lot, singing. Sparks kindled in her eyes when anybody mentioned the Holyoke.

Close to the supper hour of each day, nearing the brim of Jed's evening visit, she danced giddily about the kitchen. Humming folk tunes while setting the table for the evening meal, switching the tempo to coincide with the setting down of dishes and tinware, to the amusement of Eric and Timo. On two successive days Pa's inquiry about burnt dishes caused her flushed embarrassment. Also Pa could most definitely see, that her love filled heart had diminished her appetite.

On evenings when extra mine work delayed Jed's visit, she would sit herself at the loom, and continue her weaving until his arrival. Frequently they shared a bench on the porch, sometimes sipping porch coffee with Jed now in full mastery of sipping his coffee through a sugar cube. They would sit watching the sun lower beyond the ridge. There were times when she'd convince Jed they should go searching for lost Daisy. Or again, convincing him it would be good if they piled wood in the shed in preparation for the long winter ahead.

They would ride horseback, sometimes together on Blaze, on occasion the boys riding behind them. There were moonless nights when by light of tallow candles they walked the winding roads edged with goldenrod, talking of future days.

*   *   *   *   *

It was a perfect September day, mid-morning to be exact. At the plank table in the kitchen Petra was busy cleaning lamp chimneys. She was aware of father outside on the porch, scraping moist earth from the soles of his shoes. Coming back from the field for his mid-morning coffee which was a precious part of each day's living, never missed. The door opened, admitting a half-dozen lively flies and father. Dirt streaked his perspiring face.

He sat himself at the table, took off his tattered cap and set it on the bench beside him. Then brushed back wet strands of hair that clung to his forehead. Simultaneously Petra headed for the wash basin to scrub the black from her hands. From a cupboard she took two cups and saucers, retrieved from the hot stove top the coffee pot and proceeded to fill up the cups.

From force of habit Pa poured some of his coffee into his saucer to cool it off. After two or three sips he brought himself to discourse about the prospective potato yield, of how promising the crop looked.

There was the squeaking of wheels in the yard, now close to the window where they sat a masculine voice was heard. "Whoa!" Simultaneously the kitchen door was pulled open wide. Red faced and panting from running, Eric and John stumbled in. Their eyes told of news.

"She's here! The teacher!"

"She's got her bags 'an is gonna stay!"

Pa quickly rose, scraping back the bench on the floor. A half-dozen steps took him to the open doorway. He removed the cube of sugar from his mouth.

"Eet's Meester School Man and Mees Neeley."

Everybody scurried outside. Mr. Slocum the commissioner had already alit from the double buggy drawn by a shiny black mare, and was assisting a delicate young lady in getting down. Her skin was quite pale, possibly from spending much time indoors studying. Braids of ash brown hair were neatly twisted about her head, her face was pronounced by wide set brown eyes. Now her feet touched firm ground. She adjusted the bag on her arm and looked around and smiled, a big heart-warming smile.

Lanky Mr. Slocum extended a hand to Pa Kelso, who gripped it with his own, dirt stained and calloused. The school man's face reflected the importance of the day. "It's my pleasure to introduce Miss Neeley, our new teacher and likewise your winter guest."

"Velcom. Velcom, Meester Kommissioner and Mees Neeley. Ve been lookin' you to kom evry day. My! Dat's goot ve see you now." There was a twinkle in Pa's eye as he addressed Miss Neeley. "You gonna lik dees new job." His eyes continued to hold focus on Miss Neeley. "Long time ve vait, ve talk, 'bout ven dees goot day kom. Now eenside ve go for rest from long ride and have coffee." He cast a glance toward Eric standing stiffly by his side. "Leeft bags for Mees Neeley 'an breeng eenside."

Petra stood apart from the rest, she was introduced but added no words. Stirred by the presence of a school teacher who much to her surprise looked younger than herself.

The boys sat on the woodbox beside the stove, observing their guests sipping coffee and dunking rusks as their father did. They listened as Mr. Slocum told of the many applications received for the job, of their good fortune in getting Miss Neeley. Eric was beside himself, overtaken by the charm and poise of his very first teacher. And she was so-o pretty! He obeyed with no delay when Petra asked him to get more cream from the dugout beneath the trap door. Which consisted of a small square hole in the earth under the kitchen floor where perishable provisions were stored.

Florence Neeley's eyes drifted about, so uniquely different an environment from the kind she had been raised in. Unpainted walls, a rough plank floor adorned with parallel rows of rag carpets. All the furniture was hand made. Nails in the walls suspended pictures cut from magazines, caps and coats, pots and pans. Strips of flypaper dangled from the ceiling beams. There was a water pail and dipper on a bench by the door. And what she found out later to be a butter churn stood in one corner.

The contents of the coffee pot were drained and Mr. Slocum explained why he could linger no longer. He rose from the table and picked up his hat, gave hearty thanks for the victuals and pumped Pa's hand once more, saying that he'd be out again soon. Florence, who to this moment had been doing more listening than talking, interrupted, and thanked the commissioner for the transportation to the homestead. Pa politely excused himself, mentioning work to be done in the garden and followed the commissioner outside.

The school man seemed to be waiting for him, resting a

bony hand on a wheel of the buggy. He spoke aside. "It is important that you notify me if there is any misdemeanor on the part of Miss Neeley. I don't really expect any erratic behavior from her, but then again. One never knows."

He got in the buggy and rode off.

"Mees Neeley. Mees demeener," pondered Pa. "Vat dat man mean anyhow?"

Petra showed Florence around, outside, inside. Lastly the large upstairs area where Florence's private room was, and the classroom. Her room, cozy and bright. The classroom! Florence was dealt a blow upon sight of it, upon viewing the few and far between pieces of furniture, though she failed to show her dismay. Not that she had been nursed in the lap of luxury. A splintered table with no teaching materials thereon, an unpainted round back chair were to suffice her personal needs. Two long benches placed against opposite walls would seat the pupils. A water pail and dipper were set on a three legged stool by the doorway. A stove for heating purposes was set in the very middle of the bare floor. Chunks of blockwood were piled in the back of the room.

They stood and conversed. About the layout of the district, about the seven boys and three girls spanning ages six to sixteen who would attend the new school. The oldest, Jorn Holmstrom, who was enrolling against his desire. Florence knew not yet, that only three of her pupils understood English.

Their talk became freer and Petra felt it important that their winter guest should know about the gold mine nearby and that young untaken men were employed there. Florence didn't react. Overlooking the physical furnishings she was caught in the sheer excitement of opening up a new school. She would make it a splendid school. She seated herself on the edge of the table, in an easy way so as to not inherit a splinter.

"Petra! It's so exciting! The threshold of a new life. My dream of teaching children about to come true. I pray that I might succeed in cramming the three R's and their values into the minds of my charges." Again her eyes scanned the room. "Could it be, that a future president might rise from one of these benches?"

While busy thoughts worked her mind, Florence loosened the drawstring of her beaded purse and withdrew a pair of spectacles. She fitted them to her eyes. In new perspective she paced the room, visualizing the pupils pondering over their books. By one of the windows she stopped, she removed her glasses. Something outside had attracted her attention.

"Who's that?" she asked.

Petra moved to a near window to observe Stig, in the yard below, talking to Pa. "Why that's Stig Nilssen our closest neighbor. He lives in that little house over there bordering our property."

"Does he live alone? I...I mean, is he single?"

"Yeah. He comes over a lot."

Stig Nilssen. Big and handsome, holding so much masculine appeal. A thought crossed Florence's mind. Why did Petra bring up the subject of unmarried young men at the mine and not mention Stig? She felt Petra's eyes upon her and was quick to switch the subject. She fiddled with her glasses. "These are the most ill-fitting things. That Dr. Von Muller will be hearing from me!"

To this very moment it had not been for Florence to know that Petra, no exception to herself, stood on a new threshold of life. From the moment they had entered the classroom Petra had awaited the opportunity to release some deep seated thoughts, her fingers twitching in the pockets of her apron. She took account of herself. If the discussion were to take place it should be now. Her voice was unfaltering.

"You should know. I ain't had schooling either. Might you find time to learn me from books too?"

103

Florence was taken by surprise but failed to show it. Yet there was no need to think about the question. At her normal school graduation had she not solemnly raised her hand and pledged to teach... to the best of her ability?

A new threshold of life!

*　　　*　　　*　　　*　　　*

And the weeks passed by. The golden weeks of autumn. Every morning, sipping his mid-morning coffee, Pa was smiling big as he listened to musical refrains floating down the kitchen stairway.

> My kon'tree tees ufde
> Sweet land uf leeberty
> Ufde I seeng....

And Pa felt good inside.

When the school day ended Petra would stealthily retrieve her ruled tablet and pencil from beneath her straw mattress and pay heed to Florence's tutoring. She quickly familiarized herself with the alphabet and learned to sound the letters. She learned how to divide sounds. She started on books with big print like her brothers were using. Often while weaving at the loom she mentally reviewed her day's lesson.

With Florence it was becoming habitual while listening to Petra recite, that she would edge over to a window and gaze at Stig working his fields.

The crude classroom intrigued Jed Carter to no end. He spent time in the evenings hammering shelves on the walls to hold books and supplies. He secured a blackboard to a wall. And on two successive evenings he pitched in helping Pa and Stig build a separate outhouse for the girls.

It was the evening the outhouse was completed, when everybody was sitting around the coffee table that Florence spelled out clearly to Stig, that teachers were permitted one evening each week for courting purposes. And that night, in the quiet of her bed, she had made

104

herself believe that Stig had nodded with apparent interest.

Pa Kelso bought a big flag with the first month's rent money for use of the classroom, and set it up in the yard. And Jed Carter formed a new habit. Carrying wood and water up to the classroom.

Wood and water. Petra was more than perplexed and became somewhat concerned. Carrying up these necessities had become almost a mania with him. It was just not right, that any normal fella would be so excited about performing such chores when so many lads in the class with strong backs were available. Or was Florence becoming her rival?

Briefly Jed would be obscured by heaps of split wood near the shed. Returning with a few blocks of wood on an arm and a beguiling look on his face. The pattern of executing these chores continued and annoyed Petra to no end. Her curiosity erupted.

"Jed Carter. You're keeping something from me. I think it only right that you should tell me. Now."

But it wasn't for Petra to know. Not yet. About the steel crusher ball by the side of the shed. What her father had said regarding it. Never did Jed go for wood and water but that he stopped by the shed to raise the steel ball a bit off the ground. Nowhere as high as Pa could lift it, not as high as Stig could. But higher, at least, than the first times he tried.

CHAPTER 8
Love Does Not Run Smooth

Continued blasting at the site of the Holyoke and the far penetrating squeal of the sawmill gave evidence of bustling activity on the property. Cars rolled in and out of the tunnel every day, noisily dumping their heavy loads onto the stockpile. The South Beaver shaft was growing deeper without hitches. A building was completed to house the mill and a big fifty horsepower engine was installed and a boiler set in position.

Notwithstanding, shipment of the mill had been delayed creating disquiet among the larger stockholders and eventual restlessness in everybody connected with the workings. Trips to town to check with the rail agent as to the whereabouts of the mill became more and more regular.

It was one of those impatient, seemingly time wasting days, when Jed again stood in the musty rail station, prepared to repeat the identical inquiries he had posed the past several days. The train had arrived and was already departed. Transporting out the Good Templars who were embarking on a crusade. Passengers who had alit were gathered by the ticket window, seeking information from the agent.

Jallu entered the rail station, unsteady with alcoholic effects, and moved into the midst of the new arrivals. Jallu, who had been missing from the workings for more than a week. Though nobody showed much concern over his frequent self-proclaimed holidays. From the strange looks on the faces of those standing around Jallu and the wrinkling of noses it was apparent that the smell of alcohol permeated the air where they stood. Jallu took his turn at the window, he fumbled with coins in his calloused hands as he addressed the rail agent.

"I lik' take little vacation trip. Vat ish price ticket go Iron Paay?"

"Dollar seventy-five round trip."

"How mush go Coyuta town?"

"Fifty-five, sir."

Jallu maintained numbed focus on the coins in the palms of his hands which summed up to only half of the fare to Coyuta. "Maybe I vait go vacation next summer."

On each trip into town Jed would stop off at the company office to leave mine reports and to pick up any papers Syd wanted taken to the mine. Sometimes he'd rest a bit and josh with Syd. Occasionally he'd bring in a special piece of ore which he would leave for viewing in the barbershop window. Regularly he would check with Thor Blumstrom to see if a letter for Mik mailed from Germany was in holding. The contents of which Mik was expecting to contain the agreement papers for his forthcoming match with Hans Schimmler.

*   *   *   *   *

And so it was this day. Beginning as another ordinary trip to town, hinting of routines like the past several trips when nothing new happened. Another ride in. Another hard argument with the rail agent about the delayed shipment. Jed hitched Blaze to a wagon and took to the rutted road leading away from the mine. He must remember to pick up the special order of picks and shovels which come in. Then too, Charlie was running short on flour, and promise had been made of replenishment of stock before sundown of the day. He slouched forward in the seat, his elbows resting on his knees. He was drawn from his daydreaming only when three wolves, an old one and two young ones, crossed the road a short distance ahead.

He didn't push Blaze, there was plenty of time in the day.

His thoughts drifted to the man who lay hypnotized for the third straight day on the stage of the show house.

Huge formations of white clouds were strung over the chain of lakes. His conscience twinged, to be so lazily absorbing the fairness of the summer day with the diggers wielding picks and shovels in dark holes. He straightened the arch in his back and filled his lungs with fresh currents coming off the lake.

Now approaching at near distance was Stig, leading a colt. They stopped when they met, to give the horses a rest and to chat a bit. Jed listened as Stig told of acquiring the year old dark bay by a stroke of good luck.

*   *   *   *   *

Blaze was in good spirit and moving at a good pace. A distance of four miles from the mine had already been covered, already rounding Horseshoe Bend. Just ahead, old plank hill. Then a few miles more over mostly open country and the edge of town would be touched.

He shifted his buttocks on the hard seat.

He was half-way around the deep bend in the road when he saw the gangly lad signaling to stop. Jed reined in abreast of the youth.

"Hey falla! Could ya give us a hand!"

Jed looked around. On the sandy lake shore a dozen or more picnickers, male and female, were enjoying themselves. Most of the group wore sweaters lettered "Pedestrian Club". Food and beverages were in evidence. Sitting on the ground slightly apart from the group was a young lady, massaging her ankle. The sun cast a glint on her auburn hair.

108

Blanche!

The lad rested a hand on the side of the wagon. "A gal in our party jest twisted her ankle. She'll never make it back to town on her own. Any chance of your taking her in?"

Jed let the reins drop. He stepped down on the hub of the front wheel and walked over to where Blanche rested. Only did she look up when the familiar designed boots stopped before her.

Blanche had been out of circulation for a good number of weeks. It seemed that the summer sun had fired the red in her hair.

"Giving much pain?" inquired Jed.

She chose not to answer, but made a feeble attempt to rise. Her face winced and she fell back. Concern registered on the face of the lad. His eyes queried Jed.

"Okay. I'll take her in."

He carried her light body to the wagon and eased her onto the spring seat, all the while the palm of her hand pressing into the back of his neck.

Not far did they ride, barely out of sight of the picnickers, they were descending old plank hill when he felt her body draw close. She slipped an arm comfortably through his, lightly resting her fingers on the back of his hand. A side glance by Jed revealed much. The expression of pain shown back on the picnic grounds was no longer visible. Her mouth wore a definite smile, her features were as serene as the placid lake they were skirting. In which direction her gaze was set.

"We could picnic right over there, Jed. Just you and I."

"Picnic? What about that sprain?" His eyes held on her ankles but he found it difficult to detect which one had been twisted. "A sprain should be... attended to right quick..."

Her smile transformed to a smirk. A devilish smirk to

109

say the least. She withdrew her arm from his with abruptness, took the reins and drew Blaze to a halt. Then calmly dropped the reins to the footboard. Her delicate hands were now on the sides of his face. She turned his head until their eyes met and her fingertips brushed the hair on his temples.

"Jed Carter. What kind of a man are you... you've been too much of a stranger lately. I saw you coming from way off. I felt, or should I say I decided there and then, it was time for us to get better acquainted. There's enough fresh biscuits and fried chicken in the basket for both of us..." She tilted her head back and giggled. "Don't look so perturbed, Jed. There's nothing wrong with my ankle."

To give further evidence of no hurt she sprung to the ground and raised herself up and down on her toes. "See? No hurty! C'mon. I'll even race you to the water."

She was off, not stopping to look back, covering the grassy slope to the brim of the lake in skipping rhythm. He got down from the hard seat of the wagon. Now her form was silhouetted against the landscape. He felt for the reins on the footboard and knotted them loosely to a low bough of a birch, then reached for the wicker basket.

He made his way down the slope and followed her footprints in the sand.

The trail led around a rocky point but was easy to follow because there was a blouse, then a skirt, a petticoat, shoes, stockings, garters, chemise, drawers. He gathered them up as he hurried along the secluded shore. At the water's edge he set down the lunch basket.

"Come on in," she called. "It's cold!"

He flung off his clothes and joined her. She actually could swim! He never knew a girl who could swim!

They had a merry romp, but the cold caused goosepimples and drove them out to warm up on a flat ledge in the sun. It was more than sun that warmed them and it was a long time till they realized they were hungry. Starving! Famished! Jed got into his clothes and would have helped her but she ordered him to set out the lunch. Never did chicken taste as good.

It was a day when Pa Kelso, accompanied by Petra, made a special trip into town by wagon and so much had been accomplished. An early stop had been made at the store to drop off two hind quarters of venison, in trade for dried fish, brown sugar, candles and other supplies. Petra was delighted when Thor Blumstrom handed to her a large brown package addressed to herself - her recent yarn order! Never had her yarn orders been received in so short a time. Good. Now she could begin another weaving.

They had walked to the town hall where a hearing was being held on applications for citizenship, Pa Kelso's being included. They had lingered at the clerk's office afterward to collect bounties amounting to twenty-two dollars on two wolves killed. A stop was made at the blacksmith shop where Pa left an extra wagon wheel to have a new steal rim sweated on.. Unplanned, they had participated in an exciting auction where Pa, deciding to spend his bounty money, had been an unsuccessful bidder on a pretty brown and white cow with horns, and chain and bell attached. Homeward bound, their wagon ably drawn by a pair of young work horses, Petra was seated beside her father, prattering exuberantly. Much pleased and excited over the beautiful colors of yarn in her shipment. Pa's mind was still back in the store. Wondering. Whether Thorvald added sand to the sugar which was rumored to be one of his habits. Petra laughed it off. She could not see Mr. Blumstrom in that light. He was a God fearing man.

Her thoughts shifted. It was getting well on in the afternoon and she would miss her schooling today. But she was advancing well. Changing from printing to writing. Dear Florence. Unbelievable. That fate had

111

sent along such a wonderful teacher and friend.

The panorama at the foot of plank hill - the open grassy area between patches of woods, revealing a sandy shore and blue lake drew their gaze as if by magnetic force. Simultaneously they spotted Blaze not thirty feet off, nosing the ground. Pa pulled to the side of the road and reined in. The squeaking of the wheels ceased as did their loose jabber. Two figures fell directly in their line of vision, a man and woman, sitting close together on the shore. Jed? Petra's heart twinged. It was!

Jed Carter shifted his position, his arm curling around the waist of the woman and she responded by ruffling his hair. Something evidently quite funny struck Jed, for he threw his head back with laughter and fell back on the sand.

Petra eased her hand hold on the wagon seat and her entire body fell limp.

A ray of sunlight touched the auburn hair of the woman... it couldn't be...that female torch from town! Petra looked away from the scene which was much like precious, tender moments she herself shared with Jed.

Three days had passed, three long days since she'd last seen Jed. He had told her, and she believed his every word. That it was necessary that he help repair broken rails in the tunnel. That the job called for extra long work days. How she lay abed at night worrying about him overtiring himself.

She dared take another hard look toward the lake to verify what her eyes had seen. Jed Carter! None other than he! She jarred her head aside. Bit the inside of her lip. Prospector Jed. Who was her reason for living. Snuggled up with another girl! Strands of his fair hair, saved from when Pa had shorn him, protected in a tarnished little box, and other treasured mementos of their love were harbored in safe keeping in the big trunk in her bedroom. She'd fall asleep every night with the whisper of his name on her lips. Now the town siren was

112

rooting in her dreams. Or was it death's sting that had sapped her body of life?

Pa, with a perplexed look on his face, glanced questioningly at his daughter. He shifted his pipe to the corner of his mouth and slapped the reins on the rumps of the horses to speed up the homeward journey. Mutual silence prevailed the rest of the way.

While Pa was unhitching the horses Petra read a note left on the kitchen table. It was Florence's printing, in words Florence knew were within Petra's range of perception.

'Petra. I have gone out with Stig.
I will not be late.'

After the supper meal Eric listened through a knothole in his bedroom floor to low talking between Petra and Pa in the kitchen below. Jed's name came up time and again. There was a splatter of Finnish talk, with Pa's voice slightly raising.

"Yust you vait. Some day good Finn boy from ole kontry weel geet off train..."

That night, with misty eyes Petra sat on the edge of her bed, unlacing her shoes. All warmth of Jed Carter had left her being. Prospector! Prospecting for females as well as gold! She wished he had never come to the district. She lay quietly in bed. It would not be easy to do, but, she decided, with the new dawn she would erase from her memory the fact that she had ever met him. She would no more think of him. Ever. She lay thinking deeper. Maybe she should leave home, go to the city and work out as a maid for some rich family. But if she did that who would take care of Timo and Eric?

The dark silence of the bedroom was broken by the sound of squeaking wagon wheels directly beneath her open window. Several minutes later Florence's light footsteps were heard ascending the stairway, faint candle glow flickered in the hallway, then was heard the closing click of the latch on her door.

113

Petra buried her head in her pillow.

More hot angry tears fell.

$$* \qquad * \qquad * \qquad * \qquad *$$

It was the very next day. Close to the supper hour. Charlie would at any moment sound out the gut hammer. Jed, perched on the edge of his bunk, was polishing his boots. His stomach emitted a long low growl.

The door opened and was left open. Dan sauntered across the plank floor. "Eric's outside. Wants to see you." Dan lit up a cigarette before adding, "he's looking none too happy."

Jed's stomach suddenly felt hard, like a lump of lead. He let the unpolished boot clump to the floor. Barefooted, he left the bunkhouse. Eric had his back against a tree and was whittling madly on a stick which was taking no special shape. When he became aware of Jed's nearness he snapped shut the blade of the knife and tossed the stick into the brush. Their eyes met briefly, then Eric looked to the ground. His voice was not like his own, he choked a lump in his throat.

"..uh, Petra... Petra sent me over here. To tell you. She don't want to see you no more. Never."

Eric's words cut like a whip. Jed loved Petra like none others before. He needed her as much as the very air he breathed. She was all his happiness.

"I don't get the drift. What's the reason for all this silly talk?"

"When Pa and Petra came home from town yesterday, Pa was looking puurty mad about something. And it looked like Petra wasn't feeling good and she went right up to her bedroom. They didn't talk much at the supper table. And then last night I heard them saying about seeing you with that woman from town who ain't decent. That's what the trouble is about, mostly. I guess.

The gut hammer sounded out supper.

"I can explain everything Eric. It's quite simple."

114

"I ain't so sure my sister will listen. I know her better'n you do. When her mind's made up, it's made up." Eric picked up a broken stick and jabbed it hard into the ground a couple of times. "Gotta be pushing along back home. I said what I was supposed to."

That ended the conversation. Eric took to the path that led to the cable crossing. Jed stood quietly and watched, feet astride, arms folded. Then he shuffled back into the sultry bunkhouse and plunked flat down on his bunk. Dan had gone to supper and John was still working on the rails. Which suited him just fine. He needed to be alone. To think. For a long time he didn't budge.

Twilight began dimming the room. He tried to collect his thoughts but his mind ran riot. Shortly he swung his feet to the floor. He would go to see Petra. This very hour. And amend himself in her eyes.

He fitted his feet into clean stockings and his unpolished boots, he half-buttoned his wool shirt and plunked his hat on his head. Methodically he unhooked a lantern which hung from a rafter and took the pathway through the pine scented dimness to the cable crossing. He neared the cookhouse where a small window was pushed halfway up and from which Charlie's head stuck out.

"Tables all cleaned off and stuff put away, but not too late for a nip."

Jed didn't hear. He kept walking, past the smoking sauna from wherein he could hear the rattle of tin pails. Skidding down the bank to the water's edge he discovered that the cable seat was on the opposite shore since Eric most likely had been the last to use it. He tugged on the cable till the board seat was within reach and swung on it. Then took a moment to put a light to the wick of the lantern and hook it beneath the seat. The cable was far from free running. With each tug was heard the piercing retort of dry pulleys. He emitted a grunt of disgust. Ordinarily he wasn't one to be irked by small things, but tonight wasn't an ordinary night.

Pa Kelso would surely frown at his appearance. Petra? H'mm.... She possessed a strong mind. During discourse in which she was opinioned she didn't hesitate to take a stand of her own.

Regardless, he had to redeem himself. Nothing else mattered. He visualized activity at the homestead. The boys at the kitchen table doing their homework. Petra and Pa in the living room. Petra weaving. Pa rocking, smoking his pipe. Florence frequently stayed in her room preparing her next day's assignments. In due time Petra would retreat to the kitchen to brew some fresh coffee. At which time Pa always checked on the horses and Daisy. Then, he'd be alone with Petra, hopefully the boys having been sent to bed. He'd have a chance to talk to Petra. And she would understand.

Dusk of the evening transformed to near darkness and clouds were shifting in the sky. A half moon showed for a brief while, revealing a dank mist curling up from the water, hanging white in mid-air. He could sense the flitting of a low swooping night bird. Frequent crossings in darkness had enabled him to gauge with acute accuracy the distance between shores, and he sensed that he was almost across.

Light of the lantern radiated an ozone of brightness. Then a south breeze which had been working itself up wavered the flame and extinguished it. Or could it be? He released a hand hold on the cable and unhooked the lantern from its hook. He held it close to his ear and shook it. There was no splashing of oil.

It was not all bad, for the moon came out again from behind a cloud and light penetrated the darkness. He'd take the path along the shoreline as far as Holmstroms, from there the road to Kelsos. A bit longer than the trail through the spruce but preferable since the oil did not last.

Feminine laughter pricked his ears, voices, then his

eyes caught sight of bobbing lanterns in the woods. Good. A chance to borrow a splash of oil. Coming along the trail voices, both male and female became clearer and words became distinguishable. There appeared four shadowy forms in light of the moon. He recognized Petra's soft voice and Florence's giggle. The husky male voices he didn't choose to guess at. Maybe hired hands for a few days of potato picking Pa had talked about hiring. From the lilt of their voices it was certain they were enjoying the evening.

Jed sat motionless on the cable seat until their forms were swallowed up in the darkness, then smoked a cigarette that his fingers rolled in the dark. His mind was void of thought, he looked down miserably at the dark swirls below him. A few drops of rain struck his face but he didn't stir. Only the yelp of a bitch wolf and her pups running a deer in the swamp brought him to. He pivoted the seat and tugged on the cable till his feet touched the shore from which he had but shortly departed.

The breeze was gaining momentum and thick smoke from the sauna chimney blew in his face. As he neared the sauna the door was thrown open, emitting a burst of steam and Jallu, stripped bare, who headed for the stream. A diving plunge was heard.

Charlie was standing on the threshold of the cookhouse, a black silhouette in the light that shone from behind him. He was holding a cup of whiskey in one hand and a skinning knife in the other, muttering something about somebody helping Alex gut out a doe.

Farther up the pathway the music of Dan's harmonica infiltrated the air, spilling out a lamentful tune.

In the bunkhouse a poker game was going strong amid a haze of smoke. Pete, sitting on an empty crate was wearing a satisfied look on his face, obviously holding a winning hand. Ikey was sitting cross-legged on the floor mending a rip in a shirt sleeve. Jed circled the table, kicking an empty powder box out of his way. Eyes turned to one another and each man smiled knowingly.

"So yer lil Finn gal went to bed early tonight?" asked Nels, not lifting his eyes from his cards.

Pete played his hand and looked up from the cards he had been studying. "Maybe she found out about the skeletons in your closet? Hell is nothing like a woman scorned."

John flung his cards on the table and opened his mouth. "So it took a little back-country gal to put you in the doghouse."

Ikey looked up from his work and broke in. "Ferget 'er! She's the wrong girl fer ya anyhow. Can't read or write, so talk is. And face it man, straight on. She's still sweet on big Stig." He got to his knees to dig for something in his pants pocket. "So what matters anyhow? Ya got the town's redhead comin' yer way. And now that you two are more friendly - tell us, is she generous, or ain't she?"

Jed didn't respond. He sat on the edge of his bunk and tugged off his boots and upended them, then stripped off his clothes to his underwear and stretched out on the unmade bunk.

"A woman sure kin eat out a man's insides," mumbled John.

It had been one bad day. Jed lay on his back and thought a long while. He blamed himself, he hadn't used his head. Dawn couldn't break too soon. He'd dig hard all day with the shaft gang and time would pass rapidly and go see Petra at supper hour.

Still he spent a bad night.

*   *   *   *   *

The gathering amassments of low, heavy clouds of the preceding night had failed to generate any thoughts weatherwise. Dawn was preceded by sharp cracking in the skies, bolts of lightning flashing in the blackness, and at the set hour of rising torrents of rain smashed against the window panes of the bunkhouses. Jed partly opened the door of his quarters to see the trees being battered, gulleys of rain traversing the depressed pathways to merge with the churning waters of the Yellow Dog. There wasn't a digger who had the desire to put in a shift. Plans to transport heavy timbers to the shaft openings wouldn't hold since the incline would be in deteriorated shape.

Wretched too were moods in the Kelso domain, whose frightened inhabitants were shook from their early morning rest by the vociferous cracking in the skies and lightning flashes which vibrated and illuminated the whole house. Followed by strange noises down in the kitchen. They hastily descended the stairs in their nightwear to find the entire kitchen enveloped in black soot and rolling lids from the stove top circling the floor. All the result of lightning striking the kitchen chimney.

*   *   *   *   *

Tomorrow was today and the skies again cleared. Sixty feet down in the South Beaver Jed wielded a shovel alongside Dan, wallowing in six inches of water. No serious problems had been encountered in deepening the shaft until water began seeping in. Not uncommon in shaft openings. A pumping system was working to satisfaction, and the source of trouble had been diagnosed. It was from Beaver Lake with a four foot beaver dam at the south end that the seepage was coming from. Bill Worthington and Clem Copley were scheduled full time at attempting to find a permanent solution.

Jed's thoughts were hardly on his work. Throughout the entire morning he mulled over his personal problems. When noon finally rolled around even Charlie's fresh bread and salt pork didn't hold any appeal. Alex was cleaning some tools. His work wasn't of imminent importance and Jed suggested that he team up with Dan.

119

Jed Carter slipped back to his quarters. From beneath his bunk he dragged a sack and removed some clean clothing, then sneaked down the pathway to the sauna where he scrubbed up with a bar of yellow soap, sloshed in the luke warm water, slightly rust tinged from being left in the metal barrel overnight. He thought of what Jallu said as he soaped up. Jallu, who believed dead positively that bathing in rusty water was good for lumbago.

No time was wasted, he dressed and combed his hair with care. He eased the door shut on its leather hinges and headed for the cable crossing.

Eric was fooling around on the cable seat suspended directly over the middle of the stream. Nearby was a boat without oars. He didn't have to hunt far for a board to paddle it. The boat zigzagged as he propelled forward alternating the rowing action from side to side.

On the opposite shore he took a short cut which followed no trail. Petra! Every passing minute was drawing her nearer! A herd of deer grazing in the clearing on Stig's property failed to distract his thoughts. The wild idea struck, that he would propose to her. Today. That they would run off and get married before the week ended.

Only did he slow his pace, to regain composure, when he neared the split rail fencing marking the Kelso property. He could hear the steady striking of a hammer coming from the direction of the house. He paced the dirt road which paralleled the fence. At the road gate he stopped. Suspended on a rail by haywire was a sign, freshly painted. The letters stood out boldly on a tin background.

'NOTIS. DIS PRIVAT PROPTY. AND DIS MEANS KEEP OFF. STAY AWAY. DIS SAME AS LAW.'

He dipped his hand into a hip pocket to retrieve a bandana and proceeded to wipe perspiration from his neck. In an unpremeditated stall he reached in his shirt pocket for the makings of a cigarette, continuing to stare at the sign. Pa Kelso's makeup didn't call for anything like this. There was no doubt that the man was really triggered off. Something quite serious. He put a match to his tobacco, put a smoke ring in the air, then hesitantly took to the wagon ruts leading toward the house. His footsteps touched the ground in rhythm with the pounding strokes of the hammer. Closer now, he identified the rapping as coming from the roof of the house.

The top of the long, homemade ladder was set against the house and extended up and beyond the unpainted eavesboard. He could see Pa Kelso on the roof bent over on all fours. The pounding noise of the hammer combined with a flaring temper over the nasty repair job at hand kept Petra's father from having any knowledge of Jed's presence on the ground below him. Only when he elevated himself to send a well spent plug of tobacco to the ground did he notice his caller. Pa Kelso's usual expression had changed. His face was unsmiling.

"Vat's matter you no tak' notis sign on fence? You not read goot?"

Jed managed a one-sided smile and shifted his weight on his feet. His mind was groping for right words of approach but before he could think of fitting ones Pa's voice, stern and peppered with bitterness, again sounded out. "You got no beesnees here no more. It be very goot you go now. Else I put you up dees ladder and puush you head down dees hole."

Jed further felt the impact of Pa's temper. He hooked his thumb in his wide leather belt. "What are you talking about? What hole? I don't understand!"

"Don' you look like you don' know vat I talk 'bout. Las' Sataday ve go to town. Com' home, find trouble, like monkey-beesnees. Somebody soot da ball up mit the powder. Eet come down and make beeg hole een house roof. Dats vat say ees monkey-beesnees. Huh! No can leeft ball like man so shoot up mit da powder! Nobody fool dees man from ole kontry! I say best you not com' on dis lan' no more. Else I show monkey-beesnees mit my sotgun."

Petra emerged from the house, her work-reddened hands toting a pail of garbage. She swung her head upwards to view Pa on the roof. She wended her way to a sandy pit dug back of the clearing to dispose of the garbage. This being a daily trek. Yet having no deleterious effects, the garbage being neutralized by the fresh air with which their odors and gasses blended. She returned and set the empty pail on a porch step, then made off toward the roothouse.

A school lad returning from the outhouse to class stalled by the porch to kill time. Jed Carter began walking toward the gate.

A rig was turning into the yard with Mrs. Anderson, from town, at the reins accompanied by three stalwart women. Mrs. Anderson reined the horse to a stop as they paralleled Jed.

"Fine day, Jed!"

Jed nodded that it was.

"You just keep that mine running!"

"Still need pledges for the bell! Thought we'd cover some of this territory today."

Jed's departing response was in the form of a weak handwave. Pledges! Phooey! Out to see how a school could be run in a farmhouse. He mulled over the situation in regards to Petra. It certainly wasn't a day to get back on the winning side. He plodded back to the mine, thinking of her and little else.

The following days turned out to be nothing but grueling, dawn to dusk workdays and not seeing Petra was proving sheer misery. Any momentary notions Jed had of leaving the workings to see her were ejected from his mind when Captain Sommers spotted loose timbers in the cribbing of the shaft. It was work which commanded top priority of attention. They were short one good man, Mikko. Who had been gone for almost a week, being a contestant in wrestling matches being held in Coyuta.

It was touchy work which required tricky maneuvering of timbers in a confined area. Labor which demanded alert minds and agile bodies, tough hands straining at arms length to shift and wedge the green timbers. It was well after darkness each day, when alternating work crews could no longer straighten their backs that they climbed out of the shaft and extinguished their lamps. They dragged their spent bodies to the plank tables in the cookhouse where they wolfed down a late supper meal. Lowered the level of the whiskey keg and conversed through hazes of smoke and dragged their bodies to the bunkhouses when sleep began conquering their minds.

It was noon hour of the middle of the week at which time Mikko trudged into camp carrying three silver cups, that Captain Sommers gave permissioin to start raising ore.

Jed had given of himself as much as any man on the property. Tired and disheveled, he cared less about ore. Thoughts of Petra and his love for her kept simmering his soul. Not seldom did he look to the ribbon of smoke... rising beyond the cluster of spruce across the Yellow Dog. Captain Sommers, his features reflecting the fatigue of his men, leaned his tired body against a half-empty supply wagon. Briefly he massaged the kink in the back of his neck. All the while observing Jed, whose inner restlessness was showing.

"Hear Charlie tell this morning of being low on eggs," said Sommers. "Might be well to please the old boy and pick some up."

123

The distance from the mine workings to Kelso's homestead could be short indeed when a man put his mind to covering it in all haste. So it was this afternoon with Jed Carter. His heart had told him much these past few days. Petra had definitely moved into his life. He had discovered the depth of his love for her. And he believed she loved him still. There were those unplanned happenings some days ago. His lousy behavior. But he figured he knew Petra well enough, understood her far beyond young Eric's realm of conception. She would one of these days listen.

He passed Dolan's house which showed no signs of activity save for a grazing cow and some chickens running loose. Close to Holmstrom's he was hailed by Gus, who was tending to his old, lame horse. Gus walked to the roadside to greet him. To engage in discourse about some cousin of his coming over from Sweden, and if there might be any chance of his cousin getting work at the mine. Jed listened with polite interest, all the while his restless body shifting his weight from foot to foot.

Near Stig's property, he swept a glance at the place. He conceded for fact. Stig was really one heck of a good guy. It just being that, for quite a while back, he and Stig tred on fractured ground since both cared for the same girl.

He stopped walking. In the open field between Stig's home and Kelso's, he spotted Stig and Pa Kelso at work on a project frequently mentioned. Staking a pole line into the ground between their homes. Poles which would suspend a guidewire to keep one from getting lost in stormy winter weather. Petra was heading in their direction, her head high, a breeze brushing her hair.

Her sudden appearance was heartening... or was it?

She walked directly to where the men worked and interrupted them with brief conversation. Tools were dropped to the ground and all three headed back toward Kelsos.

124

The ensuing weeks were unbearably long. The golden leaves on the trees, the golden treasure he and Petra had imagined to be their very own, severed their attachments with each passing hour and drifted to the ground. Jed Carter for the first time in his life knew dejection. He missed Petra something terrible. The daylight work hours were bad enough, but darkness set in early and the hours after the supper meal, spent in the confines of his bunkhouse, dealing over and over a worn deck of marked cards, offered no easement to his self-imposed misery.

CHAPTER 9
Things Looking Up

It was late in the afternoon, a couple of hours before the day's work would end. Captain Sommers sat at the splintery table in the mine office, alternately working on mathematical problems and graphic charts. The answers he had hoped for were not falling in place, he scratched the back of his head with indecision.

The government weather flag in town which fluttered over the town hall had been the white one, with a black square in the middle, giving warning of the approach of cold weather. All signs of winter were coming into evidence. Northern lights, casting an eerie green glow on the northern horizon were a frequent phenomenon. Wedges of geese winging south honked overhead daily. It was going to be a hard winter, judging from the thick coats of the fur bearing animals, the sudden and early flight of night hawks to the south. The dry, hot summer certainly meant something.

Captain Sommers this very week doubled the work crew on the sawmill to insure ample firewood for the long winter ahead. Protective sheds were being built over the shafts as well as a cover over the whim. Buildings were being banked with sawdust and Sommers mulled over the good fact that three bunkhouses were nearing completion. Box stoves to heat them were already in storage. The roothouse was filled with provisions and baled hay stored for the horses.

But what had been considered minor drawbacks in the tunnel were becoming mushrooming problems with each passing day. In the tunnel the pounding strokes of the hammers and the shovelfuls of ore thrown into the cars caused circulation of dust which filtered into the lungs of the diggers. Dripping surface water kept the tunnel floor wet, and cold air had moved in causing a few respiratory afflictions. Rails imbedded upon loosely laid sills were giving under the weight of heavily loaded cars and more than one left the track.

All schemes to wit's end on how to dry the tunnel had fizzled out. Nobody brainstormed a solution that solved the problem for long.

Ventilation was becoming the stickiest of problems. Fresh air. The life of all mines. The hand operated blower set at the adit had failed to meet direct needs and had long been rejected. After which Clem Copley diagramed and worked out a solution whereby the tunnel would be left to ventilate itself by aerostatic laws. Plank boxes, airtight and measuring twelve feet by four inches square inside, were constructed at the sawmill. They were suspended along one side of the tunnel near the top to draw in ventilating currents, planned, that the impure air would be withdrawn by similar boxes suspended on the opposite wall. The boxes firmly secured upon dry cedar pegged into holes drilled into the sides of the tunnel.

Yet frequent occurrences of stagnation of the ordinary current were experienced, and the change of season and winds were causing reversals. Great difference was discernable when a blow of wind shifted direction. There were windless days, when work pushed beyond the brattice, work heavy with powder smoke, ceased to be affected with fresh air.

In the mornings ventilation wasn't too bad, when the circulation was renewed during the night during the absence of the diggers. But there was many an afternoon, and especially near quitting time, when the atmosphere was charged with smoke and the air plenty sickening. The men left the tunnel one by one, when the flames on their lamps grew large and of a pale blue color indicating the presence of air too foul to inhale. Or because they had headaches and could no longer work.

Regular testing of the tunnel was conducted with candles, and days were many when there was difficulty in keeping a light when the air was still.

In the North Beaver shaft the air wasn't much better. Guiding air currents to the bottom of the shaft was troublesome, and wagon loads of pipe which were being dumped on the property for ventilation of the shaft were running high in cost.

Problems came in bunches. The past few weeks had revealed that Clem Copley and Bill Worthington had eased off with their efforts, neglecting their responsibility of advancing the brattice to the face of the workings. Both men had been found at various times during work hours sitting by the whiskey keg. Days were uncounted when by sundown they were in drunken stupor. They took light of Captain Sommers worries, themselves considering the foulness of the air a mere inconvenience and slight enhancement of the price per foot.

The tunnel was winding deeper and deeper and fresh air was still failing to penetrate the face of the workings. Captain Sommers was on the verge of ordering an expensive blower when Mikko's inventive mind patterned one. It was a scheme completely unheard of. Operated by water from pesky Beaver Lake, it was proving a tremendous success.

* * * * *

Captain Sommers dug out more blueprints, located some graph paper and began figuring. The office door behind him squeaked open and shut. He didn't lift his eyes from his work, but pushed his hat to the back of his head and kept figuring.

Jed watched over Sommers' shoulder for a while before his few words broke the silence. "Another car laying on its side. Nobody hurt."

Captain Sommers was unstirred. Not surprised. Jed's voice took momentum. "That tunnel floor is too damn soggy to firm up any rails. We got to come up with something or we'll be sending a body home in a box one of these days." He moved to the solitary office window and stared outside.

"We're gonna try something different, pard," responded Sommers, crumbling up scraps of figure work in his big fist. "Crude but worth a try. Ever give thought that spiked boards would work as drain pipes? Suspend them by metal strappings. There won't be any mining done for a couple of weeks, but we're gonna whip this thing yet."

*   *   *   *   *

The unexpected appearance of Ed Morley at the workings bright and early the next morning, and the good news he carried with him threw a wave of excitement over the entire camp. The mill had arrived! Set over on the siding by Lil's place. A massive machine, disassembled in several sections.

It was word that had been anticipated for weeks, yet hearing the news keyed the spirits of the crew. Orders were issued to tie up work at the noon hour.

Shortly after the mid-day meal was devoured the wagons were hitched, and began to roll, as the horses threw themselves into the harnesses. The caravan wended the Holyoke Trail toward town with every man enthusiastic about loading the big mill sections. Plans were to rent out Jake's flatbed wagon, if needed.

Charlie stood back watching them go, intending to scrub up in the sauna and get to bed early.

Curious townsfolk were loitering by the railroad siding looking at the new church bell which was on a flatcar in a heavy slatted crate. It was a fine big bronze bell and they hoped it had a mellow tone, for it would touch their lives every morning, noon and evening. It would give the town a sense of unity and rhythm for the sun was often hidden by clouds and nobody's clocks were the same, those that were working. Others stood looking at the mill, amazed at the enormity of its sections, intrigued by the large Cornish pump.

"Should have ordered it long ago!" exclaimed Hank Manson, jumping down from the flatcar. He told the admiring crowd, "it's manufactured to do close work, the heart of the gold saving process."

"This baby will get the gold out of the rock," quipped Syd Crawford. "With this grinder the company will pay its way and we can start thinking about dividends."

Those who had stock smiled in satisfaction and beamed like proud owners.

Hank Manson felt a tap on his shoulder and turned to see Mrs Anderson. She was there to inspect the bell, for she was one of those who worked the hardest to get it. She had been reviewing her long campaign list of contributions and pledges but just scratched the pledge submitted by Lil, because immorally earned money would not be accepted. But Mrs. Anderson had something else on her mind.

"Mr. Manson, you yst ta man I vant see. Now ve talk 'bout sometin' dis town people don' like. Many times ve notis. Dem vagons vat belong to Holyoke Company. Mit boxes powder, hauled down town streets. An' sometimes stop by saloons, many long, long hours, mit nobody in driver's seat. Dat's vat I man, is dat you men show poor head vork."

Somebody in the crowd over by the bell was urgently calling Mrs. Anderson. She departed, saving Hank Manson the necessity of any response. Instead, he turned to direct gruff words to some rambunctious lads who were scampering over the rail cars, hollering to get the hell down from there before they hurt themselves.

A raised male voice coming from the rear of the group drowned out most talk. "Hey Mikko! Mik!" Heads turned, to see the rail agent, red faced and panting from running, holding a letter high above his head. When the agent's eyes found Mik his voice keyed in pitch... "...from Chermany! From Chermany, Mik! Vat you been lookin' for to come evry day!"

The letter! So important a missile that the agent chose to deliver it direct to Mike instead of routing it through the store mail boxes.

Mikko's blunt fingers ripped open the envelope. His eyes glowed as he read the long waited contract, concentrating on one paragraph... 'said match to take place on the 15th of December, 1864 in Ishpeming, Michigan, USA.' Mik's heart leaped. Six weeks from the day! He looked at the date of writing and the postmark, the letter had arrived in good time. Maybe, thought Mikko, a bit of strategy by Hans Schimmler, allowing little time for conditioning.

The glow on Mik's face was read by Hank Manson, he arrested his ambitious thoughts and his own features took on a relaxed expression. "First we go to Nick's for beer! Got plenty of reasons to celebrate!"

In a group they moved on foot along the tracks and jauntily trooped into the Black Bear. Everybody except Alex, who headed homeward with concern, his wife being heavy with child. Accompanied by Nels, whose home was in the same direction.

      *   *   *   *   *

In the print shop Ed Morley with arms inked to the elbows smilingly set headline type which would rock the whole district. Which news would in no time flow into the outside world.

LOCAL FINN TO MEET
WORLD HEAVYWEIGHT WRESTLING CHAMP
HERE IN DECEMBER. (In smaller print below the
headlines): Contract signed.

He wrote up a superb editorial for the front page of the POST after having a long interview with Mikko. It told of Mik's homelife in the old country and of his unmatched strength as a lad. Why he made a decision to come to America. About his phenomenal strength on the mats and his emotions on rising so fast in the sport, and his reaction to the opportunity of taking on the world champ.

Printed tickets for the match were being grabbed up at the store and in saloons all the way to Iron Bay. Necessary precautions were being taken about selling to scalpers.

*   *   *   *   *

Operations at the Holyoke were moving with increased momentum and Jed Carter found himself with less and less time for self-pity. Hank Manson and Syd Crawford were on the property almost daily. Hank assisting with technicalities of installing the mill. Syd, not knowing much about machinery but riding out mostly to keep Hank company on the trek.

The rails in the tunnel were firmed up pretty well much to everybody's relief. Though foul air continued to stagnate the excavation and the diggers were showing increased fatigue at the end of each day. Accidents were becoming commonplace, by reason of spent air dulling minds causing slowness in reactions.

The hours of daylight were getting shorter, the air was getting quite nippy and by nightfall temperatures hovered around the freezing mark. Mornings found the ground and roofs of the buildings white with frost and the stream becoming edged with ice. Pails of water left outdoors overnight were coated with thin layers of ice.

132

On two successive days cold winds sweeping in from the north carried light flurries of snow.

For weeks Nels had been far from well. He had thinned down, his shoulders sagged forward and he suffered spasms of heavy coughing. It was everybody's feeling that the powder smoke and gasses had burned his lungs for good. None of the remedies bought in town did any good, nor did any of Pa Kelso's home-brewed concoctions. Nels conceded loss of physical stamina and left the property to spend the winter at home.

Jed Carter had seen few sick days in his entire life. Notwithstanding, he lay in his bunk recovering from an aching throughout his body, presumably brought on by dripping surface water in low off-shoots. Forced to rest by Dan, who hid his boots to keep him off his feet. His worse days of sickness had passed, days when he lay drenched in sweat and oblivious of spells of slight delirium. The fever had broken, leaving him with but aching muscles to heal.

Jallu came in now and then to keep company. Jallu, who had been spending a good deal of time in town, hanging around and getting drunk with some no-good Husker who lived in a tarpaper shanty on the edge of town. A man who had worked a short time at the mine as a sorter, and quit. Jallu had been back on the job only a week when his stomach went bad again, he suffered an attack of dysentery and got a recurrence of the shakes.

Captain Sommers had long pondered. That Jallu always had plenty of money, more than his wages could reflect. He was playing a hunch that Jallu might be getting bonus cash by resorting to petty theft, not at all difficult by the common occurrence of gold in small nuggets and sights in the quartz. Sommers had even on occasion unobserved shaken the burlap sacks under Jallu's bunk to see if they were weighted with gold bearing rock.

Today Jallu had downed the last of the patent

medicine with no healing results. Now with Charlie's assistance he was experimenting with a new remedy for his ailing stomach. Pulverizing granite which showed rich in minerals and proceeding to heat the fines in Charlie's big oven.... inhaling the fumes so that the mineral values would pass through his weakened system. Muttering to himself when anybody was within hearing distance, that he hoped somebody would give him a decent burial.

*   *   *   *   *

Evening dusk dimmed the bunkhouse. Jed was lying in his bunk with his eyes closed, his hands folded under his head. He lay motionless, sleeping intermittently. There were sporadic hours when the aching would let up some. When he mentally went to work blocking a route for a rail which would move the ore from the stockpile to a town rail.

The door was opened wide, emitting its usual squeak. In came Mikko, to tell that he wouldn't be playing cards tonight since he was going to town to meet his girlfriend. With those words he departed leaving Jed to worrying a bit... that Mik had fashioned the pattern of courting this one particular girl from Coyuta quite regularly of late. Was he training enough for his match. Getting enough sleep? Mik was a man of few words, yet outside talk about the character of this certain female of his pointed out the fact that she was uninhibited.

Mik had been gone but shortly when again squeaking hinges on the door spoke out company. Jed opened his eyes and rubbed them with the back of his hand, then raised his head. Two figures stood outlined in the doorway. A match was scratched and a lantern gave light.

"Got yerself some company." It was Dan's cheery voice. Jed attempted to raise himself to his elbows but a soft hand on his brow held him down. He looked upward, to see Petra smiling down at him.

134

Petra! The most unexpected person! No woman had ever set foot in any of the bunkhouses, such ramshackle abodes. None fit for a woman's eyes.

She set a cardboard box bound with twine at the foot of the bunk. The tallow candle in her hand which had illuminated her way she put in a pocket of her long woolen sweater. Her cold fingers fumbled at the knot on her headwear.

Dan suspended the lantern from a rafter pole and hauled over a crate for her to sit down on. Then the latch on the door clicked shut and he was gone.

The flickering light caught her silky hair held in place with a comb. Her face, partially covered by the turned up collar of her sweater revealed cheeks flushed red from the walk in the cold. Her breathing was rapid, her bosom rose and fell with irregularity.

Jed was the first to find speech, but simply could speak her name... "Petra!"

"Hello Jed." Then she giggled. "You look so funny with whiskers."

There was brief, restless silence, then her hand reached out and her fingers closed on his perspiring hand.

"Dan told me today that you've been sick." Her voice was soft, as always.

"Out of my boots. But not exactly giving up on life."

"I've brought you some of father's herb tonic. And some biscuits and cheese, for when you're feeling better. ....But that's not my reason for coming."

She released her hold on his hand to brush back a lock of loose hair that fell over an eye, and to unbutton her heavy sweater. She smoothed over her full skirt.

Jed Carter was now smiling for the first time in days. Man! Her sudden presence was pure tonic!

"I trust all has been well at home?"

"Nothing at all to complain about..."

"How's Pa?"

135

"Busy as ever. The last few days he and Stig been setting in more poles for the guideline. They got to get them in before the ground freezes."

"Suppose Pa's still sore at me.."

Her eyes turned down.

"H'mm. Still convinced that I'm a bad sort of guy."

It was not Petra's intent that the evening be consumed with talk negative to happiness, and she switched the subject. "Today was pickling day. Tomorrow we string apples for drying."

"How about Florence and those kids?"

"They show up every day, even Jorn Holmstrom." Jorn Holmstrom. Her thoughts churned, mentioning his name. "Want to know something? I'll tell you. It was Jorn who blasted that ball through our roof."

A light frown cast over Jed's face. Jorn the culprit? "Sounds crazy, but I'm listening."

"All because he's suddenly gone sweet on Sarah Dolan."

"So.. how does Sarah fit in?"

"Well. Jorn never did like going to school. Until just lately he's changed his mind, when Sarah began noticing him and going out of her way to talk to him. Since then Jorn's been showing off, doing stunts, trying to impress her. Boasted one day at recess time, "You'd just better believe, cuz one of these days I'm gonna move that iron ball farther'n anybody ever has!"

Petra was convinced. "Somehow, Jed. Jorn got hold of some powder. It's just that the explosion sent the ball in the wrong direction. I've cornered Jorn about it, but he refuses to talk."

"The powder could have been some of ours."

"But my lips are sealed about the whole matter. I'm telling only you."

"How's our friend Florence?"

"Everybody's learning to spell and read, and she is helping them to talk nicer. Two of the boys are reading

136

so good that she gave them a holiday. No book work. Instead they were allowed to help father clean the barn. Last week the weather being not too bad, the Commissioner rode out with her pay and our rent money. Told Pa how pleased he was with Florence's work. Boy!" Petra giggled. "If he only knew how often she has been seeing Stig... he'd sure swallow his teeth! Fire her for sure!" Petra paused, taking another recollection from her mind and her nose wrinkled up. "Yesterday things didn't go too good. One of the girls was on her way to the outhouse and a bucket of water was thrown upon her from one of the classroom windows."

There was more to tell of, many happenings since Jed's visit to the homestead. About the school lads stirring up fights with the girls at recess time. Of Stig's three day confinement from the kick of a horse.

And Jed meant to get on the subject of Mikko's big match come December. And about Charlie's escapade last night, having to be rescued from the cable seat over mid-stream, being drunk and not knowing how to get back.

Their thoughts stopped short. Again her hand reached out and she pressed his fingers. "So how have things been with you?"

He pulled himself up to a sitting position and propped the straw filled gunny sack behind him to better support his shoulders. He rolled a cigarette and put a light to it. "Days come and go with nothing specially new happening. Waiting for another day hoping to wake up all mended. Dan levels off with me now and then. Says it's the way life goes." He chuckled lightly. "Funny guy, that Dan. Won't admit to ever having weakened to a woman but came back from town last Saturday night with part of an earring in his beard."

He reached out to crush his cigarette in a tin on the floor. His lips brushed her cheek. "Do you think your Pa can get along without you? Because I'm asking you here

137

and now... will you marry me?"

Such an utterance from Jed's lips Petra had many times dreamed of but at the moment came totally unexpected. She breathed a sigh. "I've decided that you would make a good husband."

She slipped her body onto the edge of his bunk and took his stubbled face in her hands. Kissed him as never before. She yielded to his arms, and her voice muffled on his cheek... "Jed, I love you... I love you much.."

The light of the lantern suspended above them flickered weakly, then extinguished itself.

CHAPTER 10
The Wrestling Match

Two weeks passed. Temperatures in the district stayed below freezing every day and a film of white covered the ground. Wagons on the mine property were put into storage. Horses were shod with winter shoes and sleds readied for hard use. Arrangements had been made with two Chippewas living in town to come out on snowshoes every Friday with the mail.

It was only yesterday that Mikko had gone into town to pick up a supplemental part for the mill, but was sidetracked into helping hoist the new church bell into position. With Mrs. Anderson watching close by, her big arms crossed over her bosom. Informing onlookers and passers-by "The bell vill ring evry day - at twelve noon and at six o'clock."

Descending the stairway in the small tower with the job all completed, Mikko found himself hemmed in by a group of admirers bombarding him with wrestling talk. It was that moment that alerted him, more than the nudging reminders of the Holyoke crew, that the date of the match was not far off.

And he put himself on a rigid training program. He decided for the time, to put Fredrika out of his mind. Rising before Charlie in the dark and frosty hours of each morning, he would run with varying acceleration miles along the Holyoke Trail. Lunchtime was spent

139

distance heaving a designated piece of green timber, the rings of which measured quite a few seasons. Not idling valuable training time after the supper meals, but running through body strengthening exercises in the confinement of his bunkhouse. Advantageous it was when Stig, who carried good physical weight and knew a lot about wrestling began dropping in to give Mik man to man practice. Always accompanied by Jorn Holmstrom who aspired to breaking into the sport and was taking every opportunity of learning everything he could about it.

More than anxious to contribute to Mik's physical welfare, Charlie, three times a day set before Mik only foods listed on the special training diet he and Mik had worked out.

Long after everybody was asleep Mikko lay awake in his bunk, his soul stirring with excitement over his forthcoming match with the world's cleverest mat artist. He lay quietly with eyes open, carrying silent discourse within himself. He felt no inner fear of the champ. But should he defeat Hans Schimmler... and the world heavyweight crown rest upon his head. His thoughts would revert to his parents back in the old country. They surely would be proud of him. And he would be proud to bring the crown to America.

*   *   *   *   *

The Yellow Dog froze over, and the pipes in the mill house froze solid. Clem Copley was reflecting no worrisome thoughts over the frozen state of affairs and shrugged his shoulders as though it were no big thing. Stating, that working mines in northern Minnesota hadn't been all summer work. Boasting, that there were solutions to problems of cold weather.

He took over supervising the innovative idea of grooving boards and bolting them together encasing the piping. Frost couldn't penetrate the fabricated wood insulation and the wood tubing would add to the strength of the lines.   It could prove to be a time consuming process before all pipes were covered, Copley conceded, but no alternate method of insulating the pipes had been thought of.

*   *   *   *   *

The very same week brought to light further developments. It was made known to Captain Sommers that Jallu's friend in town, Husker, whose Finnish tongue twister last name most people never wasted time trying to pronounce, had developed an animosity toward him.   Ever since the day Captain Sommers refused to rehire him at the mine, Husker had been knocking Sommers' character in every saloon.

Captain Sommers had long established himself as a man of tolerance, yet he didn't digest too well the digs and fabrications that Husker was dishing out. The day's work load at the mine was visibly heavy, nevertheless Captain Sommers made a special trip to town and found utter satisfaction in locating Marshall Malaroni. They held brief conference, Sommers telling in short of the common practice of the miners in saving nice specimens of gold for themselves, to which he had no objections. Wholeheartedly endorsing Jed's wild idea, that the pint whiskey bottle of fine gold Jed had swept off the mill could nicely be fashioned into a wedding ring.

But Captain Sommers had strong suspicions that a certain individual had gone too far with his "keepers".

Husker was home, alone, when Marshall Malaroni and his stocky aide knocked on his door and produced a search warrant.   At which sight of, and Malaroni's interpretation of, Husker dramatically doubled over as though in great pain, emphasizing his imminent need to go see Doc Billington, that he was dying. Marshall Malaroni stood firm in exercising the powers of his office, he didn't believe Husker was dying and the search began. Likely hiding places were rummaged, assorted sized sacks and containers holding what they were

141

looking for were drawn out and set by the doorway. When all areas of suspicion had been nosed out to Marshall Malaroni's satisfaction, the loot consisted of sacks of highly mineralized gold rock. Some of it quartz that had been crushed and only the richer portions saved. A whiskey bottle unearthed under a loose floorboard was filled with fine gold and a flat fish box containing very fine rock was brought to light from beneath the cookstove. Close to two hundred fifty pounds of "keepers", with Husker miraculously recovered from his dying hour and feigning ignorance as to how the booty got placed in his dwelling.

Marshall Malaroni instructed his aide to put the evidence on the sled outside the doorway. He snapped handcuffs on Husker and walked him to the lockup to await examination.

*   *   *   *   *

The last wire received from Max Grubenstein stated that Hans Schimmler and he would be arriving in Ishpeming on December 13, two days prior the scheduled match.

It was the day marking Hans Schimmler's arrival. Leaning toward the noon hour. Train number 7 was running late again, the tracks being covered with heavy snow.

A small group of townsfolk were gathered at the depot, most of them stomping their cold feet on the ground. Two sturdy lads had the honor of supporting a large banner "America Welcomes Hans Schimmler". Uniformed members of a brass band milled around rubbing their hands together to keep the circulation in their fingers.

When from afar the bell of engine 7 clanged her arrival and was seen puffing billows of black smoke into the sky, hords of people came running from diverse directions to swell the group already on hand. By the snow-coated platform the wheels of the belching steam engine screeched to a slow stop. All attention was focused on the one passenger car. Within minutes of stopping the door was pushed open by a trainman who stepped down, followed by two young couples, then a mother carrying a baby bundled in fur. A bespectacled man of middle age and medium build, wrapped in a full length raccoon fur coat, nimbly alit and introduced himself as Max Grubenstein to the man standing nearest the rail car exit who was none other than saloon keeper Nick. A huge figure completely filled the doorway of the rail car - Hans Schimmler! Awe struck the crowd. The brass band struck up.

Hans Schimmler turned his body sidewise to descend the three steps to the ground, such move being necessitated by the width of his shoulders and hulk of his body. The crowd looked on in wonderment, mouths agape. There were loggers in the immediate area who were considered to be giants of men, but at the moment Hans Schimmler loomed larger than any.

Hans looked down upon Nick, he shot out a massive hand and began pumping Nick's hand, establishing a bond of friendship, whereby the band director motioned for the music to stop. Hans' bass voice broke the still air.

"I presume you to be Mikko Rymponen's agent?"

Nick was caught short of speech. Never had be communicated with a person of eminence. Taking the cigar butt from his mouth and almost blurting out "Mik ain't got no agent", he held his tongue when the glorious thought struck. Mik had all along proved himself worthy of an agent though he couldn't afford the luxury. Nick broke his hand from Hans Schimmler's grip, he erected his stance and straightened his necktie. He locked eyes with Schimmler.

"Dat's right - Rymponen's agent." He returned the cigar stub to his mouth, and in a move of heretofore unseen dignity reached down for the two valises which

143

belonged to the men, then continued discourse in his new self-appointed role.

In the background the new church bell rang out the noon hour.

Which reminded Nick that it was time for victuals. "Maybe you hongry now? We fixa you up good in hotel." The engine bell began clanging and puffs of smoke blackened the air. Hans Schimmler couldn't hear and Nick repeated himself. Hans smiled his approval. Nick broke a pathway through the crowd, Jorn Holmstrom assisting with the valises, and led by blaring brass everybody trooped toward the Chippewa Hotel.

For a few hours that same afternoon, and extended hours the next day Hans Schimmler executed warm-up and limbering exercises in Blumstrom's storage building which was comfortably heated and officially set up for the match. A storm shed had been added to the entranceway to conserve heat. Inside the building, a twenty foot diameter circle, well defined, was thickly covered with sawdust. The lighting had been improved, it being an evening match, and rough bleachers had been erected.

Betting was getting heavier in the saloons with proprietors of most of the establishments holding the stakes.

*   *   *   *   *

That very afternoon at the Holyoke, had not Ikey and Dan been blazing trees to be felled to mark a rail bed, things might have turned out entirely different. As it was, their keen eyes were quick to detect the approach along the Holyoke Trail of a horse drawn sleigh carrying three occupants. A sharp bend in the road brought the sleigh near where they worked and the horse was drawn to a halt. The whiskered, straight-faced man at the reins hollered out to Ikey who was nearest the sleigh.

"How much farther to the mine?" His voice carried an

144

overtone of grimness. His frowning face certainly meant something.

Ikey relaxed his hold on the axe handle letting it slip through his hand to the ground, he advanced toward the sleigh with Dan following him. They walked into the icy glare of a beady-eyed tight-lipped woman snuggled under a robe beside the driver, whom they took to be his wife. Their eyes flicked to the pretty face of the occupant in the rear seat, who was near buried beneath a bulk fur robe.

Fredrika!

Her face was unsmiling.

Mikko's Fredrika! What... Dan's thinking was cut off when once again the driver growled out his original inquiry. "I say, how much farther on to the Holyoke Mine?"

Already Ikey sensed that all was not well. "Yer lookin' fer somebody special?"

The man's lips moved, there was some hesitancy within, not sure he should answer. Then uncontrollably he blurted out, "Mik Rymponen..." The anger in his two word delivery sounded out real trouble. The man was hot under the collar. And these days Ikey and Dan knew, Mik shouldn't be troubled. Lack of any response provoked further irritation in the man.

"Case you don't understand clear, it's Rymponen the wrestler I'm looking for. Who knocked up our Freddy. So there's things to be talked about, like a wedding."

Never in his life had Ikey evaded the truth or uttered an outright lie but now he did. "Mik left fer town yes'tiday. Said he'd be stayin' in town till the match is over. Think ya kin find 'im down at Blumstrom's place."

The fabrication took effect and Dan and Ikey breathed in relief. It sent the unhappy party back towards town, away from Mik, who was no more than a quarter mile away heaving green timber.

Only leaving Ikey perplexed, that his conscience didn't

even bother him.

Daylight hours in this northern region were short in December and when dawn came the next day which was Saturday the 15th, it was well past the hour of eight. Sunrise settled into a clear crisp blue just as the Farmer's Almanac foretold.

By noon hour Main Street was stirring with above normal activity, with sled and cutters moving in diverse directions, with everybody tending to matters of business usually left for Saturday night, but by necessity, fulfilling their needs earlier in the day since twilight would find every male inhabitant in the district waiting to witness the match. The populace on Main suddenly swelled when the special train that started in Chicago puffed into the station, releasing nine coaches of ticket holders who had come to enjoy what promised to be the most spirited wrestling match ever held in America. Now hundreds of people were roving the snowy streets, many patronizing the saloons. Most everybody stopping in at Blumstrom's general store to pick up a free souvenir, a stamped tin plate commemorating the event, and to be favored with handbillings announcing the event, giving all rules of the match. Likewise people entered the store for the purpose of recording their guess as to the day and hour the large candle displayed in the store window would burn out, which prize would be ten dollars cash.

Free calendars were much in demand, and when Blumstrom's supply became nearly exhausted he ceased giving out but one to a family.

The warehouse was filled to capacity an hour before match time and ticket sales at the door were cut off. Turnaways later were calculated to have exceeded three hundred, though none were Holyoke men who cut their work day early in order to get to town in good time.

Now Marshall Malaroni let the door open once more, to admit Ed Morley, equipped with writing materials under an arm. Ed worked his way to the vantage point which had been reserved for him near the edge of the sawdust filled circle. Already written on his note pad were interesting items of news obtained from brief prematch interviews with each man in his dressing room. Which rooms happened to be the ladies' and men's fitting rooms in the general store.

Nick entered the building thirty minutes before match time with Mikko following him close behind, then Jorn Holmstrom with clean towels draped over an arm and carrying a bucket of water. Rousing cheers and hoots of support for the local wrestler had scarcely died down when Hans Schimmler made his impressive appearance. Striding toward the sawdust ring, his handsome head held high, he sported black knee britches and regulation loose canvas jacket. Contrasting Mikko's garb which consisted of tight black trunks and regulation jacket.

A platform scale which had been transported from Jake's livery, considered to be the most accurate in the area, had been set up at the ringside. Each contestant weighed in, said weights attested to by both Nick and Max Grubenstein, who made a late entry, and by the two impartial umpires and the match referee from Chicago. The referee, who carried an immortal name in wrestling, was sixty-five years of age and in his wrestling days recognized as champion in America. He was a referee not to be denounced, having met 536 opponents during his mat career.

Ed Morley jotted something on his notepad.

Now a dignitary from Detroit, a political aspirant for governorship of the state advanced to the center of the ring and made a speech, entirely irrelevant to the evening's event. When his abbreviated oration came to an end music furnished by the Sons of Sweden brass band filled the air. When their rendition ended and was applauded, the two umpires and referee entered the ring as did the two contestants from opposite sides.

A gong struck. The referee moved into the center of the ring and introduced each wrestler and gave his respective weight, which fact ejected surprise among most everybody this big Hans tipped the scale at a mere fifteen pounds over Mik. It was announced that the match would be catch-as-catch-can, without handicap, to go the best two out of three falls. Match scoring would include total points.

Mik and Hans Schimmler advanced and shook hands, then pranced back to where their respective agents stood ready to serve them. Ready with water pails, towels and supply kits. The contestants kicked off their shoes to bare feet and began warming up with body twists.

The starting gong sounded. Each man fell into a low crouch and warily advanced with open hands. Almost immediately they were tugging at the canvas jackets and forcing one another about the ring. The crowd was more than ready for fast action. Rumor had been that Schimmler had talked of throwing the Finn boy twice in 75 minutes.

Partisans for Mik began to holler out with cheers of support as the agility of Hans Schimmler was quickly revealed, when rapid change of holds were quickly executed.

There was shuffling in the thick sawdust. Pushing and pulling, dancing around, tackling and tripping, each man bent on achieving the first fall without wasting time. All to the increased roars of audience participation when a good move was made. Over they rolled, over and over in the sawdust, their hair becoming full of it. Nothing big happened up to the halfway mark in the opening bout, when neither man risked nothing foolish.

The pulse of the crowd quickened when Schimmler managed to wind his powerful arms around Mik, lifting him high and throwing him hard on the sawdust. He leaped upon Mik with dead weight. With hard work Schimmler managed to force a hip and a shoulder of his challenger to the sawdust but it wasn't enough for a fall. Mik wriggled out from underneath, sawdust was kicked about. Schimmler began proving himself an extremely aggressive wrestler. He executed a neat side head lock and a trip, Mik's knees bent and one hand touched the floor. Foul! Groans of disappointment were drowned out with increasing shouts of encouragement to Mikko.

Mikko read Nick's signal of two minutes left to the round and went to work harder. Briefly he had Schimmler face down, eating sawdust, but Hans explosively broke free from the arm lock. Sawdust flew thick, all to be seen was arms and legs of both men. Mik's hand again touched the sawdust and an official fall was recorded against him.

Hans Schimmler pranced to the side of his manager, winning the first fall in twenty-eight minutes and forty seconds.

Schimmler passed consent through the referee to allow the official five minute rest period permitted between falls but Mik's pride carried a reject to the offer.

Whereby the gong sounded and Mik came out with a flying tackle. Schimmler outmaneuvered him again, causing Mik to miss his target but before Schimmler could stabilize his feet Mik spun around and had him dancing on one leg. Schimmler's hands were tight on Mik's neck in a near choking hold, there was a retaliating illegal kick which brought admonition to both men from the umpires.

Hans Schimmler was displaying phenomenal strength in body to body wrestling, twice he put a bear hug on Mik and lifted him into the air. Now he was working stubborn Mik down to one knee. An umpire quickly moved in to break holds, the contestants shook hands and fought again. Mik was definitely the underdog, Schimmler was proving his superiority. Frequently his big fist held onto the front of Mik's jacket like a closed vice, he pushed Mik and pulled him, but Mik was hanging in there. Thinking 'he's no bigger'n them green logs I heave at the mill'. Over and over in the sawdust they rolled, Schimmler executing an escape, again both men leaped to their feet. There was body contact and a rending tear and Mik was minus a sleeve.

The gong sounded. Both men were breathing hard and agreed to rest the official two minutes permitted between bouts without a fall. At which point the brass instruments of the Sons of Sweden vibrated the air with a patriotic selection. Jorn greeted Mikko with an open towel, he rubbed down his idol and wiped off sawdust adhering to his wet skin. He shook the sawdust from Mik's hair, all the while Nick pouring advice into Mik's ear. The gong rang for continued action.

The voice of the crowd began clamoring for Mik to "Do something! Do something! Flatten him!" And that's just where Mik took over. From that point on the night was all Mik's. Some later gave due credit to Nick, for whatever words of advice he poured in Mik's ear. Whatever, Mikko was revealing an edge in sheer stamina, his pain rending lock holds on Schimmler were causing sweat to roll off the champ's body. Mik's lightning-like moves blended with acute timing, his agility in tripping began troubling the champ who was red-faced and hard panting for wind.

In sixteen minutes and five seconds Schimmler lay squarely on his back in the bounds of the ring. Mik had won his first fall!

Hans Schimmler welcomed the five minute rest allowed in the rules. Shortly after the gong sounded he again was flying through the air like green timber. Regaining his feet he retaliated with a kick above the knees and the umpire gave severe warning. Mik failed to dodge a flying tackle but nevertheless was hanging in good, knowing at this very point he was no less than equal, if not superior to big Hans. The count stood one apiece on falls. On total points Mik gave no thought. Now a rash dispute erupted between the two men over something that the crowd missed, when each man stood with arms drawn offering to strike. The referee quickly moved between them, offering protection against forfeit to the stake.

Action resumed. Mik twisted Schimmler around and kicked his legs from beneath him. He grabbed Schimmler's collar and one arm and turned him head over heels, with the crowd roaring like wild men. Schimmler managed to rise, but Mik executed a neat trip and Schimmler's shoulders hit the floor for his second fall.

Explosive cheers shook the building.

The two umpires and the referee huddled over the score table for a full three minutes before the referee broke to the middle of the ring to raise high in victory the brawny arm of the young Finn, who had settled beyond doubt that he was the best. Jorn Holmstrom sprung up from the sidelines and leaped onto Mik in embrace, beating hundreds of Mik's backers who rushed into the ring to congratulate him.

The brass band struck up and the crowd began pushing toward the door, some shoving for rapid exit to collect last minute bets from fast escaping scoundrels who chose to elude payment. Once outside Ed Morley quickly separated himself from the wild crowd, taking the short cut from behind the storage building to the church where he sounded out the bell in victory. Then hustling himself to the print shop where he went to work setting up type by light of midnight oil.

Straight to the Black Bear saloon the cheering, raving diggers trooped, in broken ranks of twos and threes, to celebrate Mik's victory. To promote a fitting celebration. For such honor as Mik had brought upon himself, to the town and country it wouldn't matter at all if some shifts were lost.

Ikey lagged behind in the thinning crowd. By the side door of the mercantile store he loitered. Mik should be shortly emerging, fully changed, and the honor would be his of escorting Mik to the saloon.

His pleasant thoughts were disturbed when a figure separated from the waning crowd and came rushing at him out of the darkness. Now the glaring face of the man was so near his own that the garlic smelling breath was far from appreciated. The man nailed a fierce grip into Ikey's shoulder.

"Where is he? That scoundrel!"

One good look at the man's face was all Ikey needed.

Fredrika's father! Seething in boiling rage. And the celebration blast at the saloon getting in full swing! The man rapped a clenched fist into Ikey's chest.

"Your friend Mik Rymponen, that wrestler. Where is he... where is he! Tonight for sure me and him will talk about a wedding for Fredrika. Or half-purse to Freddy for damages." Ikey noticed that it was a pair of open handcuffs he was dangling in one hand.

Ikey's thoughts moved fast. "Ya.. never caught up with him yesterday?"

"Chased all over this bloomin' town looking for him. Don't even know what in the hell the damn scamp looks like. Couldn't even get a foot in the wrestling place tonight."

A chill tingled Ikey's spine when from the corner of his eye he saw light reflecting from the side door of the store building. He dared a look and breathed in relief.

"Mister. You betcha I kin help ya... There he is... that guy over there comin' outa the store building. Don't let 'im get away!" Ikey pointed out Hans Schimmler, standing alone, who had just emerged from the side door of the store. "Mister... give it to 'im good, everythin' he's got comin' to 'im for what he did to your Freddie!"

Mik was hoisted to the bar top in the saloon and toasted a thousand times that night, and victory booze was guzzled there all the next week.

With only Jed making a deflection. A day's trek to Iron Bay to seek out the town jeweler. On the outskirts of Iron Bay a couple of urchins dragging sleds gave directions. Go halfway up the steep hill alongside the lake, the shop is on the left side of the road.

He tied Blaze to the hitching post in front of the shop, entered, and bided his time before the display counter since a female customer had entered the place just ahead of him. He took immediate cognizance of the jeweler-optician. Why! Son-of-a-gun! He was the fella who'd staked his new boots in that back room poker game, Jed's very first afternoon in this town.

Jed waited his turn. He watched the optician's deft hands ply the tools of his trade, bending the bows of the woman's spectacles, the nosepiece just slightly. Satisfied with a more comfortable fit, the woman took her departure.

"I see your luck's been holding out at the card tables," quipped Jed.

Briefly the jeweler stood in frowning silence, not recognizing his customer. Curiosity loosened his tongue.

"What grounds you got for making talk like that, stranger?"

"You're still wearing those boots you once lost to me."

The jeweler's outburst of laughter and Jed's ribbing about the incident last spring proved the man was possessed of good humor.

It took not long to negotiate the business Jed had on his mind. He left with the jeweler the pint whiskey bottle of fine gold he had stored up, with the knowledge it would be sent away to be cast into an engagement ring and matching wedding band.

*　　　*　　　*　　　*　　　*

A special edition of the POST blazed headlines of Mik's great victory - LOCAL FINN DETHRONES WORLD WRESTLING CHAMP, and lengthy front page columns told in glorious detail how the young logger trained for the match by heaving timber, adhering to daily consumption of a bowlful of kirmopiima, and mentally conditioning himself by daily meditation in the sauna.

The day's story didn't please Marshall Malaroni as much as it did everybody else, since the news item stuck on the back page, asking for recruits to form a new brass band of which he would be the director, was not read or seriously absorbed by many, since nobody approached him about joining. Talk was all Mik Rymponen.

Newspapers throughout the country blazed out headlines about Mik's feat, and the train chugging into town the next Saturday carried in a news photographer from Chicago, who came to take pictures of the new champion. But Mik could not be located. He never did return to the mine. It was from Syd Crawford in the company office in town, that a slice of information was obtained, which Syd thought was something generally known. That two days previous Mik had stopped by the office to collect all of his pay, stating that he was quitting his job and leaving the district. Mumbling something on his way out about not being ready for marriage.

CHAPTER 11
Christmas

The peace of Christmas Eve reigned over the countryside. Under early evening moonlight Pa Kelso on snowshoes, his sons and daughter behind him on homemade skiis, trekked single file to the site of mother's snowy grave where they set a burning white candle.

The Holyoke was strangely quiet, the crew having abandoned camp, days back, to be with their families for Christmas. The only activity was the movement of Charlie and Pete in the cookhouse cleaning up on leftovers from the supper meal, and Jed scrubbing up in the sauna.

Jed followed the custom of the Finns in the area. He came out of the sauna naked and red-skinned and took a quick roll in the snow before slipping off to the bunkhouse. He dressed in a new shirt, new trousers, shrugged into his warm sheepskin jacket, turning up the collar, and pulling down the earflaps on his cap. With planned thoughts he hitched Blaze to a sleigh, retreated to a shed and returned with a set of brass bells which he tied on the shaft. Another trip back to the bunkhouse, and he tossed on the sleigh seat a bearskin robe. He slid onto the cold seat, pulled the peak of his cap low on his brow and lightly slapped the reins on the rump of Blaze.

The night was clear and cold. A silver half moon hung

155

high in the pale sky. The bells rang sharply and the runners squeaked on the frosty snow as Blaze trotted along the logging road beside the Yellow Dog. Jed reined tight, guiding her in the direction of the Kelso homestead.

At not too far a distance could be heard the howling of a coyote.

The ride across the ice of the Yellow Dog and across Dolan's snow meadows took not long, though a rut almost upset the sleigh. He passed the Dolan home which was in total darkness, passed Holmstrom's likewise darkened, and Stig's home, dark. The road opened up now. In no time flat he'd reach Kelsos. He removed a chopper mitt off his hand and felt in his sheepskin pocket to make sure his gift for Petra was resting safely.

Whisps of wood smoke, pine scented, curling from the two chimneys of the Kelso home penetrated his nostrils. Alongside the house, now, lighted candles on the Christmas tree reflected through the frosty windows. Blaze stopped by the open porch without reining. Homemade sleds with big wooden runners gave indication the neighbors were visiting. As Pa Kelso had mentioned was traditional on Christmas Eve. Timo's face appeared in a window, his small nose flattened against the pane. Before the bearskin could be cast aside the kitchen door was flung open by Eric, whose keen ears had long detected Jed's arrival. Eric stepped out onto the porch, his hands tucked in the warmth of his britches.

"C'mon in!" His voice was cheery. "We been watching and waiting for you. Everybody else is already here!"

Everybody but Stig, despite the fact that he had received a warm invitation. But circumstances being as they were, Stig mulled over one evening in his home while rubbing wax on the skis he had hand crafted for Petra. It would be best to go away for the holidays, spend some time with cousins in Chicago.

156

Jed mounted the four porch steps and followed Eric inside. He stood at the doorway tapping his one boot against the other knocking off the crusted snow, wiping them on a worn carpet laid down for that purpose. Joyous chatter and laughter reverberated throughout the house. The kitchen floor was strewn with straw, which he quickly found out was an old Finnish custom. Grinning, he responded to greetings shouted to him in English, Swedish and Finnish tongues. Jackpine was crackling in the cookstove and the warm air was permeated with a blend of cut balsam and boiling coffee. A sprig of mistletoe was hung in the doorway of the living room, wherein he could see the Christmas tree, erect on two crisscross boards and adorned with red apples and colored candles clamped to the boughs.

Timo was circling the kitchen table, eyeing the beautiful decoration set in the center - a big loaf of bread with real ears of corn sticking out of it. Singing to himself oblivious of listening ears....

"...up on the house top, cleek, cleek, cleek,
down troo the chimbley with good St. Neeck..."

There was creaking on the stairway leading upstairs, the fast tripping descent of two feet in black button shoes. A white petticoat showed, a red skirt with bright embroidery around the bottom. Petra. Wearing a white blouse with high lace collar and puffy sleeves, and a big smile.

On the bottom step she paused, her eyes starry. Though she wasn't really surprised at Jed's presence. Countless times, after darkness fell, she had moved from one window to another, downstairs and upstairs, peering through the frosted panes looking for signs of his arrival. She pranced across the kitchen floor.

"Was wondering if you'd ever get here!" She touched her hands to his arms, raised herself on tiptoes and put a kiss on his lips. "Merry Christmas, Mr. Prospector..."

Now there was that certain expression on her face, an

157

expression he had learned to half interpret, which told him that she had connived up a new scheme.

"We've decided that you should stay on a few days as our guest."

Stay on! An unexpected invitation it was. "Well, really. I really don't..." His words were loose strung. Pa butted in to put emphasis on the invitation. Finnish custom it was, for families to take in a guest for the Christmas season.

Petra laid her hands upon his shoulders. "Don't you try to decide. It's been agreed that we won't take no for an answer. Florence has gone home for the holidays. If you don't stay... why, we'd be all alone."

A warm and generous invitation it was. Certainly appealing to any man whose loved one was sheltered under the very same roof. Further deliberation of the issue was interrupted when Pa moved a corked crock of apple cider from the sideboard of the cupboard to the bench by the doorway. He took his cap and coat from a hook behind the door in preparation to going outside.

Fine. Just fine, thought Jed. Now. He addressed Pa directly. "Wait outside. I'll be right out."

Pa Kelso went outside. He waited as requested. He didn't comprehend but he waited. Jed circled the living room, everybody was needed outside. Everybody? Everybody? Even the ladies? Eyebrows arched, brows frowned with curiosity as heavy outer coats were removed from nails on the kitchen walls.

Petra was feeling concern. That mysterious, beguiling smile was growing on Jed's mouth. The identical smile she so often attempted to decipher.

Outside Pa Kelso was busy puffing on his pipe., trying to get it to burn, only to look up and see his guests pouring out of the house. Jed reached up to the eave of the porch roof and broke off an icicle, which he proceeded to snap into short bits. He cleared his throat, he addressed Pa directly but spoke loud for all to hear. "I trust that you're

158

a man of your word."

Pa took his pipe out of his mouth. "Vat you mean? Man uf vord? Vat dees all 'bout anyhow?"

Jed's head jerked a bob in the direction of the woodshed, he moved part way along the hard pathway leading toward it. Then looked back, to see that everyone was not following.

"Come on! This way!"

The snow on the side of the woodshed in which direction he broke tracks lay undisturbed by man. Directly under the tiny shed window, windsweeps, and the overhang of the eave had kept the snow from piling too high. He stopped. He proceeded to kick the snow around, swinging a boot in a sweeping motion till he struck the firmness of what he was seeking. The crusher ball. He fell to a knee and with his chopper mitts brushed off the loose snow. The challenger, now... if ever.

And everybody was beginning to comprehend.

Jed straightened himself, he peeled off his sheepskin coat and handed it to Pa. And Pa quickly joined him in spirit.

"I gif three chance tonight."

Jed shook his head negatively. "One chance." Fierce determination began burning within. "One chance. Like any man gets."

He flexed the muscles of his arms and bit the inside of his lip. he started to remove his choppers with the thought of insuring better grip with bare hands but decided against it. The steel would be too frigid for bare hands. Though again, the choppers could prove slippery since they were brand new. He stood for a moment flexing his fingers inside the mitts. Again he loosened his arm muscles, his chest expanded, contracted. He straddled his legs, working the loose snow under his boots till his feet held firm on the ground, then bent down and took a good hold on the ball.

159

His biceps bulged under his shirt sleeves. The ball gradually elevated from its resting place.

Every muscle in his body tightened. There could be no split second pause. Higher, higher, higher the ball was raised till it paralleled his chin and Pa's eyes. Jed's body held rigid like a shaft of steel.

There were gasping oh's of surprise.

"My! My! I don't believe!"

"Goot boy, Ched!"

There was the clapping of hands in approval.

Only Jed's eyes shifted, to read Pa's face. Visible by light of the moon, it showed pleasure and surprise.

"Goot! Cheen high. Yust same I leeft, Cheen high!"

The entire performance took but scarcely a minute, yet the strain was already paining his wrists. He couldn't hold up the sphere any longer.

He let the ball crash to the ground and his muscle slumped to limpidness. He closed his eyes. He'd done it! Doggone! He'd done it!

And all had witnessed.

He felt Pa putting the sheepskin coat around his shoulders. "Now eet's vot Petra say."

Jed Carter made no attempt to hide his big smile as he and the boys bedded Blaze down for the night..

Everybody scurried back into the warm house and hung up their coats, then settled themselves comfortably in the living room chuckling over the solid kiss Jed bestowed upon Petra beneath the mistletoe. Pa Kelso removed the huge family Bible from its resting place on a shelf. He drew his rocker close to the light of the fireplace to better see the print, and read aloud passages from the Book.

And all listened intently.

Later there was lighthearted conversation, followed by an exodus to the kitchen for consumption of coffee bread, Finnish cheese, raisin soup, coffee and tea. Back again to the living room for the opening of gifts, something which the restless boys, if they had their say so, would have scheduled as an early evening priority. Following tradition in the old country, food would be left on the table until Christmas was over.

Moments were when the flames in the hearth flickered bright on the carpet where Petra sat, lightly thinking about the beautiful pair of skiis in the porch which Stig had crafted for her. Again, touching the heart-shaped nugget secured to a gold chain about her neck. A gift from Jed. It was the exceptional find, the nature created love nugget retrieved from the river bed last spring. Jed knowing at the moment of its discovery, that it must have been created for one most special.

CHAPTER 12
Winter's Power

It was mid-January. The morning hours of an ominously dark day. In the mine office Captain Sommers shoved aside his half-written report to the stockholders, deciding he would need Bill Worthington's assistance in completing it. He had stopped Bill on a pathway an hour back, where they had lightly discussed the report. Clear-headed Bill was for a change, with a mind to business, separating from his carousing partner Clem who was still in town on a bender.

Captain Sommers pushed open the door to recognize young Jorn Holmstrom standing outside, about to enter. Jorn knew it was poor policy to long detain a busy man. He advanced no farther but right there stated the reason for his presence. He would like to apply for a job.

Captain Sommers invited Jorn into the office and motioned for him to sit down.

"What kind of job you looking for?"

"I'm strong enough to mine."

Jorn's answers to rapidly fired questions were for the most part unhesitant.

He had quit school. Well, just didn't like school. Age? Sixteen. His mother had disapproved his quitting, but his father didn't care one way or another. Yes, Miss Neeley had disapproved. Read? Little words, not the long ones. Write? Write? Not very good...

162

In a vest pocket notebook Captain Sommers jotted Jorn's name and told him to check back in a week. Together they exited the office, Captain Sommers going in search of Bill Worthington, to ultimately find him behind the powder shack tippling a bottle of whiskey.

Late that afternoon the first blizzard of the season began raging in from the north. Well before quitting time the crew abandoned their work and forged through the blinding gusts in the direction of their bunkhouses. Their clothing, eyebrows and beards, moustaches, were quickly whitened with snow, and by the time they reached their separate quarters the northeaster was blasting even worse. They tugged open the bunkhouse doors to enter. Wet clothes were peeled off and dry garb sought out. Wet mackinaws were placed close to the stoves to dry out, and wool stockings and paired boots were slung over pole beams to dry.

In due time most everybody was physically comfortable. But the news of the morning warmed nobody. Every man on the property had been aware that the stamp mill wasn't doing what the manufacturer claimed it would do. It was too large. It couldn't be kept going at full capacity without receiving all of the poor as well as the rich rock accessible in the veins. The heavy metal shoes which crushed the ore were breaking every week. Other parts broke under stress. In the blacksmith shop hands were working around the clock repairing parts permitting no time for sharpening drills and tools or repairing other metal work. Special trips had been made to Coyuta and Iron Bay in search of substitute parts to replace those which gave out much too soon. The mill had been down for two weeks, awaiting shipment of a new pulley from the manufacturer.

Captain Sommers managed to keep a level head. Since the ice on the stream was not strong enough, he kept his idled men busy hauling logs with travois from both sides of the Yellow Dog which would be used in erecting more permanent buildings.

But this morning. A wire was carried in by Ed Morley which he knew to be important, which stated that the mill was an imperfect one and that another would be shipped immediately.

Captain Sommers entered the bunkhouse where Jed bedded down, tugging the door shut behind him but not before an ugly gust of wind covered a portion of the floor white. Here most of the men congregated to deal cards, the bunkhouse being larger than most and definitely warmer. Captain Sommers dropped to a bench along a wall and stared at the floor for a prolonged time. Sporadically his head shook in dejection. He got up, opened the door of the stove and aimed his chew in. He began releasing his thoughts.

"Sure, the millhouse was built big enough to add more machinery. But cripes. Didn't think it'd go this way. And that bloody wire didn't say who's going to pay for the second mill."

There wasn't a man in the bunkhouse who could come up with a half-heartening response. Pete was settled in his bunk, trying to keep his mind on a book. He wasn't with it, he stuck his reading beneath his bunk and rolled over on his stomach. Ikey flung his cards to the tabletop and dropped out of the card game. He slapped a hand on his thigh, tilted back on his box seat and reached over for the bundle of newspapers which Ed had left in the morning. Dan and Curt were huddled close to the red hot stove in the middle of the floor, working over chews of tobacco in their cheeks.

Captain Sommers utterances were penetrating each mind, plenty deep.

Dan and Curt heavily pondered things over in silence. There were more matters to be talked about. But it wasn't the right time. Deciding that their tightened muscles needed movement, they pulled their mackinaws

164

down from the pole rafters and went outside where they swallowed the cold night air. They could make out Charlie's light, still burning, and suddenly felt the need for a tin cup of whiskey.

*   *   *   *   *

The Holyoke crew was seated at the plank tables in the cookhouse devouring a supper meal of rabbit and venison, with Charlie in his hour of glory refilling victual bowls as fast as they emptied. The outside door was pulled open. Pa Kelso appeared in the doorway , his mackinaw and cap coated white from the fresh falling snow, and trailed by Timo and Eric who had refused to stay home. The tension on Pa's winter-red face and the unsmiling faces of the boys told the diggers that all was not well.

Pa's eyes searched around, he advanced to where Jed sat and told it all, quickly, his mind too preoccupied to be concerned with taking off his cap or loosening the tight button on his coat collar. He addressed Jed directly, though he had no objection that others should hear.

"Got news vot ees not goot." He sat down beside Jed, resting his hands on his knees. "Three days now Petra be seeck een bed. Mit high fever. Her eyes them have glassy look. She eat notting! Notting! Too-day she be vorse, ver-ry seeck. I plenty vorry." He broke his speech to wipe moisture from his eyes. "Meeses Holmstrom lady come every day. She help. Mees Neeley say dees afternoon, an' I know dat be right, she say Petra belong een doctor's hospit-toal. But vat I do? Road ees not open, heavy snow I no can open queeck. Maybe take vun veek." His chin began quivering. "Vun veek, maybe too late! Ched, I know not vot best do."

Pa took a sip of the hot coffee Charlie had poured for him.

The bowlfuls of beans along with rabbit and venison were rapidly diminishing, yet every man had been listening.

165

There was no extended conversation among the men when Pa Kelso finished telling the reason for his mission, merely brief communications across the tables. Nods of mutual agreement. For the Holyoke crew there was nothing to decide. They were able bodied men who could tow some sort of a rigging to town.

They put it straight to Pa, to go home, not to worry. That by early morning they would have a skid built on which Petra could lay comfortably. She would be towed to Doc Billington's quarters. That he should go home and tell Petra of what was planned for early morning, and to get himself a little rest.

It was midnight, exact, and the tow skid was completed. A seven foot by four foot rigging with wide runners of pine and a bed of split cedar. Boughs of balsam were cut and carried indoors to dry overnight.

The four men who would tow the skid partook of breakfast along with the rest of the crew at the regularly scheduled post-dawn hour. Having a few hours to spare and it being Charlie's birthday they surprised him by clearing off the dirty tables. They were anxious to get on with the day's task they committed themselves to, though no consideration could be given to an early morning departure. Foolhardy it would be to expose a fevered person to sub-zero weather. It wasn't till mid-morning, with temperatures on the rise, that a bed of balsam was laid on the skid and covered with Mrs. Holmstrom's thick batted quilt and Petra laid thereon. Blankets were layered over her and tucked in all around.

It was Curt, Dan, Jed and Ikey who manned the ropes, each with snowshoes bound to his feet. As previously agreed upon, they swung over to the snowshoe trail leading to town which metered two miles less than the Holyoke Trail though the first mile was difficult travel. Windfalls needed to be bypassed. One-half mile was uphill. Downhill slopes were numerous which necessitated two men dropping back to handle the rear

166

ropes of the skid, to keep it from gaining downhill momentum and to deter sidewise skidding.

Not much ground had been covered when notice was taken that Petra had shaken loose some of her blankets. Again she was tucked in, regardless of the discomfort of her feverish condition she needed to be kept covered. Two glassy eyes were all that could be seen of her well covered head.

There was a rest stop. When mackinaws were unbuttoned and very limited conversation held with Petra. Mostly abbreviated queries. How was she feeling? Was she comfortable? Her weakened voice requested a drink of water which was trickled into her mouth from a canteen. The men quenched their own thirst. Cigarettes were burned short, with that, earlaps were turned up and again the ropes manned.

Another check stop was made. Petra had fallen asleep. Sleeping? Ikey didn't want to say what he feared but took a look for himself. She twitched under the coverings causing Ikey to breathe with immediate relief.

Progress was being made at an improved pace when for a prolonged while all four manned the front ropes. Then sporadic coughing which seeded continuous coughing caused cessation of their light, insignificant discourse. Was she inhaling too much cold air?

Petra pulled aside the covering from her mouth, her weakened voice uttered a request. "Maybe I could be propped up a little?"

Nobody figured it could do any harm. Mackinaws were shed and placed under her shoulders, her head. It seemed as they propped her up that her eyes were regaining focus. her request for more water was taken care of and her coughing subsided.

The remaining distance yet to be covered, over the frozen lakes and some cleared land had been anticipated to be easy pulling, but warming temperatures complicated matters. The snowshoes began breaking through the crusty surface. Petra was alert enough to notice and be concerned. "How much farther to go?" she asked.

Ikey's quick response was not entirely within the scope of the Ten Commandments. "We'll be picking up the road pretty quick."

They reassured her that everything was fine, they were having no problem. Though now even the sleigh runners were beginning to break through the crust.

Near the wooded edge of town was heard the snorting of horses. An empty lumber sled was sighted heading for town and the towers hollers out for attention. The driver heard. Stopped. The towers unbound the snowshoes from their feet and lifted the skid onto the platform. That done, they jumped on to ride in the rest of the way.

Petra was definitely looking much better, evidently the fresh air having much to do toward her improvement. The look in her eyes told she was grateful for what had been done. Stopping in front of Doc Billington's house the driver asked about their getting back to the mine. Indicating he would be returning that way.

Jed chose to linger at the office-hospital to await Doc's diagnosis. Agreed upon, that he would meet the three in the Black Bear.

Not long after he entered the saloon, his eyes brighter and wearing a genuine smile.

They trudged onto the mine property shortly after the supper tables had been cleared, though Charlie was happy to oblige with heated leftovers. Word circulated the bunkhouses that Petra was going to be all right but that she would be confined at Doc's quarters for some days. Jed crossed the clear ice of the Yellow Dog to the homestead to bring the cheering news. And a tear escaped Pa's eye as he listened.

*   *   *   *   *

Of the thirty-one days in the month of January, twenty had been of stiffening frigidity. February took another dip with temperatures dropping yet lower and heavy blankets of snow fell with unprecedented regularity, as far back as anybody could recall. No mail had reached Ishpeming for two weeks, and local Indians, using snowshoes and dogsleds were attempting to make a breakthrough to Iron Bay.

At the Holyoke the workers knees knocked together as they plodded the deep, narrow pathways which twisted about the site. Scaling the bluff to the South Beaver shaft was out of question and regular use was being made of the roundabout road to the top of the bluff. Good portions of many work days were being spent struggling to keep the Holyoke Trail open. Yesterday, for the first time it became impassible. The whim was shut down since all horses were needed for plowing.

All pipes on the property froze solid.

In the late afternoon Captain Sommers glumly entered the side door of the cookhouse and as he expected, found most of the crew tasting the contents of a whiskey keg. He fumbled with the buttons on his mackinaw, shook it off his broad shoulders and tossed it over a barrel. He kicked shut the draft on the hot stove, then dropped to a plank bench set against a wall. He fumbled with his pipe for a while, shaking the ashes from it, cleaning it out. He muttered loud enough for everybody to hear.

"Cripes. Every damn pipe froze solid. Be weeks before we'll be moving any ore from the looks of things. Sure as hell the stockholders are going to make some bloody noise."

It was Nels who found the courage to speak, for himself, Dan and Curt, the nucleus of the shaft crew. Nels, who had regained his strength and returned to his job just a few weeks back. He unpocketed his hands to open the door of the stove and spit in his chew.

"That ain't all. There's more bad news nobody is gonna like to hear. Might as well say it now so everybody kin hear." Nels turned, to direct his attention more directly to Captain Sommers. "Since the forty-five foot mark we been mining the vein at one-quarter its full size. Three days back it turned over. We've tried like hell to follow it but no bloody luck. It's hurting to say. Dammit. Looks like the shaft has petered out."

*   *   *   *   *

The officers got the bad news the very next day and called for mining experts and geologists to inspect the property. Several came out during the ensuing week, some staying on two or three days while running tests.

Most of the experts agreed, that there was plenty of gold in the bluff for profitable mining, but that the vein in the South Beaver had been disturbed by volcanic action. They advised that the shaft be abandoned and the ore removed through the tunnel. Increased tonnage could be derived by dropping a level, and drifting. One expert asserted himself with a completely different viewpoint, in short, convinced that the vein in the South Beaver shaft had merely "jumped".

*   *   *   *   *

The supper hour was plenty dark and one would have been unable to locate the cookhouse had it not been for the lamplight shining through the windows. A special meeting was being held on the property. Called for right quick after the bad news broke out, which by the same token violated the bylaws covering the calling of special meetings. The door of the cookhouse was opened and shut an uncounted number of times. Straight-faced stockholders were present who had failed to attend regular meetings, including a few who had last week refused to pay their installments. The discomfort of sitting on plank benches and up-ended boxes, or even standing, played little on their minds. They listened with intent to what Hank Manson was saying, digesting everything he said with concern.

Hank Manson wasn't a man to conceal facts. He talked of the situation in the tunnel. How as work advanced in depth expenses had increased in an unexpected manner. He did not pass lightly on the matter of powder fumes fouling the air, slowing the movements of the men. Cutting down on production.

There grew fright in the eyes of some of the stockholders as he passed on the recommendation of the mine experts, that the shaft should be abandoned.

There were interruptions, the men expressing opinions of their own. At times the talk became heated.

Hank Manson wasn't through. "Two stockholders unable to dispel troublesome thoughts regarding our method of operation, and being unable to attend this meeting, have asked that I speak for them. They express criticism in the general workings of the mine, as often is the case in ventures that are not attended by a profit at an early stage in operation. They cite the working force as being top-heavy — in their exact words 'too few miners against one superintendent, one captain, two engineers'. Their concern being that there is not proper distribution of muscle, that surface expenses are exorbitant. And also most perturbed on hearing word about town that a segment of management is consuming spirits during working hours. These stockholders are seeking verification of these reports.

Hank talked on, pausing frequently to set the facts clear in the minds of his listeners. "We've had opinions expressed tonight on what might be best at this time for all concerned. It has been the expressed conviction of the majority present that winter operations are biting into the funds of the company with no appreciable progress. Therefore, I should like to make a motion, since a majority of investors are present to validate a vote. That operations be suspended until spring when the future

171

process will be rapid and less costly. At which time we will intensify operations and further explore for more pay chimneys.

There was some movement of bodies and shuffling of feet, turning of heads for exchange of added thoughts.

"Everybody in favor raise his right hand and say 'aye'." Hank's eyes swept the room as hands went up. He gave a slight nod. "The ayes have it." With unexpected abruptness he adjourned the meeting.

Those who had been sitting got up to straighten their backs. Some smoked, in near silence. Those who spoke said little.

Hank Manson edged over to the pot bellied stove, he poked the fire, and kicked the draft shut with the toe end of his boot. He moved to a window and stared through the half-frosted panes into the outer darkness. His hands searched his pockets and found a cigar, he clamped it between his teeth and scratched a match with a thumbnail. The tobacco was burnt hardly at all before it was discarded in a pail of sand.

Jed Carter detected in Hank's mien something different. Hank wasn't his real self tonight. When he put on his fur hat and buttoned up his mackinaw and went outside, Jed bided time for a few uneasy minutes, then donned his own sheepskin and slipped out of the cookhouse.

A north wind was cutting sharply causing the bare branches to creak in the wind. Jed's eyes pierced the darkness. He could make out a figure standing at the edge of the ice sheltered stream.

"Manson."

"Who is it?"

"Jed." Strides were taken along the frozen bank and now Jed stood at Manson's side.

"Looking for me?" asked Manson.

"Yep. Something's wrong. Something's bothering you more than a little."

172

"You're imagining. Everything's fine." But Hank Manson's voice was not like his own.

"Your face was creased with trouble."

"What did you think of the meeting?"

"Just about what I expected. You did a good job. Put everything right on the line and still kept chins up. Paul Witters by me was doing some nail-biting, but he does that even when his dog has pups. Sure, we'll give her tar again in the spring. Just like you said." Jed paused. "Now that preliminaries are over we can talk man to man. What's troubling, Hank? What's wrong? What are you holding back?"

Hank Manson looked straight down at the ground. "Nothing. Things are going to work out like we discussed at the meeting."

"You're not going to get much sleep tonight if you don't talk to somebody. I wasn't born yesterday. You shot one barrel at the meeting — now shoot both and get it all off your chest."

Hank was reluctant to talk but felt relief from the offer. He closed the distance between them. "It happened again yesterday in the office in town. A couple of stockholders wanted to look in the books to check operating costs. Syd was reluctant about releasing them. It's been that way for quite a while now. Nobody can get near the account books. Ask to see them and he gets annoyed. You can take it from there.

The door of the cookhouse on the knoll above them was opened, and some of the men came out. Hank put a hand to Jed's shoulder. "Better get back where we belong."

Captain Sommers took to the pathway leading to the bunkhouses with Jed following not far behind. Captain Sommers stuffed his pipe as he forged ahead. He paused, to put a light to the tobacco, and exhaled smoke between words. "You know. That decision to shut down till spring was the right decision. Best to just ride out

173

this cold weather. Can't make any money when costs are out of proportion." He relit his pipe which had extinguished itself. "I'll break it easy to the men."

The diggers were lazing around in the largest of the bunkhouses making small talk. Waiting to hear what went on at the meeting. Sommers made it short.

To the crew the news wasn't all that startling, every man knowing that the handicap of frozen pipes had made progress next to impossible. John managed a smile. "Hell. A man needs to spend a little time with his family."

Dan wasn't complaining. He hadn't seen his girl since Christmas time. Jallu and Pete looked at things in another perspective. Now Pete was talking. "You know. Me and Jallu really got no special home to go to. We sort of hang on to the idea of batching it right here."

*   *   *   *   *

Neither had Jed Carter any intentions of leaving the site. It wasn't the desire to unbury a fortune. He knew that gold itself built dreams, crumbled them. That the worth of man is not measured by the contents of his purse.

Man seeks his own life course. Deep inside he was beginning to interpret the magnetic power of this wilderness. Days in this isolated country were more than measured time. He was shaking off the veil covering his mind and beginning to comprehend the meaning of life itself.

He lived enchanted with the changing elements of all seasons, he loved the rippling blue waters, the bright skies and the stars, the valleys and fields, the cry of the night hawk, the howl of the wolf and coyote. He loved Petra.

And his whole being had matured, to possess a new richness of spirit which was worth more than gold.

*   *   *   *   *

The weeks passed by, and amid the silence of the naked woods winter laid a thicker and thicker white blanket over the silent machinery.

CHAPTER 13
The Murder

It was one of those brisk winter mornings with the temperature hovering on the ten below mark, the saplings and tag alders white with rime. When the snow squeaked and creaked under each footstep taken and hot breath vapors hung in the air. Over the entire landscape lay a cover of new snow, severed only by a long narrow black gap in the Yellow Dog.

Jed bent down to check a strap on one of his snowshoes. It was tight enough. He straightened up and shifted the pack on his shoulders. A domineering wind was sweeping from across the Yellow Dog, he wriggled his cap on his head so that the earlaps fitted snugger, then reached for his rifle which was leaning against the bunkhouse. Certainly the traps set on the edge of the swamp should produce something this morning. Only yesterday tracks had been all over the place, and he had liberally baited the traps with fish and rabbit.

He perked. To the sound of hooves clopping on the winter hard ground, closing in, the sound of a horse being ridden full gallop. Around the last bend in the trail appeared the mare and horseman. Dan! Still charging in at full speed. Very near, Jed flicked a broad handwave. With no return of the greeting Dan reined in and dismounted, his mare snorting steam from her nostrils.

Bad news was stamped all over Dan's countenance.

"What is it, Dan? What's happened?"

Dan's words came out in choking spurts. "It's Syd Crawford. He's dead. Murdered last night in cold blood."

Dan's words lashed deep. Jed's hold on his rifle was unconsciously eased, the barrel slipping through his hand till the stock met the ground.

"Syd! He didn't have an enemy!"

Dan shook his head from side to side, not a muscle in his face moving. "He's dead. Cut down with a bullet."

Jed leaned his rifle against the wall of the bunkhouse and in the same motion slipped the pack from his shoulders. He knelt to release the snowshoes from his feet but shock of the news sapped his coordination. A feeling of lightheadedness took hold, things began blurring before him. His fingers fumbled with the straps. When the snowshoes were released he straightened himself, stuck the shoes upright in the snow and went into the bunkhouse. Dan followed. Jallu and Pete were shaken out of sound sleep. They sat on the edge of their bunks, half-asleep, trying to absorb Dan's ugly message.

Jed's lips barely moved. "How did it happen?"

"They don't know yet. Syd was working late last night. It was young Jorn Holmstrom, who has been banking the fire at night who found him lying by the safe in a pool of blood. Shot in the head. He lived only a couple of hours."

"Robbery?"

"Appears so."

"Any clues?"

"Pair of pliers Jorn found near the body."

Dan's ride out had been hard and exhausting, his heart was heavy and his words few. He moved to the side of the crackling stove and weighed the contents of the blackened coffee pot in his hand, then poured himself a cupful of the hot contents.

"Jorn has even been mentioned as a suspect," muttered Dan.

"Jorn! God, no!" sputtered out Jed. He circled the room, gathering his clothes and rolling them into a tight bundle which he secured with a strap. He stuffed a few odds and ends in his packsack.

He brushed crusts of bread from the table top, opened the door and threw them out for the birds.

"I'm riding back with you Dan. Going to help hunt down whoever notched his gun on Syd. And right now I'll tell you, it's not Jorn. I won't quit the hunt till I see the killer hanging." He paced the room once more. By the window overlooking the winter-dark Yellow Dog he paused. "We'll go around Petra's way and tell her the rotten news."

*   *   *   *   *

They trotted their horses as far as the Y in the road where "Old Ish" maintained silent vigil, then eased the horses to a walk. Ribbons of wood smoke from shops lining Main spiralled skyward. An increased number of people were stirring about than on the average winter morning. Many clustered in small groups conversing, their faces grim.

They kept to the side of the road to allow clearance for passing vehicles. A sizeable group of townsfolk was gathered in front of the Holyoke office, some with their faces pressed against the windows trying to make out the scene inside. They slid down from their horses, only to be barred from entering the building by Marshall Malaroni who stood guard at the doorway. With a voice of authority he affirmed that nobody was allowed in the ransacked, bloody office. Nobody, irregardless of affiliation with the company.

They trotted alongside the livery, the horses blowing thick clouds of steam from their nostrils, turned the bend in the road. Then shortly reined in the horses before the unpainted square building which housed the Ishpeming

POST. Wind driven snow had wetly plastered one side of the building white, likewise most of the lettering on the swinging sign was white.

They knotted the reins on a hitch in front of the print shop. At the doorway they stomped the snow from their boots. The door of the shop was swelled tight. Jed put a shoulder to it and pushed it in.

The room was comfortably warm, though the air was heavy with the smell of fresh ink. The thumping of a machine in a back room could be heard. In the small front office where they stood, bundles of newspapers were stacked on the floor. The headlines bore deep —
HOLYOKE OFFICIAL MURDERED IN OFFICE.

Ed Morley was bent over the hand press in the back room. When he heard talk in the outer office he lifted his head. He shut down the machine, located a rag and proceeded to wipe his hands clean as he came to the outer office. He removed the visor which shaded his eyes and set it on the counter of business. Ed's face showed strain, his eyes narrow and weary looking. He bent an elbow on the counter.

"Never gave thought to such foul doings in this town. I grant there's a few rough characters around. But didn't think we harbored a killer.... the town people are pretty nervous...." Ed's eyes were glued to the newspapers stacked on the floor. "Sure hated to set up those headlines."

"Anything uncovered?" inquired Dan.

Ed shook his head sidewise. "Nothing. Marshall Malaroni claims to have a few leads, to have latched on to a suspicion. But he's tight lipped, doesn't want to put anything in print." Ed Morley stopped talking, he closed his eyes to rub his eyelids. "Mrs. Crawford is taking it real hard. Doc Billington and the Reverend have been at the house all morning."

"Any talk about an investigation?" queried Jed.

"Understand they're out looking for a jury right now.

179

Got to move fast with this type of crime. A jury will need every bit of information while it's still fresh in the minds of those who last saw Syd alive. An inquest might begin tomorrow, so word's going around."

In the course of their conversation several townsfolk came in to pick up a newspaper. Mr. Slocum, the school commissioner, dropped off a writeup telling need of a higher school tax. A rosy cheeked lad entered the shop. With no interruption he loaded a bundle of newspapers onto his sled outside the doorway.

Jed reached for a loose POST on the countertop. He rolled it up and stuck it in a pocket of his sheepskin coat. He looked at Dan. "Time to be moving. There's things to be done."

Dan exited the shop with Jed close behind him. Ed trailed them out, coatless and bareheaded but wearing his frayed shop apron. He buried his hands in his trouser pockets for warmth. A soft, feathery snow was settling on the manes of the horses and the saddles. Jed located his choppers and proceeded to whisk the snow from the saddle. Momentarily he stood, with a hand on the pommel. Directly he addressed Ed. "You'll find me at the Chippewa should you need me. Plan on being in town for a while to do some looking around."

The cold was causing Ed to shiver. He tapped one boot against the other. "We stand on common ground," he responded, then went back into the shop. Jed vaulted into his saddle but Dan held ground.

"There's an empty bed at the boarding house. It's a whole lot cheaper than hotel living."

It wasn't what Jed had in mind. "Will be keeping loose hours which isn't appreciated at the boarding house." He picked up the slack from the reins and turned Blaze around. "Keep alert. If you latch onto something pass it along."

Dan nodded. "As you say."

Jed Carter stood at the rail which fronted the

Chippewa Hotel, alone now. Several months had passed since he'd slept here. The chain of events since his arrival last spring swept through his mind in rapid motion.

His meditation was cut off when the door of the hotel was pushed open and Blanche emerged. Disheveled and glassy eyed she was. Hatless, with her long unbuttoned coat dragging the snow on the porch. She broke past him onto the road, failing to register recognition, being definitely in numbed stupor. Muttering words were heard, "...damn it, damn it all... the cheap son of a bitch."

He walked through the door left ajar. Inside the hotel, with the door closed tight behind him, he looked around. It wasn't a bad place to lodge. The building was solid, there were no boarded up windows. A large waiting room furnished with unmatched furniture served to convenience the lodgers, as well as numerous itinerants who showed before and after train runs. The sleeping rooms were decently furnished. Clean. Though conversation leaked audibly through thin walls which partitioned them off, and it was not uncommon to be awakened from sound sleep with undesirable noises and commotion.

He could smell coffee cooking in the back kitchen, that probably being the reason for the registration counter being vacated. He set his bundle of clothing on the countertop and again scanned the surroundings. A bewhiskered old man, appearing to be of means, was seated low on the couch perusing the POST. A man he'd never seen before was enjoying a pleasant sleep in a horsehair chair, snoring loudly, his stomach rising and falling with each snort emitted. Jed pressed the service bell.

Virginia responded. Emerging through the kitchen doorway carrying a steaming coffee pot in one hand and clutching empty cups in the other. She viewed her client causing her eyes to sparkle and her face burst into

181

radiance.

"Glory be! It's Jed Carter!"

Virginia's father owned the Chippewa Hotel but Virginia helped him out by doing most of the cooking and waiting on tables. Though Jed had chatted with her but on three different occasions he had taken a liking for her. Because of her pleasant mannerism. Mostly, because she knew where to draw the line when discussing with patrons their personal life and activities. She was not a person to digest raw language and when occasion necessitated she let it be known.

She filled two cups with hot coffee, sliding one toward Jed. "Still drink it black?"

"You have an excellent memory." He raised the cup to his lips, the coffee was too hot for drinking and he set the cup down. "Might you fix me up with a room for a spell?"

"Sure can." She cocked her head sidewise and shrugged her shoulders tauntingly. "We put up with worse guys than you." Her eyes shifted to the register book. "And just how long do you intend to stay put?"

"Can't really say."

"Single or double bed?"

"Double."

A smug look crept over her face. "Should I even ask. All men take doubles." She turned her back to check a chart on the wall. "Am going to put you in number 6, right off the waiting room. A bit noisy at times, but it does have advantages."

Jed drew a mouthful of coffee and swallowed it, appreciating the extra good flavor. He withdrew from an inner vest pocket a wad of greenbacks. "Receipt me one week in advance."

She had him sign his name on a ruled sheet in the registry, retrieved a cigar box from underneath the counter and stuffed in the money he gave her. "If everybody would pay in advance the books would be so much easier to keep. Some of these rowdy woodsmen are never paid up... and those fast talking salesmen...!"

There was the sound of footsteps descending the stairway, at the turn in the stairs there appeared a man gripping a black case. Virginia lowered her voice. "Oh hush, here comes one now."

Each stair answered to the weight of Dr. Von Muller. Suave appearing he was, and sporting a trimmed pencil line moustache as his badge of manliness. At the stairwell he set his carrying case on the floor, took time to wind a long woolen scarf around his neck and to flash a toothsome smile at Virginia while his roving eye covered as much of her as showed above the countertop. "Not the best kind of weather for selling door to door, but we'll not let the rude elements of winter keep people from enjoying better vision." Dr. Von Muller's talk was rapid.

"Sounds like you really like your work," quipped Virginia.

"A-ah, yes! No boss. I conduct business to please myself. Travel in good style, lodge in the best hotels." He picked up his optician's case and headed toward the doorway, his head high, his shoulders back. His walk reflected a certain dignity.

Virginia suddenly remembered. She whisked something from beneath the counter and scurried toward Dr. Von Muller. "Just a minute, Dr. Von Muller. This lens. Mrs. Anderson dropped it off yesterday afternoon, said that you had left it at her house."

Dr. Von Muller's thanks were attended by a low bow. The door slammed shut behind him.

"I'll stick to blasting and mucking," muttered Jed.

*　　　*　　　*　　　*　　　*

The morning was yet dark when Jed Carter rose from a restless sleep and hastily dressed. He swallowed a bowl of hot buttered oatmeal which Virginia ladled from a big pot in the kitchen, washed it down with plenty of coffee, all the while reading of Syd's murder as Ed had written it up in the POST. Which story covered the entire front page of the newspaper. He looked for, and found, verification of word repeated around town, that the inquest would open this very morning.

He arrived at the town hall well in advance of the hour to find that the small frame building was already crowded with well over one hundred people. Once inside the rectangular shaped room he caught sight of Dan, resting his back against a wall. Jed squeezed a route to Dan's side. Dan had little to say, but stood quietly, with arms folded.

Both men's eyes searched the room. Close friends of Syd's were in attendance and many stockholders in the Holyoke. Jorn's mother and father sat together, showing strained faces, not communicating. Other faces were recollected just vaguely, as maybe having been casual introductions at one time or another. Present also were a number of spectators who were total strangers.

The thought seated alike in both Dan's and Jed's minds. Among these assembled townsfolk and innocent faced strangers, was one Syd's assailant?

The hands of the clock on the wall crept close to the hour of ten. A door communicating with an added room in the rear was opened by Marshall Malaroni and Judge Horace Tittlebaum, who had been summoned in from Iron Bay to conduct the hearing entered the room. His underweight body was clad in an unmatched suit, he looked prematurely old for his forty years. His bulging eyes were prominent on a stock face. Yet most people assembled were impressed, since his status of employment put him in a favorable light. Also, it being a known fact that persons with prominent eyes had a great command of words and were ready speakers.

Judge Tittlebaum carried himself with an air of self-importance. He made his way to a plain wooden table in the fore part of the room and in a move reflecting professional training seated himself behind it. He rolled his big eyes to the left where a row of ten serious faced

184

jury men sat erect in round back wooden chairs. He sought something in the stack of papers before him, selected two papers. His drawling bass voice sounded out.

"As Judge of this district I hereby open the inquest into the death of Sydney Crawford."
The quiet of the room broke with a choking sob from Mrs. Crawford.

"I'll have roll call of the jury." He read the names, stumbling on the pronunciation of many, contorting one name so badly the said jury man momentarily failed to respond to his name. When a full jury was recognized by each 'here' he certified their presence by endorsing his signature on a paper in his hand. Judge Tittlebaum surveyed the jury. "Were any of you gentlemen acquainted with the deceased?" All but two raised their hands.

With that Judge Tittlebaum jotted down a brief note in an open book before him. He looked out to the audience filling the room. "This is the first hearing of the murder case of Sydney Crawford, town of Ishpeming, who met his death as the result of a supposed robbery." Once again he directed his attention upon the straight faced men sitting alert in the jury chairs.

"You have been selected to inqure on behalf of the people by what cause Sydney Crawford met his untimely death. After hearing testimony from witnesses at or near the scene of the crime on the fatal night, and from other persons who have information of value, you will make every effort to identify the person or persons who committed this atrocious, cold-blooded crime, and to deliver to me, a fair and just verdict. No false compassion must sway you, nor shall you be pressured by outside influences. We are here to protect our townsfolk, protect life and property. I have been informed that witnesses are in attendance to present testimony. We shall proceed with the questioning.

185

"I request Mr. Stanley Eland come forward to take the witness stand."

Stan Eland knowing he would be summoned moved to the fore part of the room without hesitancy.

"Raise your right hand - "I promise to tell the truth, the whole truth and nothing but the truth so help me God."

Stan Eland stood erect and steady while he repeated the oath.

"Your full name, sir."

"Stanley Reginald Eland."

"Mr. Eland. Will you please tell this court the nature of your work in this town."

"Negotiator for sales of land and quick claims."

"Is it correct to understand that your place of business is in the same building where Sydney Crawford was employed?"

"That is correct, sir. All my business affairs are conducted in a one room office which shares a common wall with the Holyoke office."

"How well did you know the deceased?"

"We became close friends when our work brought us together. We visited frequently in one another's office. Fished and hunted together."

"And how would you describe the character of the deceased?"

"Syd Crawford was held in high esteem by everybody who knew him. He had strong family ties and followed the principles of Christian faith."

"On any occasion when you were in his company did he give you reason to believe that something was troubling him?"

"No sir."

"When did you last see Sydney Crawford alive?"

"On that fateful Monday night I worked a little later than usual on a bill of sale. I wasn't sure of the hour, but I figured it was near seven o'clock when I went to Syd's office to check the time."

"Did you see his watch?"

"Yes, your honor. Syd always carried one."

"Did you exchange further words with him?"

"Yes. I mentioned about our both putting in a lot of overtime lately, and that maybe we should take a couple of days off to go hunting. But he didn't react too strong to the thought."

"Did you observe anything different than usual in his manner that night?"

"No, sir. Nothing. He was his usual happy self."

To this point in the questioning the frozen countenance of Judge Tittlebaum hadn't cracked. With unexpected abruptness he stated. "That will be all, Mr. Eland."

Stan Eland returned to his seat in the front row of the room. The Judge called the second witness of the day and the spectators glued their eyes on young, muscular and handsome Jorn Holmstrom, who likewise rose from a front row seat. He stumbled forward, stood before the Judge and repeated the oath under nervous tension.

"Your name, young man, and your connection with this case."

"Jorn Holmstrom. I tend fires in some of the buildings in town. One of my work places is the Jamison building."

"Would you tell us of events on the night the deceased met his death?"

Jorn fidgeted, he could feel the boring eyes of everybody in the room upon him.

"Do you desire that I repeat the question?" asked the Judge.

Jorn mustered enough inner strength to move his lips.

"It was a cold one, that night. I hung around the pool room a while, shot a few games of pool. Then went to work banking fires at the places I work. The Jamison building is always my last stop. But it was so cold that I decided to sleep in the building all night 'steada footing it back to my friend's house in the freeze."

"And while you were performing your chore that night in the Jamison building, did you see Sydney Crawford at any time?"

"Sure. Saw him when I come in. I poked around in his office a while looking at gold samples from the mine. That was around ten."

"Did you talk to him at that time?"

"Yeah. We chewed the rag for a while. He was telling me about a new drill that jest come in, telling how it worked. I remember he said something about too much night work lately and that he was going to start spending more time with his family. I left him to go bank the fire and must of fallen asleep by the stove. When I opened my eyes I noticed the lights still on. Went to Crawford's office, but couldn't see him."

"You say the lights were still burning?"

"Yeah. In both rooms."

"Please continue."

"Well... I stood by the door, couldn't see him so I went to take a look in the small office room. He was laying on the floor by the safe. Blood coming from his head. I was pretty sure he was dead. The way he laid, his arm twisted under his body and his mouth open. His eyes were glassy and staring at me."

"And you had heard nothing resembling a shot previous to this?"

"No. Must have been sleeping pretty sound."

"What did you do then?"

"Was damn shook up. I run over fast as I could to Doc Billington's house and told him to get on right over to the office. That Syd Crawford was dead. Doc told me he'd be on the move and that I should run and get the Marshall."

"Did you notice if the safe doors were open or shut?"

"Never noticed. Too shook up to look around."

"Might there be any other information of importance that this court should know about?"

Jorn thought, but briefly. "When Doc Billington and

188.

Marshall Malaroni were bent over Crawford I noticed a pair of pliers on the floor by the table leg. Never seen those kind of pliers around the office before. I picked them up and handed them to Marshall Malaroni and showed him right where I found them."

"Any other details?" queried the Judge.

Jorn nodded his head negatively.

The Judge turned a paper over. "Your testimony is sufficient for now. You're dismissed."

The third character witness was called upon. He lumbered forward to take the oath.

"Your name?"

The man hesitated. There was a prolonged silence.

"Your name, sir. You're under oath. No alias."

"Rushton Sylvester Biggers from the Salsburg location. Everybody knows me as 'Rush'. Some call me 'Big Rush'. I own da pool room on da Main road."

"Mr. Biggers. I would like to have you tell the jury exactly what you told the Marshall on the day after the murder. Every detail you can recall on the night of the crime."

Rush was ready to talk. "It wuz one of doze Monday nights when the pool room was dead. Guys 'round here don't go out much on Mondays. Seems dey spend all da dough on week-ends an' cash is low first part of da week. Ya know how it goes. Like da young lad here sez, the night wuz a bloody cold one. Only a few guys in my place, shootin' da bull, and dey leave early. So I put on my sheepskin and locks up."

"And what time would that have been as closely as you can calculate?"

"It wuz past twelve-thirty. I locks up and heads for the location like I do every night. I go past the Jamison buildin' an' down the south road. Well. That night I goes by the Holyoke office. Lamps all burning bright but don't see nobody inside."

Judge Tittlebaum chose to interrupt. "Mr. Biggers.

Did you notice through the windows, was the safe open or closed?"

Rush moistened his lips with his tongue, his mouth twisted.

"You're only here for questioning," reassured Judge Tittlebaum.

"The safe was setting open and the office was wide open. Jest like it was open fer business. Books on the tables, papers around. Syd Crawford been working puurty late the last coupla months. I figured he wuz somewhere in da place. Ya know, sometimes I'd go in an' shoot da bull wid him fer a while. Well, anyway I don't see him so moves along. By the side of the building I hear voices, an' sees a coupla guy talkin' an' when dey spot me dey stopped talkin."

"Did you recognize the men?"

"One. Crawford. An' he kinda turned sidewise when I looked his way like he don't wanna notice me."

"And the other man?"

"Couldn't see his face in da dark. But he wuz bigger than Syd."

"What did you do after that?"

"Kept movin'. Lil even seen me go by her place."

Lil. A female whom Judge Tittlebaum had heard much about. Judge Tittlebaum cleared his voice. "Her name will not be used in these records. ...As it stands, Mr. Biggers. Since you have stated that you positively saw Sydney Crawford at that particular time, it appears that at this point you were the last person to see him alive. Since you are a key witness in this case I ask that you not leave town till the inquest is closed. You are dismissed."

The hands on the pendulum clock on the wall moved ahead and the questioning of witnesses went on. A man called Jim O'Reilly took the stand. After proper administering of the official oath Judge Tittlebaum began interrogation of the man.

190

"Exactly what do you do for a living?"

"Train man. Run Number 7 out of town every other morning."

"It is understood that you have some information which might throw light on the solving of this brutal killing?"

"The boarding house isn't too far from the Jamison building. I hit the sack early that night because I was due to pull old 7 out the next morning. Usually I sleep darn sound. But that night I slept restless, had dozed off and on a couple of hours when I heard a shot. Must have been about midnight. Jumped out of bed and looked out of the window, thinking there was some trouble outside. Couldn't see anything, so went back to bed."

"At what approximate time would you say the shot was fired?"

"If you are asking me to calculate close... I'd say .. that shot was fired at midnight or right after."

"Very interesting information. Is there anything else you might enlighten the jury on?"

"No, your honor. Nothing more than that what I just said."

"Thank you for information bearing of importance. You are dismissed."

The Judge turned to address the straight-faced jury. "The court has heard the first witnesses in this case. I move for adjournment for the day. There will be no hearing tomorrow since funeral rites will be held for the victim. The inquest will be resumed on Friday at the hour of ten in the morning."

Jed Carter lingered outside the town hall, his hands tucked in his sheepskin pockets, puffing cigarette smoke, keeping a casual eye on Jorn Holmstrom who was engrossed in conversation with his parents. When they broke up Jed made his approach toward Jorn.

Jorn's anguishing voice was pleading. "You don't think they're going to try to nail this on me? God, I didn't

191

do it!"

Jed flicked his cigarette into the snow. "Nobody knows anything, Jorn. I just waited by to tell you, if you need any help, got anything to say in private look me up. Anytime. I'm staying at the Chippewa."

With that Jed started walking away, only to look back after a few paces. "If you're ever in need of a warm bed you can use mine."

*　　　*　　　*　　　*　　　*

The next morning as soon as light broke Jed Carter rose from his bed in the hotel, he washed and shaved at the crockery basin in his room and put on his best clothes. He lingered over a breakfast of hot oatmeal and black coffee since there was no need for great haste, then left the hotel and sought the shortest route to the church. A strong wind prevailed and the cold was intense. A block from the churchyard Mrs. Anderson and Mrs. Lindstrom crossed from the opposite side of the road and fell in beside him. When they arrived at the churchyard they found it crowded with horses and sleighs.

Men and women in black funeral clothes were silently entering the log church. Jed followed them in. The place wasn't overly warm though a hot stove would soon offset the chill.

He sat motionless at the end of a rough pine pew, briefly his eyes set upon the closed pine casket in the front of the church. He lowered his eyes to the floor. He could see before him Syd's radiant face. Syd, who so loved life itself. Who lived every hour of each day to its fullest measure of happiness. Now it was over. The life on earth he so cherished.

The door behind him was opened and members of the Order of Woodsmen of which Syd was a member solemnly filed in, trailing in cold air. The bell in the tower began to toll. Words uttered by Mrs. Anderson in the not long past repeated themselves in Jed's ears. "It vill reeng for funerals."

Now voices of a half-dozen choir ladies vibrated the air.

> 'Yes we'll gather at the river
> The beautiful the beautiful the river
> Gather with the Saints at the river
> Which flows by the throne of God.'

Reverand Culbertson, in a long black coat, rose from a chair adjoining the choir ladies and read some passages from the Book. He proceeded to talk about the life of the deceased, his character and habits, all the good he had done during his walk on earth, and sorrow of his untimely passing. How he now rested in peace. He talked of the necessity of constant preparation for eternal life by a course of right living, and smilingly referred to Syd Crawford as such a man.

He moved alongside the pine casket. He rested his palms upon the cover and closed his eyes.

"Earth to earth... ashes to dust..."

Jed Carter closed his eyes. Ashes to dust.

The bell began tolling. The pallbearers left their pew, and carried the pine box past the misty eyed mourners to lay Syd in eternal rest.

*   *   *   *   *

Judge Tittlebaum rapped the gavel sharply on the tabletop. "Order is requested for the second hearing of an inquest into the death of Sydney Crawford."

"First witness... Dr. Aloysius Billington."

Doc Billington worked his way out of the corner where he had been crowded into. He took the oath. The Judge promptly began his questioning.

"Under oath you swear that you are a fully licensed and practicing doctor of medicine?"

"I swear that is correct your honor."

"Dr. Billington, we would like to know just what happened after Jorn Holmstrom gave you the bad news."

"When I reached the scene I took the pulse of the victim and found him to be yet alive, though unconscious... contrary to what young Holmstrom thought. Judging from the nature of the wound and tremendous loss of blood I knew the man didn't have much of a chance. Right then Marshall Malaroni bolted in followed by Jorn Holmstrom. The Marshall and I moved the victim to my home where I did all I could to save him. He died at four in the morning, living about three hours after the shooting.

"I performed a post mortem examination and found that the bullet entered the head two inches above the right opening of the right eye. The course of the bullet was nearly horizontal, deviating slightly upwards and backwards. Part of the bone was carried by the impact of the bullet to the back of the head and the bullet was lodged there."

"Dr. Billington. Did the post mortem examination reveal anything?"

"The body carried no trace of any sort of disease."

Briefly the Judge held silence while recording a few notes on the doctor's testimony. "Thank you Dr. Billington. The court appreciates your presence and your providing a medical report for the records. Your testimony is sufficient for today."

It was Marshall Malaroni who was sworn in next, and the Judge continued his intensive questioning of those called to testify.

"As town Marshall, will you relate to the jury the events which took place after Jorn Holmstrom summoned you."

Marshall Malaroni's big eyes rolled in his head as he proceeded to recount his moves on the fateful night. "Ten minutes after the lad reached me I was at the scene. Saw through the window Doc Billington bending over a body. Before I went in I stopped. To check out some tracks in the snow by the doorway. Two fresh sets of footprints, leading to the west side of the building."

"Were you able to get a cast of those tracks?" inquired the Judge.

"I was successful, your honor." Marshall Malaroni inhaled deep and his chest expanded with pride of his achievement. He took a look toward the jurors to reassure himself of having their complete attention. "After leaving Doc's house I rushed back to the scene of the crime and took casts of the prints. One set checked out right away... they matched the boots worn by Syd Crawford."

"On this fact you are positive?"

"Absolutely sure, your honor. It's my opinion that somebody had been hanging around outside, watching Crawford, and somehow Crawford was on to something and went outside to check."

"And the other set of tracks?"

"Haven't had enough time to determine to who they belong."

"Did you search the clothing of the victim?"

"At Doc's house. In Mr. Crawford's pockets was a key, a handkerchief, pocket knife and tobacco."

"Did you find a pocket watch?"

"There was no watch."

"Mr. Crawford always carried a watch."

"No watch was on him."

"Marshall. Did the scene indicate a scuffle?"

Marshall Malaroni nodded negatively. "No signs of any such thing. The victim was not messed up, nothing showed arm to arm struggle."

"Did you take notice if the safe was open, or shut?"

"The cast iron safe was wide open. Papers messed all over the place. Completely ransacked."

"Did you observe the position of the body?"

"Failure to do so would disqualify me as a law man. It appeared to both me and Doc, that Syd Crawford was sitting at a small table by the safe. Blood and particles of brain matter were on the wall near the table and at a level corresponding to the head. A revolver with an empty chamber was close to the body. Doc and I smelled the weapon and we agreed that it had not been long fired.

The bullet found in the head of the deceased has been checked and it corresponds with the caliber of the revolver."

"Marshall Malaroni. Have you in the course of your investigation given any thought to the possibility of suicide?"

"Speculation as such has to be included in the investigation. But we are bypassing this theory for now. Had this been an act of suicide, marks would have been visible. There weren't any. We ran tests with a revolver of this same size, firing at a piece of meat from different distances and it proved, that the scalp and eye area would have been marked if the revolver had been held at close range."

Judge Tittlebaum shifted his body, he opened the one drawer in the table and withdrew an object.

"Marshall. I would like a statement from you regarding Exhibit A — this pair of pliers Jorn Holmstrom picked up at the scene of the crime."

"These are classified as long nosed pliers. They are smaller than average in size. The type fishermen use for tying flies. I have examined them under my magnifying glass but couldn't pick up anything special. Except to say they show wear. Been used a lot."

For the time being Judge Tittlebaum was satisfied with Marshall Malaroni's testimony and dismissed him. He rapped the gavel. "The hearing is adjourned for the day. The inquest will be resumed next Monday."

The church bell was ringing out the noon hour sharp and clear. Jed Carter lingered outside the town hall, as perplexed as most spectators who poured forth from the building. Most minds were in accord - there were details bearing weight on the case which needed to be cleared.

Jed took note. That it was mostly the same people this day who had attended the first hearing. There was Nick, Ed Morley, some of the Holyoke men, stockholders, Blanche. Reverend Culbertson appeared now, as did Dr. Von Muller, and Mrs. Anderson.

The crowd dispersed in diverse directions with tongues rippling with what had been heard, leaving but a few lingering. Blanche held herself apart from those remaining. She was clad in a black fur coat buttoned to her chin with collar pulled high concealing part of her face. She wore a matching fur hat, high black leather boots. With dainty footsteps she covered the short distance to where Jed stood. The essence of an exotic perfume quickly penetrated his nostrils. Now her gloved hand was resting on his arm.

"So a man has to get murdered to get you back into town. Can't figure any red-blooded man preferring snow drifts in the north woods to warm comfort in town."

Jed's lips were buttoned, his reponse was but in the form of a smile. The few people who had lingered walked away. Blanche retained her thoughts until none were within hearing. Now she asked, "Where are you staying?"

"At the Chippewa."

The door of the town hall was pushed open and the Judge and a few of the jury men emerged from the building. Her hand squeezed his arm. "Convenient enough. Let me be your guest. Anytime." She raised herself to the toes of her boots and brushed her lips on his cheek... "Anytime.."

He stood alone now. A look skyward, a south wind was rippling the government flag on the roof of the town hall and he suddenly was aware that the weather had taken a change - to say for the better. Rays of the sun were hot enough to cause long icicles which decorated the eaves to drip in patterned rhythm. Where travel was heavy the road was sloppy with slush. His thoughts, for maybe the

197

hundredth time this week were of Petra. He quickly calculated. There were enough good hours left in the day to ride out and see her. To tell her about the latest events and how the inquest was going.

He slushed his way to the store where he found a dozen customers inside waiting for mail which Thor Blumstrom was busy sorting. Jed bided his turn, then pointed out a box of chocolate coated peppermints in the glass showcase which he had Thor wrap up with brown paper and store string. He made a diagonal cut to the hotel where he stayed only long enough to devour a large bowlful of stew and to compliment Virginia on how good it was. And to retrieve from a hidden place in his room the diamond ring, beautifully cast from Holyoke gold, which he carefully buried in a deep pocket.

At the livery he was surprised to find nobody around. He saddled Blaze and led her outside. He scrounged around for a scrap of paper, located a paper bag and scrawled out a note to Jake, should he return and find Blaze missing, and stuck it in a crack of the sliding door.

His uneasiness of soul stirred by the frustrating hours of the past several days eased up as he paced Blaze northward, through the blend of dark naked hardwoods and green of the pines. Boughs on the firs were trimmed generously with loose snow from which winter sparrows flitted back and forth. From time to time he noted tracks of rabbits, and the smaller markings of the weasel.

It was mid-afternoon when he made the turn through Kelso's roadgate. Stig was approaching on foot from the opposite direction towing a homemade skid supporting two milk cans. Greetings were exchanged. Jed listened as Stig told of his frozen water pump and what he was doing about it. How in the meantime he had to haul water.

Jed reined in Blaze by the open porch and dismounted, he waved a greeting to Pa doing chores by the barn. Time was taken to admire two snow angels. Fashioned

198

no doubt by schoolgirls, who would lay on their backs in unbroken snow, moving their arms up and down to make wings.

Petra was in the kitchen, surrounded by muffins and browned loaves of fresh bread from the oven. Her face was flushed from the heat of the stove, her brow beaded with sweat. Her mouth fell ajar when the outer door opened and Jed entered behind Eric, who was returning to the classroom after a trek to the outhouse. Jed! Never was it that her pulse did not increase upon seeing him, more so with his arrival at an undesignated time. She daubed dry her moist face with the corners of her apron, she rushed into his arms and he closed her mouth with a kiss. Only did he release her when young voices and laughter were heard, the rattling of tin lunch boxes and thumping of feet down the kitchen stairway. School being dismissed for the day.

Supper was held up till Jed emerged from the sauna. There was venison, browned potatoes and golden carrots which had been carefully attended to by Petra with a sprinkling of assistance from Florence. He ate hungrily, and had to admit, that it had been an awfully long time since he'd tasted anything half so good.

"Petra! he exclaimed after swallowing a mouthful of food. "Your cooking is great. The very best!" But did he not yesterday tell Virginia the very same thing? His heart dictated. Petra was the best cook, Virginia second.

Pa Kelso couldn't wait to share the good news. That citizenship papers had been granted the family. Adding with deep pride, that they now were "Americans".

There was the gathering in the living room after the supper dishes had been cleared away. With everybody hungry for news about Judge Tittlebaum's hearings. They sat bug-eyed, as Jed related in length up to the minute details on Syd's death as derived from the inquest. Pa allotted time for only two games of checkers, played by the boys bellied on the worn carpet by the fireplace. No championship game tonight. Pa prodded them to bed earlier than usual, his face radiating love as he listened to them clump up the stairway. Florence excused herself, saying that test papers needed to be graded. Shortly Pa mentioned undue fatigue, he added firewood to the box stove and checked the drafts, and followed his sons to bed.

It was well past midnight and the house was very quiet. Now relaxed on the floor by the fireplace, the reverie of Petra and Jed was broken by no sound save for the crackling of the burning logs and occasional hissing of sap in green wood. For intervals there was but loving silence, Jed's head resting comfortably on her bosom, her fingers combing his hair. Though it was difficult for Petra to keep her eyes off her left hand, with the flickering radiance of the fireplace sparkling the diamond embedded in a gold ring, so tenderly presented after all had retired. Embedded in Holyoke gold, but Jed yet held his secret.

*   *   *   *   *

The inquest was in its third day and the man in the witness chair was Hank Manson. His face reflected a pallor unlike his own natural coloring and fatigue was evident in him. He identified himself to the Judge and jury and told of his affiliation with the Holyoke Mining Company. In decided contrast to the preceding days, Judge Tittlebaum's face showed some spark and his character took on new fire. He lost no time in riddling Hank Manson with sharp interrogations.

"Mr. Manson. In what capacity was Sydney Crawford officially employed by the Holyoke Mining Company?"

"Syd Crawford was elected to the position of secretary-treasurer of the Holyoke Mining Company at the organizational meeting of the company last May, and was holding that position at the time of his death."

"Then one might assume that he worked in a very

200

exacting and satisfactory manner?"

"Very much so. Which leaves me to question a portion of .Mr. Bigger's testimony of last week... when he stated that after leaving the pool hall on that grim night... that he saw the safe open and Syd not in sight. Syd was very particular about locking the safe when he was not close by. I maintain that he was too precise a man to have left the safe and office open and gone outside at that time of night."

"Mr. Manson. To repeat the last part of my question. Did Mr. Crawford perform his duties in a satisfactory manner at all times?" The Judge was gaining momentum in his cross examination. It was observed by spectators in the fore part of the room that Manson was breathing deeper.

"He did. Except to say that in the past few months he was drawing himself into somewhat of a shell. I thought it might be fatigue from overwork that was catching up with him."

"Aside from what you observed - a slight personality change, let me repeat my original question. Did Mr. Crawford perform his work satisfactorily at all times?"

Hank Manson looked to the floor. The query was beginning to bore deep. He spoke without raising his eyes. "For the past few months Syd was reluctant about releasing the account books. To me, to stockholders or anybody who had a right to review them. It was a disturbing matter... inability to get at the books, having to take Mr. Crawford's word regarding our financial condition, rather than seeing the figures for myself."

"Have the account books been examined since his death?"

"An audit was completed yesterday."

"And the report... was it accepted to the satisfaction of the officers and stockholders?"

"The audit report shows a shortage in the cash account of $1800."

201

Hank Manson's statement electrified the air in the room. There was rippling of tongues, but most spectators sat in stunned silence. Judge Tittlebaum reached for his gavel and pounded the tabletop once. "I ask for complete silence in this room so that the questioning can proceed." Attaining pinpoint silence he readdressed Hank Manson. "Is there more to the audit report that should be revealed?"

"We generally kept several hundred dollars cash on hand to meet quick demands. On the day Mr. Crawford was murdered the audit showed there should have been $1100 in the cash box. Yet that same afternoon Syd had to write a check drawn on the local bank for $30.00 to pay the office rent. I wish to stress one point to the jury. That the practice existed, of advancing cash to many of the men on the payroll. But advanced monies would always be deducted from their pay. We have located a few advance slips. But, should more be uncovered, the cash shortage would be less."

"Was Mr. Crawford himself in financial straits?"

"That I doubt very much. His personal life appeared financially sound. Can't say I ever saw him wasteful with money."

"Are there other pertinent details you feel the jury should know before you take leave of the witness stand?"

"No sir."

Judge Tittlebaum scribbled a few notations on a piece of paper. He dismissed Hank Manson from the stand.

Some faces in the audience twisted with perplexity when the Judge requested Bart Fauquier to take the oath and testify. Bart appeared unduly calm, he rose to his feet and lazily advanced to the spot Hank Manson just vacated.

Bart was sworn in.

"Might you enlighten the jury about your operations in this area?" requested Judge Tittlebaum.

Bart's face was deadpan. He shifted a matchstick

202

from one side of his mouth to the other. His words drawled out. "Proprietor of the South Arm."

"Mr. Fauquier. What are your feelings about the death of Sydney Crawford?"

"He's dead. Nicely buried. We'll all go... what else is there to say?"

"Had you no respect for Mr. Crawford?"

"Here today... gone tomorrow... that's life."

"Mr. Fauquier, do you know anything at all about this case?"

"I don't know nothing. Nothing at all. I got nothing to talk about to you or to this here jury."

"Reports have circulated about the area that your concern has been hard pressed for funds, of late, and that you are in financial difficulties."

Bart didn't like the statement. His face crumpled up. "Mister Judge. My money matters ain't nobody's business but my own."

"Isn't it true that the bank has been pressing you lately for payment of notes?"

"You got no grounds for sech talk."

"And isn't it true that just last month you were refused additional loans from the bank. That maybe you and Mr. Crawford were in consultation about money matters outside the Holyoke office on that fateful night?"

The question stirred a few jury men who leaned forward in their chairs. Their movements caused irritation in Bart. He turned to face them, his face twisted in defiance. "It's a lie. This Judge man don't know what he's talking about!"

The rap of the wooden hammer resounded throughout the room demanding complete silence.

"Mr. Fauquier. Do you carry any inner reaction about the operation of the Holyoke? Has there been, let me ask, hard feelings on your part toward those affiliated with the company. Remember, this courts asks that you speak the truth."

"Hard feelings! You're damned right! They stole my men."

"Would you be kind enough to trace for the jury your whereabouts on the evening Syd Crawford met his death."

"I don't think I can hardly recollect."

"Come now. Think hard. I'm sure a man of your intellect can quicken memory on events that night."

Bart reacted. He smiled. The unexpected compliment pleased him. He moistened his lips with his tongue and kindled his memory. His tongue became free. "Well, now. By jove, Judge. I suddenly do recollect a few things. Sure, sure... as a matter of fact I was in the Black Bear saloon. Enjoying some of my favorite beverage."

"Which is a stone's throw from the Jamison building. And you lingered at the saloon, exactly how long?"

Bart shrugged his shoulders. "Don't remember that part too good. Maybe three, four hours."

"Did you leave the saloon, for even a short while?"

Bart was beginning to show some uneasiness. "Nope."

"You're sure about that?"

The question thoroughly annoyed Bart. "What are you trying to do to me?"

"Mr. Fauquier. Identification has been made of two sets of footprints near the scene of the crime. One set has been definitely established as the prints of Syd Crawford. The other set of prints corresponds with the boots you are wearing."

Bart's face hardened. "You're trying to frame me. Put the bite on me. You don't know what you're talking about, saying strong words to agitate my nerves..."

There was mumbling throughout the room about Bart's uncouth manner, and Judge Tittlebaum pounded his mallet. "Everybody shut up or we'll clear the whole room!" He again addressed Bart. "One final question, Mr. Fauquier." Judge Tittlebaum rummaged through the drawer in the table and produced an object. "Exhibit

B - this watch which fell out of your pocket during a scuffle last week in the Black Bear. Does it belong to you?"

A quick glance at it, and Bart was satisfied. "It's my watch, all right... so you're the guy who had it. Been looking all over for the damn thing!"

The Judge's eyes searched the spectators and came to rest upon Syd's widow. "Mrs. Crawford, will you please step forward for just a minute."

Mrs. Crawford rose weakly, the shock of her husband's death had sapped her of strength. She took a deep breath and falteringly moved to the fore part of the room, a silk handkerchief pressed to her grief-strained face. She was tall, quite slender. Possessed of sharp cut features and dark hair which was graying at the temples. She bore characteristics of grace and refinement. Now she stood before the Judge, her tired eyes fixed blankly upon him.

"Mrs. Crawford, please take a good look at this watch."

Her trembling hand reached out for the watch, she held it gently in the palm of her hand, she pressed the stem to pop open the case.

"It looks very much like one that belonged to my husband." Her voice broke. Her hand groped for a nearby chair and she slumped into it. Now she was sobbing hysterically, her face in her hands. Marshall Malaroni's eyes rolled sidewise and he quickly left his vantage position near the jury and moved to her side. He retrieved the watch and handed it back to Judge Tittlebaum, then whispered something to Mrs. Crawford, assisted her up and escorted her out of the room.

Judge Tittlebaum once again focused his attention on Bart. "You're dismissed. But it would be well if you would stay within easy reach of this court. We may find it necessary to call you again." He rapped the gavel. "Hearing adjourned. The jury will recess until Wednesday morning."

Judge Tittlebaum was escorted out of the courtroom by Marshall Malaroni, but returned shortly to the near vacated room to pick up his reading glasses. Jed's approach was direct.

"Your honor. I ask permission to view Exhibits A and B."

Judge Tittlebaum's response was wordless, he merely reached deep in his pocket for a key, unlocked the drawer in the table and produced the pliers and watch.

The small pliers Jed turned over and over in his rough hands. They were clean, no dirt or grease was embedded. X2 was engraved thereon. He set them down on the table. Then studied the heavy gold encased timepiece, first the front casing, then the back, noting the twelve embedded ruby jewels perfectly encircled thereon. He pressed the stem to open the case, noted the black Roman numerals, and the second hand. He snapped the case shut and returned the exhibits to the Judge.

It was evening of the same day. The bell on the church whined out six o'clock and the hour found the Holyoke diggers congregated around a cigarette burnt table in the Black Bear, hashing out events of the day. The crew was near complete, save for Nels. And Curt, who had gone to Iron Bay to pick up his bride who was arriving by boat. Thick smoke curled the air around the table and hung heavy about their heads. They were an unusually quiet bunch tonight. The testimony heard this day was far more numbing than the sub-zero weather outside. It was hard to believe, and digest, what they'd heard in the morning from Hank Manson's own lips... shortage... account books... cash shortage. True or not true. It was spice enough for the town's newsmongers.

"I jest don't swallow it." muttered Dan. "Syd wasn't that kind of a fella."

Ikey set his empty glass down. "His purse was stuffed green before he took the job. He didn't need money."

Jed was tilted on the back legs of his chair, balancing a foamy mug of beer on a knee. He didn't bat an eyelash when he spoke his thoughts. "Face it you guys. Hank's the sanest character in this district. He got the figures straight from the books."

"I can't shake the idea but that Bart figures in on this mess."

"If Syd needed money, he wouldn't have taken ours."

"I talked with him on most every trip into town," added Jed. "He didn't carry the colors of a till dipper."

"One guess right now is as good as another."

The evening hours devoured themselves... more beer... cash shortage... Syd.. more beer.

"The clues might lead to nothing."

"Still don't think that killer is far out of reach."

Jallu fully agreed. "Point 'im out and I'll shoot 'im on the spot."

"I'd like the chance of putting 'im outa gear," growled Ikey.

It was plenty late when Jed left the saloon, alone, and plodded down snowy Main Street toward the Chippewa. His sheepskin coat was unbuttoned. He had left his cap in the saloon and light snow which was swirling over the frozen town settled in his thick hair. His eyelids were growing heavy, his eyes smarting from smoke... cash shortage... pliers. His mind was crammed with confusion.

Something had to give, he thought, pretty damn soon.

He entered the hotel and tugged shut the door making sure the latch had caught. Once inside, he stomped the snow from his boots, only to look up into the smirking face of Jorn Holmstrom, who was on his way out.

"You made me offer of a warm bed. It didn't really have to be a hot one." Jorn pushed open the door and left.

Wisecracking kid, Jed mused as he passed through the deserted waiting room, illuminated by a night light burning behind the registration counter. Near the threshold of his door he hesitated, then stopped short. Dim light filtered from under the doorway... or was it his room? He looked up, to read 6 painted on the middle of the upper panel.

He lay a soft hand on the doorknob, turned it slowly and pushed the door inward.

The lamp burning low on the shelf did not radiate bright light, yet enough to reflect upon Blanche. Her coat and hat had been shed, she was seated by the table with her head thrown back, and clutching a half-emptied glass of liquor. Jed eased the door shut behind him, he decided there and then that she was a bit under the weather.

"Thought you'd never show up! Been waiting for you to join me in a nightcap."

He shook off his wet sheepskin and hung it on a bedpost, then sat on the edge of the iron bed, lowered his head and ran his fingers through his hair, shaking out the melting snow. His eyes rested briefly on the table, on the bottle she had brought with her.

"Wasn't expecting any company. Been waiting very long?"

"Time doesn't matter when the guy is worth waiting for."

She set down her glass. Reached for the bottle, uncorked it. Filled a second glass which she totteringly presented to him, then took another swallow of her own drink.

"Who gave you my room number?"

"The registry book is right on the counter. Don't worry honey boy. If it will make you feel better the waiting room was empty and nobody saw me come in. And, by the way, how come your door was unlocked?" She lowered the contents of her glass in rapid degrees and filled it again. Only then did she note Jed's drink still untouched. She stood up, and with an unsteady sweep of an arm raised her glass to the level of her drooping eyelids. "To Jed Carter! The only man I've wanted in my whole life." She put the glass to her lips and upended it.

Jed released a thin smile and raised his drink in response. "Cheers. Cheers to Miss Blanche!" With that he downed the liquor.

From the crack of dawn to the present late hour the day had been long and full, with plenty to think about, no rest for the mind. Now the warmth of the room contrasting to the cold outdoors was bringing on uncontrollable fatigue. There were soft thudding noises, and through his smarting eyes he saw Blanche's buckle slippers on the floor. With uncoordinated moves she rose from the chair she had been seated in and advanced toward the bed. Now she was sitting beside him, smiling wickedly. She slapped a hand on his shoulder. "Cheers. Cheers to the both of us!"

He sat not long. Got up and set his empty glass on the table. The small wheel which controlled the light of the lamp was turned back and the room was dimmed to near darkness.

His steps toward her were slow, at the foot of the bed he stopped. His hand reached out to the bedpost and he removed his sheepskin, tucking it under an arm.

At the threshold of the open door he turned and looked back at the curvaceous creature sprawled on his bed. "Goodnight, Blanche."

But he wasn't sure that she heard.

*   *   *   *   *

A blustery 30 degree below morning slowed the pulse of the town. Jed Carter closed tight the door of the Chippewa behind him and headed toward the town hall, to attend the fourth hearing in the past seven days. A merciless north wind was picking up loose snow off the street and thrashing it through the air. Few pedestrians were in sight, no vehicles were moving. He held his sheepskin collar over his mouth to warm the air he was inhaling, to avoid collapsing a lung.

Dan emerged from the general store, hailed him and they joined company. Rumor from diverse sources had been strong that final testimony was to be heard. That the jury might render a verdict.

As expected, the penetrating freeze confined previous spectators to their homes effecting but a half-filled courtroom. The hands on the clock turned the hour. Marshall Malaroni opened the door to the rear addition and routinely ushered in Judge Tittlebaum. The Judge moved to his chair of honor and rapped the gavel but once, opening the session without wasted words. "I'm told that all witnesses are present. We shall proceed."

"Jorn Holmstrom. Please return to the witness stand."

Jorn! Jed Carter's heart took a thump.

Jorn appeared more at ease than his first time on the stand. He raised his hand and repeated the oath. The Judge looked gravely at the clean-cut youth before him and motioned him toward the witness chair. "Sit down, young fella." He shuffled papers before him. "It has been brought to my attention that there are further details regarding this crime which you would like to reveal to the jury."

"Yes sir."

There was low talking among the spectators and the Judge impatiently rapped for order.

"Why did you hold back information last week when you stood before this jury?"

"I was afraid."

"Afraid... afraid of what? Some person or persons who might be threatening you?"

Jorn's lip twitched. "No, jest plain scared. The whole thing is so creepy."

"We'll proceed. Am I to understand correctly that you have details regarding this crime heretofore unfolded, which should be revealed to the jury?"

Jorn was ready to talk. To clear his worried mind, get

210

it over with. "That night Syd Crawford got killed. On my first stop in his office he was bent over his work table, studying a little black book, marking some pages with a pencil. He seemed kind of puzzled about something in that book. He didn't even make me feel welcome."

"Please continue."

"Uh-h. After I banked the fire and right before I fell asleep I thought I smelled smoke. Like paper burning. Got up and went back to Crawford's office. When he saw me standing in the doorway he slammed an account book shut and came towards me, asked me if I needed something. Made me feel like I was bothering him. When I walked away he stood in the doorway and watched me."

"What happened then?"

"That's everything. Got nothing more to tell."

The details merited thought. The Judge wrote more notes and then dismissed Jorn. Now his bulging eyes searched the audience and focused on Rush Biggers and Bart Fauquier sitting side by side. "Mr. Biggers. The jury desires that you take the stand for reexamination."

Rush didn't like what he heard. Though he'd known all along that he was subject to recall. He made no motion to rise, but darted a questioning look at Bart who was nonchalantly gnawing on a matchstick. Bart's ultimate nudge was far from docile. He growled low. "Go ahead. But don't use a loose lip. Don't let that old fogy pull anything out of your head."

Rush would much rather it would have been Bart called to the stand when he once again found himself facing Judge Tittlebaum, who motioned for him to sit down.

"Mr. Biggers. We are seeking..." Rush brashly interrupted. "Call me Rush. That's what I'm called, don't cha remember?"

"Very well. I'd like to raise further questions about your moves on the night of the crime. To be specific -

Monday night of last week. You stated at your first appearance on this stand that after midnight you locked up the pool room, walked by the Jamison building and saw the lights burning but saw nobody inside."

"Right, Judge. You got it clear."

"Might it have been that through the window you saw the safe wide open, and being familiar with the layout of the place you entered and committed robbery. That when Syd Crawford returned unexpectedly you became startled upon being caught red-handed and your identity known to him. That you grabbed the revolver you knew was concealed on a shelf and shot him, and then placed the weapon near the body to indicate suicide?"

Rush lunged to his feet. "Yer full of hot air. Trying to frame me! Al da time I thought ya wuz gonna give me a nice piece of talk. Ya can't find nobody who done it so ya pick on me!"

"Would it be unfair, to have you take the blame alone? Maybe it was that you had an accomplice?"

"Yer using words I don't understand."

"Possibly you had a partner in crime whom you don't want to involve?"

Rush looked to Bart for moral support. Bart had changed color but was controlling himself. Once again Rush's eyes bored into Judge Tittlebaum and his expression began to harden. Rush decided that he would not answer the question.

"How long have you known Bart Fauquier?"

Nohow did the query meet the liking of Bart, who sprang to his feet. His heavy eyebrows met and resentment of the question began smoldering in his eyes. His face twisted into a knot and his nail blackened fingers became fisted. From the midst of the spectators he roared out, "Jest mind your own business, Mister Judge, and I'll mind mine."

Throughout many years Judge Tittlebaum had tried hundreds of cases and had taken lip from nobody. He snapped out a sharp retort. "That'll be enough from you. Sit down and keep quiet or I may have to ask you to leave." His attention was turned back to Rush. "I'll reword my question. "Are you an acquaintance of Bart Fauquier?"

"He drops in my pool place. I got da only pool tables in town."

"Might I assume that he was both patron and friend?"

Rush was definitely ruffled. "Everabody's my friend. 'Cept I'm not so sure about you."

"Might the picture portray itself more clearly, since it has been determined that the second set of tracks in the snow outside the office have been positively identified as matching the bootprint of Bart Fauquier. That you two had carefully planned this robbery, but plans fell apart when Mr. Fauquier failed to detain Mr. Crawford long enough outside the building?"

Rush was hot under the collar. "Ya got nothin' on me. Ya need proof. Evidence... is da word. Evidence. Ya jest ain't got none."

"We'll leave that for the jury to decide. Witness dismissed."

Rush stormed back to his seat.

All witnesses had been heard.

Judge Tittlebaum rapped the gavel once, twice. He turned to address the jury. "Gentlemen of the jury. Over the past several days you have heard testimony of witnesses connected with the demise of Sydney Crawford. I request your adjournment for deliberation, and ask that you return to me as soon as possible, a just verdict."

A half hour passed, an hour. Marshall Malaroni stood sentry before the door behind which the jury deliberated. An hour and forty-six minutes had passed when a written communication was passed out to Marshall Malaroni and advanced by him to Judge

213

Tittlebaum. The message was read. Whereupon Judge Tittlebaum whispered words into the Marshall's ear.

With his glove-covered hand Marshall Malaroni opened wide the door leading to the deliberating room. Members of the jury returned in single file to their rows of chairs, their faces saying nothing.

Silence prevailed. The air was charged with tension. The only motion in the entire room was created by Ed Morley who was twisting a pencil in his hands which would scrawl out headlines for the POST.

Judge Tittlebaum faced the jury men. "Gentlemen. Have you reached a verdict?"

The church bell could be heard ringing out the noon hour when the foreman arose. "We have, your honor. It is the decision of this jury that Sydney Crawford met his death by a revolver shot in the head, inflicted by a party unknown."

Applause collided with scattered hoots of dissent. The outside door was sprung open and spectators bolted out to spill the verdict to the outside world. Some lingered in the courtroom, in small groups, to exchange final words.

Dan and Jed shuffled out, neither reflecting emotion. The verdict wasn't a surprise. It was the only one the jury could give. There hadn't been evidence enough against anyone, and suicide was ruled out.

CHAPTER 14
Case Solved

There was a raw dampness in the air and though it was but mid-day the temperature had already begun to dip. Jed dropped the earlaps on his cap and buttoned his sheepskin to the neck. Back down Main he plodded, alone, vapors of each warm breath funneling into the cold air. A perplexing case it had turned out to be. One day the pattern seemed to be evolving to a clear pattern, the next day it would wash out. Only in the past few days new details in the case had come to light, details unknown last week. He was convicted on one thought. The murderer had to be someone familiar with the office and onto Syd's work habits. With lights burning he must have been fortified with a steel spine.

He heard his name being called and turned, to see Jorn Holmstrom running to catch up with him. They continued along together. In front of the bank Jed chose to stop. To observe Marshall Malaroni tacking a hand printed sign on the front of the building. It could hardly be missed by any passerby.

$1000 REWARD

The town of Ishpeming will pay the above reward for the apprehension of the murderer or murderers of Sydney Crawford who was shot in his office on the night of Monday, January 9, 1865.

By order of the Citizens Common Council.

215

"Can't make out all of the words. What's it say?" asked Jorn.

"Thousand dollar reward for turning in the killer."

"That's all it says? All that printing?"

"That's it.', in a nutshell."

Moments later, waiting by the railroad tracks for a passing train, Jorn raised his voice to offset the clacking noise of wheels on iron rails. "Jed. Couple of weeks now I been thinking..."

"Yea."

"If Miss Neeley still has my study books I'm going to go back to school."

At the Y in the road Jed took a glancing sweep at "Old Ish", now cloaked in ice and snow. He lifted his eyes to the face of the iron warrior and the thought churned in his head. "You know who did it, "Old Ish". If only your silent lips could speak."

*   *   *   *   *

The following weeks the district remained in a deep freeze with sub-zero weather which didn't even break at the noon hour. Few people moved about in the streets. Even the sturdiest who bucked the cold, mostly for the sake of securing provisions, felt the pain in their lungs from deep breaths of cold air. Few lingered on the streets to converse, but hurried home to huddle by the warmth of their stoves.

Jed's treks to the homestead became more regularly patterned and it was often, when dark skies or suspicious squalls forbode stormy weather that Pa Kelso insisted he remain overnight, longer, if necessary. A man would only be asking for trouble, time and again Pa repeated, by underestimating the forces of nature in this north country where storms dropped even the hardiest into wintry graves.

Jed's every stay at the homestead stored cherished memories within him. He was content, as were the Kelsos, in the solitude of the rugged countryside, and he desired no release from its powerful grip.

Yet there were uncounted days when he needed to cover ground in and around town. Creating a pattern of activity which varied but little. He made frequent treks over to the POST, to talk things over with Ed whose usual appearance was in a soiled shop apron, hands and arms half-black with ink.

Jed made it a point to develop verbal communication with most every patron of the Chippewa. He loitered around the store which was the center of daily life. At Sam's barber shop, and at the blacksmith shop where he watched shoeing of horses and steel bands being secured to bottoms of sleigh runners. Listening all the while to every word spilled.

Iotas of information he stored in his mind. Sam had made an unusually big investment in railroad stock. And Thor Blumstrom had told Ed Morley, which word Ed passed along, that Rush had placed an order for a half carat diamond stick pin with a traveling salesman. Jake wasn't tending much to business anymore. Though he seemed to have plenty of loose cash evidenced by his buying rounds of drinks in the saloons. At the livery just yesterday, fate had drawn Jed upon an occurrence of prime importance. Finding Jake peering through a cheap scope set in a knothole on the north side of the livery. Where one's vision diagonally fell in line with the Holyoke office. Jed asked no questions. Pocketing the scope, Jake offered no explanation of what he was doing.

If Rush carried suspicion about Jed's sudden addiction to pool cues he never let on. But for Jed Carter the pool hall was a place to relax, challenging Jorn at the pool tables almost daily. Never bent on being a winner but remembering everything his ears gathered. Attempting to interpret Rush's split personality, his effort at a lukewarm friendship, then again evasive of any conversation. Yesterday Rush had hurried to the front door to deter Bart's entry, they had engaged in

217

unbroken hushed talk.

Habitually Blanche loitered in front of the pool room after darkness, courageous enough to peer through the window at the patrons inside. Seeking to create an evening friendship with one who might appear to have a surplus of cash.

Hours were dwindled in the Black Bear saloon, where uproarious card games were common and marked cards spelled doom. Bart made regular stops there, sometimes gulping down a drink or two and quickly leaving. Occasionally remaining to buy a round for friends at the bar. Dr. Von Muller who hadn't been doing much peddling was becoming a steady patron of the joint. Of late he was unkempt and unshaven. Secluding himself in a corner, keeping more or less to himself.

Swig put in an unexpected appearance at the Chippewa this morning, unbelievably sober, to rouse Jed from sound sleep. Most surprising, the full bottle expanding his mackinaw pocket containing but cherry bark juice. Jallu wasn't a man to put business before pleasure, but he had the presence of mind to pass along that the rail agent had sold a ticket to Marshall Malaroni, a one-way ticket to the east coast from where he would sail to Italy. That Malaroni would be leaving within a few weeks.

"He don't make that much mazoola to go traveling," said Jallu. "Somebody being real nice to him?"

"Why would he want to go back to a country that branded him?" questioned Jed.

So it was. More often than not that Jed returned to the Chippewa late each night, or in the early morning hours to snatch a few hours sleep. Sometimes having to nudge Jorn over to get a share of the bed. There were times when fatigue caught up and he'd sleep nearly a whole day away. Many hours he lay awake with thoughts churning his mind.

The following day wove out a routine pattern, save for

the appearance of Captain Sommers at the saloon during the course of the evening to pass word to the diggers who happened to be around that weather permitting, the mine would be opened up at the end of the month. The next day, March 8 was well circled on Jed's calendar. An important day in Petra's life, it being her name day. According to the Kelso family heritage, name days carried greater importance than birthdays. Though as Pa had explained, name days and birthdays could be the same day, though in Petra's case it was not.

Jed's only stop on the morning of the 8th was at the store, an hour after Thor Blumstrom had opened up for the day. A half-dozen customers were encircled about Widow Lindstrom, appreciating a very large egg she held in her hand which Jed heard tell, that it was laid by one of her plymouth rock hens, that the egg weighed a quarter of a pound, and was the best performance of any hen in her coop.

Thor was busy behind the counter measuring a quantity of flour and rice from bins against the wall, ignoring the few townsfolk who were waiting to pick up their mail. Jed interrupted Thor and made known his scant need, to which Thor responded with a thumb pointed in the general direction where the box of greeting cards was shelved. Whereas Jed headed toward the back of the store. sidestepping kegs of nails, sacks of beans and boxes of dried fish. He moved over a barrel of butter. Near the shelf holding bottles of patent medicines he located the greeting cards. He scanned a few and quickly took preference to one with fancy printed lines full of sentiment.

'A violet by a mossy stone
Half hidden from the eye!
Fair as a star when only one
Is shining in the sky.'

The skies were foreboding. By the slaughter house it

219

began to snow, a soft, wet snow and he heeled Blaze to a trot.

From the moment Petra's wide-awake eyes met the pink dawn she anticipated Jed's arrival. Disappointment would register deep if he did not remember her name day. She reflected. He could have easily enough forgotten. It was way last summer when they had talked about birthdays and name days. At midday she conceded that the ominous dark and low sky could be reason for not traveling. Florence dismissed school early, the weather looking like it was.

Jed veered in at the roadgate. Her eyes sparkled. He didn't forget!

The greeting card, hand painted, with feathers and lace and fancy words in print! Briefly Jed stood in wonderment. Her lips seemed to move when she scanned the printed lines. Or had it been an illusion? How she tremored with happiness when he fitted on her wrist the sterling bracelet, with both their initials inscribed on the inside. Florence sat by, sharing Petra's happiness. Only to suddenly remember that she should go see Stig, to borrow a mail order catalog. She put on her boots, her coat, felt in the pockets for mittens but instead withdrew her eyeglass case which she set on the table. She pulled on a stocking hat and made a hasty departure along the packed guideline trail.

Jed's hunch of the morning, premonitions of a change in weather began coming true. The light falling snow was becoming thick and heavy and gusts of wind sweeping out of the northwest suddenly increased in velocity, savagely churning the big flakes through the air. Within a half-hours time a storm was hammering the district. Small outbuildings on the property were lost to visibility, the big barn could barely be discerned.

Pa finished tending to the horses, he milked his cow Daisy. Then battled his way back to the house handling with extreme care Daisy's generous donation. He stood in the doorway of the kitchen, virtually a living snowman.

"Vat? Mees Neeley ees not een house, you say!" His normally pleasant expression took on a look of appall. He was slow to unbutton his coat, to shake it off his shoulders, as though maybe he shouldn't. Beside the cook stove he stood rubbing his cold hands above the lids, frowning, saying nothing. Purely distressed with the fact that Florence had ventured outdoors.

Supper meal served shortly didn't go down too good with Pa. The howling winds rattled the window at his back, mostly he didn't like the sight of Florence's vacant place across the table.

Petra read her father. "Don't worry, Pa. She's safe and sound. She surely made it to Stig's place before the storm broke."

But the growing worry in Pa's mind and the oncoming darkness was too much to bear, without trying to do something about it. He pushed back the bench and got up. "I go valk guideline. Maybe she have trouble an' no can make all vay."

Petra knew. As did Jed. That when Pa made a decision no amount of talk, however rational, could change that decision. Accordingly, Jed swung his foot over the bench and got up. He told Pa, "I'll go with you."

Petra sprung to her feet. "Me too!"

"Oh no! You're staying put right here!" It was an order from Jed, something she seldom heard. She offered no argument.

Excitedly Timo and Eric sat by watching their father and Jed ready themselves for the venture, unaware of the risk involved. Heavy outerwear was donned. From the cupboard Pa took a tin box which he filled with wooden matches and put in his mackinaw pocket. He strapped on his Colt 45, noting in the meantime Petra pouring oil into two lanterns they would carry. She put lights to the wicks and closed the sliding drafts on the bottom. Outside on the snow covered porch snowshoes were strapped on, each move watched by faces pressed against the windowpanes.

Face coverings were pulled up so only eyes showed. Their bodies leaning into the wind, they broke tracks to the guideline pole abutting the sauna. Pa chose to take the lead and handgrips were taken on the lifeline. They pressed on, staying close together, the guidewire sliding through their double mittened hands. Seven poles had been counted when Pa stopped. The snowshoes had been sinking right from the start causing him to become prematurely winded. In need of rest. Already they were completely encompassed in stormy darkness save for the lights of their lanterns. Even the beacon light of the homestead could not be detected. Jed set down his lantern and pulled down the wool covering from his face. With hands cupped to his mouth he shouted into the darkness ahead..."halloo... halloo.... halloo....."

He waited. Only the violent winds responded. He covered his face to eye level.

It was not long before Pa picked up his lantern indicating he was ready to proceed. Heads down, shoulders bent forward they pushed on. Roughly an additioinal fifty feet. Again Pa stopped. Startled! The guidewire wasn't passing through his mittened hand! Jed closed the few paces separating them. Pa turned his head and pulled down his face covering to enable him to communicate. He raised his voice to combat the winds.

"Sumptin' wrong!"

Combined lantern lights revealed but a short length of guidewire extending beyond the ninth pole.

"Vire ees broke!" Pa eyed the snapped end. "No rust. Eet break not long ago." The radius of lamplight failed to reveal the other end of the wire. Under snow no doubt. A snapped wire, an abrupt ending to their endeavor. There was no alternative but to reverse direction, but not before shouting with full lung power..."halloo...Florence halloo, halloo......"

The ears of the cruel storm heard their calls and responded by extinguishing Pa's lamplight. New tracks were broken, the first ones being completely blown over.

Close to the fireplace they sat that night watching the flaming logs disintegrate to ashes, while on the opposite side of the room the crackling box stove gobbled up block wood. Minds were not at ease. Thoughts were interrupted with winds rattling the windows and whipping the walls of the house as if testing the strength of their structure.

A thin layer of snow had swept beneath the kitchen door, whereby Petra located an old carpet which she rolled up and lay at the threshold. She hung a worn jacket on the doorknob to seal off another draft.

Florence's name kept sprinkling their conversation. Jed and Petra sporadically convinced that she was safe and sound in Stig's house. Or that she could have taken earlier shelter in his roothouse. Pa was not a bit at ease and he let his thoughts be known. Florence never had been exposed to a vicious north country storm. Physically, she wasn't real strong. And another thing, she hadn't worn enough protective clothing. But then again, he had to admit, she possessed a good head. She thought clearly.

Pa gave admonishing advice to the boys before sending them off to bed. "You talk nottin' 'bout dees ven school commissioner man come here. Say nottin'. Else Mees Neeley lose her yob!"

Timo's young mind did not totally comprehend, but he would obey his father's request. Eric thought he knew what Pa meant. In bed Timo lay quietly with folded hands, minutes later his soft voice moved his lips..."and God, please bring Miss Neeley back safe cuz we need her. She learns us so good."

Petra who had been standing outside the bedroom

doorway entered the darkened room and lay old coats over the boys for added warmth.

All night long the wind continued its fierce wailing and rattling of windows. Everybody slept lightly, except the boys, with Pa getting up during the night to feed wood into the fires. Jed at rest on a day bed near the fireplace, doing likewise, telling Pa to go to sleep, that he'd tend to the fires.

Pa Kelso rose in the five o'clock darkness, his ears telling him that the storm was still raging. He dressed quietly by candlelight, softly descended the stairway to the kitchen. The room was unduly chilly. Miniature snowdrifts lay on the window sills and the window panes were fuzzy with frost. He kindled a fire in the cookstove, put on kettles to heat water, then sat close to the crackling stove, and smoked his pipe while the room took heat.

His sons unlike his daughter were born early risers. With the oncoming of daylight they came scampering down the stairway, clad only in their long underwear and wool stockings. Only to stand, flabbergasted, when they discovered the kitchen windows half-covered with snow. With Pa's strict words, to get dressed, that the floor was too cold to stand on even in thick stockinged feet, they thumped back upstairs in obedience.

Sleep could not be extended for anybody in the household once the noisy twosome had bounced out of their bed. Jed, half-awake anyway, and lured by the aroma of perking coffee, got up from a partial night's rest near the fireplace. Upstairs Eric was shaking Petra's iron bed, and Timo was shaking Petra, telling her to get up, to see how much snow had fallen. To their dismay she wasn't budging, they told her that coffee was ready.

Breakfast consisting of fried eggs, toast smeared with wild strawberry jam, cardamon rolls and coffee tasted plenty good. Yet appetites were tempered with continued concern over Florence. Though assured by Timo that worry shouldn't be so deep, that he had prayed for her.

Jed failed to hear Timo's last remark. His eyes were set on Florence's spectacle case still resting upon the table. Twice in the recent past Florence had mentioned need for tightening the nosepiece of her glasses. He thought. Just like he'd seen... like he'd seen the jeweler in Iron Bay fix that woman's...

His countenance took on a deadening look, Petra asking if he felt not well.

Throughout the restless morning hours, one after another would push the storm door partly open, to stick a head outside, to perceive with his own eyes nothing visible past the porch. No signs of the storm letting up. Conversation touched upon ramifications of the storm, about the safety of the neighbors, the need to check on the horses and Daisy. The big job of opening up the roads. In midafternoon Pa and Jed, already feeling housebound, ventured outside in an attempt to clear a path to the barn. Determinedly they wielded shovels in the blinding squalls, reshoveling the pathway only to see it rapidly fill in.

The storm showed its vehemence all day, and for a second night. Only in the morning hours of the third day did the winds cede their power and the snow quit falling.

Jed shoveled the windblown snow from the porch and cleared off the steps. He leaned the shovel against the porch railing and watched as Pa withdrew an upright measuring stick from the snow.

"Vun eench past four foot," Pa announced, and with his pocket knife notched the mark on the stick.

"And you said that last winter's...snowfall.." Jed's words cut off. Something on the landscape caught his attention, his eyes caught fire and his mouth broke into a big smile. And the boys, inside looking out, their heads sandwiched between the kitchen window and the curtain, must have seen the same. The door flew open and they burst outside, bareheaded and with coats unbuttoned.

"Pa! Take a look over there!" Jed's finger pointed out the direction.

Crossing the field was Stig, on snowshoes, and not far behind him was Florence, awkwardly advancing on snowshoes. The first time for Florence! The boys eyes popped. Miss Neeley walking on snowshoes!

Stig waited so Florence could catch up with him, when she did he again proceeded to break trail. Twice he backtracked, to reach out a hand and pull her out of the snow.

Suddenly Jed Carter found himself just standing there, breathing freely of the fresh air, raptured with the white purity of the new landscape. Should he ever leave the area, he thought. Not that he intended, but should he. The beauty of the unbroken white panaroma before him would forever be framed in his mind.

Stig and Florence were at close range and Eric and Timo wildly waved greetings. Pa and Jed likewise signaled welcome. They were met by the sauna. Eric fell to his knees and unfastened the strappings on Florence's snowshoes. One, then the other she shook off.

Breathing a bit heavy, Florence still radiated her warm smile, yet revealed a shadow of embarrassment detected from her inability to lock eyes with anybody. Petra was now standing in the open doorway with an ear to ear smile. "Don't everybody stand out there and catch cold. Get in where it's warm."

On the porch Jed edged beside Florence. He squeezed an arm around her waist and produced a devilish grin. "You forgot the catalog, teacher."

Three days of hard plowing, demolishing drifts five to eight feet high in places, and the roads were open again. With that Jed saddled Blaze and rode off back to the half-buried town.

226

It was well after the supper hour when he arrived at the livery, to find Jake, contrary to catching snatches of sleep, actually working. Forking hay for the horses by lantern light. Jake stopped his work, to tell of a man shot dead last night at a gambling table. To tell of one of his best horses dying. And to thrash over details of the storm, telling of several teams of horses being completely worn out after a few hours of heavy plowing, even using two teams to a plow. Jake decided more work needed to be done and Jed had reason not to linger. He tethered Blaze in a stall, and trudged through deep snow back toward Main.

He passed Lil's place, reflecting its usual dim light. Most of Main Street stood in darkness. Good, the store was still open judging from window lights reflecting upon the new fallen snow.

He pressed down on the latch, lightly rattled the locked door of the store. Then peered through a frost free section of the window. He could see Thor Blumstrom behind a counter busy counting his day's cash intake. He removed a chopper mitt and rapped sharply on the glass to get Thor's attention.

Obligingly Thor unbolted the door, locked it behind them.

"No sense keeping open when everybody's snowed in up to their necks."

Jed tipped his hat to the back of his head. "Don't plan on detaining you," he said moving directly to a counter where numerous catalogs were stacked. "Just need to take a quick look at a couple of catalogs. It's important."

He ran a finger down the "o's" in the index pages while Thor Blumstrom moved about the store extinguishing the kerosene lamps. O - O - Optician's kits. Specific pages of three catalogs were scanned. Answers to one question in mind were identical.

A nucleus of Good Templars, immune to rash changes of weather stood like sentries outside of the Black Bear.

Blanche emerged from the saloon carrying a bucket of beer in ungloved hands. Jed tipped his hat and received in return a cold shoulder. He entered the door she left ajar.

At the bar he raised a boot on the footrail. He felt in his pocket for some silver and slid it across the bar. "Beer, Nick!"

Nick didn't hear. In a guarded voice he was telling a stranger how to get to Lil's place. Subsequently Nick diverted his attention to some men, their big bodies tight against the bar, telling in their heavy foreign accent, how they had searched for days for a friend believed lost in the storm pelted woods, and just learned that he had left the country for Sweden. The end of the story became inarticulate when a half dozen inebriated loggers attempted to harmonize in song.

The door was being opened and closed, with a steady influx of patrons trailing in cold air, and the place was getting noisy. Loud mouthed characters, deviating from middle of the road language were hollering and whooping it up. Laughing uproariously, taunting one another with insults. Yet maintaining separate tables according to their nationalities, still refusing to blend as oil and water.

Sporadically voices lifted in song. Jed raised his voice. "Nick! A beer!"

Nick finally heard. He responded in haste, wearing an ear to ear smile.

"Been out of town a couple of days, Nick. What's new? And what in the hell is this racket all about?"

Nick skimmed a wiping rag over the top of the bar. "Don' you no hear? Malaron' gonna go back to ol' country? Beeg party. Evrabody lika Malaron' an' no lika see go."

Jed's eyes scanned the room. "Tomorrow you'll have to put the place together."

Nick nodded in agreement. "Dem guys gonna hav' one

228

helluva time cuz Malaron' no arresta nobody tonight!"

Somewhere in the middle of the room somebody was hollering for Nick. But Nick yet had news to impart. He put the palms of his hands flat on the bar edge and leaned over to pass on something of importance. "Beeg news tooday, Jed. Da meeses say dees morn - nudder bambino on da way."

"One a year," grinned Jed. "Nice going."

Nick nodded negatively. "You ferget? Two las' time?" Nick measured himself a small drink of whiskey, swallowed it and drank a chaser of water. He took his wiping rag and disappeared in the midst of the crowd.

Jed tasted his beer, he turned around and leaned his back against the top of the bar. None of the diggers were around.

The smoke in the place could have been cut with a knife, yet through the thick of it he caught sight of Dr. Von Muller, alone, slouched over a corner table. Jed abandoned his beer, he had reason to talk to the peddler. Locating a vacant chair he carried it over his head to where Dr. Von Muller secluded himself. He was sitting in moody silence, already having initiated another bender. His eyes were heavy and bloodshot. His arms rested on the table to provide support for his body. The suit he was wearing appeared to have been slept in more than once. Jed minced no words.

"You look grubby for a salesman."

Dr. Von Muller's head bobbed an erratic pattern, his bleary eyes staring into space. He groped for the bottle before him but Jed pushed it aside. "You don't need any more of that stuff." There wasn't much fight in the peddler and he didn't argue the issue.

Patrons at a near table began singing at full lung power, and bursts of guffaws broke out from another. Jed pivoted his body to observe the doings. He caught glimpse of Marshall Malaroni, unsteady on his feet from too much drink.

229

"Noshin' like having a good time before leaving," mumbled Dr. Von Muller.

Jed pricked his ears. He tilted his hat to the back of his head and crossed his arms and a leg. He kept his eyes on the merrymakers. "Didn't quite hear you."

Dr. Von Muller raised his husky voice. "Deschided to have myself a good time. Latsch night in town. Noshing like having a good time..."

Jed held his eyes on the crowd. "What the hell, stick around a while. Country here is hard to beat. Fresh air, four seasons.." His eyes followed the barmaid.. "women.."

Dr. Von Muller's voice tightened, he wasn't too drunk but had imbibed enough to become ornery. His mood was challenging now, he pounded the table with a protesting fist. "Yer too young. But ya'll learn. Takes a few lesshons." His words broke off, he upended the liquor glass clenched in his hands to drain off the remaining drops. In a defiant voice he babbled on. "Where's your blue-eyes babe? Out making love wish shom logger?"

Jed rubbed his thumb on his chin. A corner of his mouth curled upward. "I'm sure of my Petra. She never gives me cause for worry."

Dr. Von Muller's voice became still grimmer. "Yer buffaloed. Young ones you can't trust! Take you fer what'cha got. Then you don't see them no more... jest like Blanche... the little bugger."

Blanche! Her name struck like a bolt out of the blue. Jed concealed his shock, yet the ring of her name continued to vibrate his ear. He reached in his shirt pocket for a bag of tobacco and fumbled at the knot on the string. There was no variation in the natural tone of his voice when he spoke. "Maybe you don't figure her right."

Dr. Von Muller sat up a bit straighter and a drooling, grimacing sneer appeared on his face. He slapped a dirty palm on the table top. He snorted, and new bitterness released itself.

"Oh-h, I've got her number! A fat pocketbook and she hangs on like flypaper. Low on cash and she vamooses." He stared into his empty glass. "Red-headed son-of-a-bitch, jesh wants money..."

A barmaid was drawing near carrying a full pitcher of beer in her hands. "Service needed at this table?"

Jed shook his head negatively. "We're leaving." He rose, and pulled Dr. Von Muller up by an arm. The barmaid ejected surprise.

"Stick around! Why! The party's jest a-starting to roll!"

"My friend's had enough."

Jed headed toward the outer door, nudging Dr. Von Muller ahead of him. Outside, the Crusaders had given up their stand surprisingly early for the time of night, and the street was near deserted. The only moving creature was a hound dog that appeared from nowhere and sniffed at their boots. They shuffled along in the darkness, their breath hanging vapors in the night air. There was no conversation, the only sound was the scrunching of their boots in the snow.

Outside the hotel there was unlooked for activity. Three men on the hotel porch were struggling with weighty trunks. Another man wrestling a trunk from a sleigh beckoned Jed for a helping hand which was given.

Inside, Virginia and her father were scurrying around, checking accommodations for a dozen cold-numbed men and women. A young mother huddled two youngsters and a whimpering baby close to the pot bellied stove which glowed red in the middle of the waiting room.

Two large trunks had to be sidestepped in order to reach the stairwell. Jed's weight creaked each step as he ascended the stairs to the upper floor, with Dr. Von Muller stumbling ahead of him to the frowning disdain of women patrons. Dr. Von Muller led, halfway down

231

the dimly lit hallway, he stopped by a doorway. Fumbled in his pockets for a key, and after several unsuccessful attempts located the keyhole in the door.

The room was pitch dark as was to be expected. Jed struck a match and held it eye level, he scanned the room for a lamp. There was one on a near stand, smudgy with soot, but the flame of the matchstick heated his fingertips. Another match was scratched, the wick of the lamp ignited and the flame adjusted.

Virginia would have been hot under the collar had she been aware of such untidiness. Dirty clothes were heaped over the furniture, empty liquor bottles had been discarded underneath the bed.

Dr. Von Muller released his weak hold on a bedpost and sank into the mattress.

Jed paced the floor once, twice. He glanced over his shoulder to see Von Muller sprawled across the bed, with eyes closed. Only then did he fall to one knee, and quietly release the snap locks on Dr. Von Muller's carrying case.

A quick scan showed the contents to be in immaculate array, divided sections in the bottom holding lenses, frames, test charts, sundries. Instruments and tools of the trade hung in ribboned loops against soft velvet lining the cover.

There were no pliers. Catalogs listed the contents of all optician's carrying cases to include small needle nosed pliers. Such as he'd seen the jeweler-optician in Iron Bay make use of. One ribboned loop was empty.

He removed a small screw driver and squinted at the coded X2. Read another instrument, X2. He stuck them in the appropriate loops and noiselessly latched the case shut.

The needle nosed pliers were missing. And Dr. Von Muller dared not purchase a replacement, knowing he'd be a dead duck!

By a makeshift table he stopped to arrest his attention to objects thereon - some cancelled mail, several pairs of broken eyeglasses. A...a gold watch. Again he glanced over his shoulder to check on Von Muller. He reached for the timepiece. It was heavy, gold encased, with ruby jewels embedded on both sides. He popped open the front casing. Satisfied, turned the watch over. His eyes glued near the stem, where two ruby jewels were missing from polished settings.

His body numbed. Crawford's watch! Had not Syd been dismayed that day in the office when he discovered that two rubies had dropped out!

His jaw closed tight and he could feel a light creeping of sweat on his forehead. A hard lump grew in his throat. He stood motionless, for what might have been minutes, again he studied Dr. Von Muller, in dead sleep. He slipped the watch into a pocket.

Now he was sure.

He extinguished the lamp and quietly exited the room. At the threshold of the closed doorway he stood, biting his lip, his tension rising to a razor sharp edge. Von Muller was their man... the old boy, asleep in the room behind him, did in Crawford.

Shuffling feet were ascending the stairway and Virginia's voice sounded... "I'll rap on your door early enough in the morning so you won't miss the train..."

Passing Virginia on the stairs Jed sensed that she was wondering about his never before seen presence on the upper floor. Downstairs, he slipped into his darkened room, leaving the door slightly ajar.

Facts of the evening stood clear. Marshall Malaroni would by now be too drunk to make a legal arrest. Von Muller had talked about leaving town and a train would be pulling out at six in the morning. One cigarette after another was burned short with a mental block put to half-heard talking of the adjoining tenant and his female companion which penetrated the thin wall. He paced the room, then dragged his packsack from beneath his bed, unbuckled the straps and removed a weapon should

233

protection be necessary and shoved it inside his belt.

He waited. Until well past the midnight hour when the waiting room became near deserted. His tension became surmounting. He vacated his room to play a hand of cards with the one remaining patron who had been engrossed in solitaire. Shortly, fatigue of a hard work day overtook the man and he sought the comfort of his bed. Jed settled himself in a horsehair chair set in a dim corner, he spread an edition of the POST over his lap and leaned back in pretense of sleep.

The hours passed slowly. The clock on the wall behind the counter chimed the quarter hours, the hours. Two o'clock. The clock ended the last chime of three. The saloons must have closed for the night, he figured, when at closely spaced intervals inebriated lodgers drifted in. With each opening and shutting of the door could be heard the wailing of the wind. Three-thirty. Virginia's father passed through, clad in a flannel nightshirt and wool stockings, holding a hot water bag against his paunch. The only sound during the next hour was the click of a door latch. Blanche, slightly under the weather and disheveled, emerged from some room beyond his. She found her way to the outer door and disappeared into the darkness outside. The night wore on and his eyes were growing heavy with sleep. Through the windows he could see it was still pitch black outside. But a few more hours and dawn would break, bringing a long waited day.

A day of reckoning.

A stair creaked. Or was it the imagination of a fatigued mind? Or a siding board which had popped a nail in the cold? He shifted his body to relax a cramped muscle, again his heavy eyelids closed shut.

Creak. The sound again pricked his ears, he opened his eyes and fixed them on the dim stairway. His breathing seemed to cease as he listened to slow, deliberate steps descending the stairway. Another step

234

creaked. At the turn in the stairs there was complete quiet, for what might have been a full minute. Three more steps, and the figure of a man emerged, descending with cautious tred. In one hand he held a case. Jed eased the newspaper from his lap to the floor. He rose and moved along the shadowy wall to the foot of the stairwell.

The wooden stairs continued to sound out the descending weight of the man. When his feet touched the floor Jed emerged from the dimness to block his path. He stood face to face with his saloon partner of last night, washed, and surprisingly neat.

"Going somewhere, Dr. Von Muller?"

The sight of a person, a voice breaking the silence of the early dawn hour startled Dr. Von Muller. He twitched, simultaneously his right arm shot forward brandishing a revolver. It was not a light weapon and his hand trembled with its weight, yet it was aimed plenty on target. Jed shuffled a foot and now felt the muzzle of the gun touch his chest. Von Muller's straight mouth grimaced to a snarl.

"You took the watch! Your death means my freedom."

To Jed's great benefit, Lady Luck paid a call. The clatter of pots and pans in the kitchen diverted Dr. Von Muller's attention and Jed took advantage of the split second break. He executed an arm twist which Mikko had taught him. Von Muller winced and fell backwards on the stairway, the revolver flying from his hand and hitting the wall with a thud.

Virginia came running out. She cast a perplexed look at sick-faced Von Muller, on his back, his eyeglasses hanging on by one ear.

Jed spoke out before Virginia could fire her question. "I'm hauling him in for the murder of Syd Crawford."

With the paleness of shame on his face Dr. Von Muller sullenly slouched in a chair in the jailhouse, his wrists linked together with handcuffs. "Pliers," he was heard to mutter. "Hooked by a pair of pliers." Only a few people were permitted to enter the jail - Ed Morley, Reverend Culbertson, Hank Manson, Jed, a few men who had served on the jury. Then the door was barred and the safety bolt secured. Marshall Malaroni stood guard inside the doorway.

Word of an arrest ripped through the town and the group of people standing outside the jailhouse began swelling. Dr. Von Muller's head hung low as he told his story, all of it, and he was listened to without interruption.

"The fella you knew to be Syd Crawford spent his early years in Omaha, Nebraska working in my father's bank under his real name - John Rogers. On the day when auditors of the bank discovered Rogers' accounts pointed to embezzlement of funds he disappeared.. and was never tracked down. Last summer when I stopped off here to do some business, I recognized him. He had aged, his features somewhat changed, but I knew it was John. Still wanted in Omaha for embezzlement. I talked with him secretly several times. At first he denied being Rogers, then finally admitted I had him trapped. He often cried in my presence. I felt kind of sorry for the guy,, respected here, a good home, family.

"He paid me to keep quiet so that he could retain his serene life. But when my money got low I always knew where there was more to be had. A week before... he died... he gave me two hundred and told me it was the last. That he didn't have any more, never to come back. That I'd gone far enough. That sort of annoyed me since my female companion had expensive tastes. I needed money on the night he met his death.

"He was sitting at the table working on books. He flared up when I entered the room. Grabbed a gun from a drawer and jumped up, threatening to end my life. Saying he'd fix me once and for all. We grappled.. the gun went off. When he slumped to the floor I set the gun near him, grabbed from the safe what my pockets would hold. I took one look back. His pocket watch was dangling from a chain... I unsnapped it."

All the while Ed Morley was writing the torrid news of the morning. He stuffed the scribbled pages into a coat pocket and had Marshall Malaroni unbar the door allowing him exit from the lockup.

"Is there anything more to add to this confession?" asked one of the jury men. Dr. Von Muller slowly raised his head. He nodded negatively.

A paper and quilled pen were shoved into his hands. "Will you please sign this confession." Marshall Malaroni was beckoned from the doorway. "Lock him up!"

Jed Carter vacated the jailhouse along with the other men who had witnessed Dr. Von Muller's confession and elbowed his way, straight-faced through the babbling crowd outside. Fatigue from the long sleepless night was beginning to gnaw at his body, and to friends and others who hailed him, or tugged at his sleeve for information on what happened inside, his words tersely repeated themselves - "the eye glass peddler Von Muller has confessed."

The news flowed down Main ahead of him.

He cleared himself of the crowd. Zigzagged the slushy, manure spotted street and headed straight for the general store, dodging horses and sleighs along the way. It was there, as he had hoped for. Kelso's sled. Squeezed alongside others in front of the store. Utter disappointment would have injected itself into his being had it not been sighted, knowing that Pa Kelso came to town on Thursdays for provisions, if the weather was good.

Timo and Eric were standing outside looking in the store window, their backs to him, engrossed in a guessing contest. Trying to guess the number of beans in the big bottle in the window in hopes of winning the displayed rifle. At the very moment Pa Kelso came out of the store balancing a hundred pound sack of flour on his shoulder. With uncanny movement of ease he flipped the sack into the back of the sled, then went back into the store.

Jed's tense body relaxed when from across the road he heard his name called... Petra!

They had much to talk about and Pa raised no objection to their riding back home together. Luckily Jake had a spare cutter not committed to anybody. Blaze was harnessed up.

They passed the familiar log houses, passed the slaughter house, the sleigh creaking over the dry snow. They skirted the small ice covered lake. Petra, sensing Jed's quiet inner mood, talked little of the break in the case. Nearing the small white cemetery, where a few snow covered crosses protruded above the snow, Jed's limited conversation trailed off. He reined in and sat motionless for a full minute, staring at a white mound not far off the roadway. Syd's resting place. He set down the reins. Without spoken word he got out of the cutter and trampled through the unbroken snow toward Syd's grave, oblivious of Petra following in each sunken bootprint.

A pine slab coated with crusted snow marked the head of the grave. With a chopper mitt he gently brushed the snow from the slab. In silence he read the freshly carved inscription.

Erected to the memory of
Sydney Crawford
Aged 40 years 16 days
A tender husband
A faithful friend
Felled by a bullet of a gun
Gone but not forgotten.

Petra read and understood each precisely carved word and she quietly absorbed the complete message. No word she missed. Now a tear embedded itself in the corner of an eye. No word she missed.

She let Jed read it aloud to her. Not yet ready to reveal her secret.

There wasn't much going on around town during the next few days due to a lot of bad weather, Jed choosing to more or less just stay in and relax at the Chippewa.

Virginia's stew served at noon time had been the best ever. Now, hands in his pockets, he stood looking out of one of the front windows. There was nothing special to hold one's attention save for Marshall Malaroni legging it up the Chippewa roadway. Delivery of the POST was late presumably because Ed Morley was having trouble with the press, having spent a good part of yesterday at the blacksmith shop trying to get a part brazed.

Marshall Malaroni entered the Chippewa, closed the door behind him and stomped the loose snow from his boots. The immediate presence of the very person he was seeking made his mission most easy. With his mind on the strait-laced business at hand he reached into an inner pocket of his uniform jacket and withdrew an envelope. Smilingly he turned it over to Jed.

"From the Common Council for a job well done."

With the blade of his pocketknife Jed slit open the sealed envelope. He withdrew the contents - a bank check in the sum of $1,000 made out in his name. An unprecedented quiet overtook him before he turned to address Virginia, now appearing through the swinging door of the kitchen. "How about some hot coffee for the Marshall?"

On the countertop Jed endorsed his name on the check, on a note pad before him he scrawled out a brief message.

Mrs. Anderson
Treasurer, Church

Please accept the enclosed. It is my desire that monies owed on the bell be paid off. Anything left over to be retained in the treasury.

Jed Carter

He stuffed the check and note into the original envelope and handed it to Marshall Malaroni. "I'll be giving the Council my personal acknowledgement of their kind gesture. And, if on your way back you'd give this to Mrs. Anderson."

CHAPTER 15
New Pulse at the Holyoke

After months of ice and snow, spring began to dispossess winter's captivity of the land. The snow began to melt under the April sun and with surprising suddenness fair weather prevailed.

It was a fine morning, cool but warming, when the Holyoke diggers, after abandoning loaded wagons bogged along the Trail trudged into the mining camp. Crows raved noisily in the tall pines. Here and there new tender leaves were breaking the soft bark of the alders, shoots of green punctured the sandy soil. Wintergreen berries were in evidence and fragrant trailing arbutus was again in its glory. Warblers and thrushes sang like flutes across the Yellow Dog as they wove their nests.

Looks of determination were legibly written on the faces of the crew, individually and collectively they were possessed with a powerful inward drive that would permit no more rest. A change in supervision had been made, every man working under the total supervision of Captain Sommers, Bill Worthington and Clem Copley having been fired.

The river ice broke up and floated away. A boom was put across the landing and part of the crew was put to hauling out logs with horses. Days blended into weeks with a surprising smoothness of operation. The wagon road was widened out and mud holes were planked.

Supply wagons began making regular trips into camp. The whim was moved back to the North Beaver where its need was greater, a strong wood ladder was constructed and attached to one wall of the shaft. Tracks in the tunnel were reinforced with closer spaced sills. The second mill was installed with meticulous care, and an expert connected with the manufacture of the machine arrived to superintend the mill work himself. The squeal of the sawmill resounded through the valleys.

The Holyoke was alive, humming with life! Dangerous, dirty and backbreaking work for most of the crew. But it was what they all wanted. Dan, happily married, sang to himself as he went about his business. Jed was finding it more difficult to concentrate on detailed work in that a month hence, he and Petra would wed.

It was an hour before daylight. Jed Carter quietly vacated his bunk and donned his better clothes. He ate a leisurely breakfast with Charlie who with diversified queries aimed at the reason for wearing better attire. When the east sky began to release daylight Jed saddled Blaze, and in the crispness of early morning took the Holyoke Trail to town. Spring runoffs had overflowed portions of the Trail, he altered his course and veered Blaze to winding side trails, at times following no trail.

All considering, the miles were covered in favorable time. Past the slaughter house, past the log houses. By Partridge Creek, wide spread, where two barefoot lads who had discarded their heavy outer clothing probed the churning currents with long sticks. In front of 'Old Ish' he encountered Mrs. Anderson, her mouth low in the corners, prodding two frisky heifers before her.

In general, the town seemed to be still half asleep.

He secured the reins to a post and took time to scrape the mud off his boots before entering Stan Eland's land office. Stan was opening shop for another day's business, raising the two windows and propping them with slats to let in the fresh air.

"Top of the morn!" exclaimed Stan. "You're in town pretty early. Business or pleasure?"

"Mostly business." Jed smiled quietly. He sat backward on a wooden chair, propping his arms on the back. From the breast pocket of his shirt he took a scrap of paper and proceeded to smooth the wrinkles from it. "This advertisement you ran a while back. On the Ansli homestead up north... if your price is still holding I'd like to negotiate purchase of the property. Would kind of like to surprise Petra with a paper of ownership on the place."

"So, its Petra for sure!"

"She's the salt of the earth!"

Stan Eland was all for doing business since land sales had slackened off considerably in the late winter months. He moved to a work table in a corner and returned with some papers and a section map. He sat down at his rolled top desk facing his client and unfolded the map and located thereon an X. He thumbed through the papers, withdrew a sheet and unfolded it to full length. Briefly he scanned it on one side, then the other. "Title is clear enough... $300 will initiate and close a bill of sale."

Jed worked his hand into an inner pocket of his vest and withdrew a soft pouch. From it he shook out a solid roll of greenbacks. He moistened a thumb and peeled off the designated sum from the roll. His lips curled to a smile. "Receipt me. Before someone comes in and offers you a bit more."

It took but little time to fill in the blank lines on the legal paper. They both signed their names, as did Mrs. Anderson who was on her return trip from the pound and hailed in to attest to the inking of both signatures. The document was embossed with a seal. Jed Carter fingered the paper, it felt good to the touch. He pulled the brim of his hat low on his brow, as was his habit when things were going well. "Take care, man. Don't go breaking any more bones. We'll be expecting your presence at our wedding."

The day was yet young and Jed was glad for there were matters to be tended to. Petra had stayed overnight at the dressmaker's house and it was a planned event that he would meet her there around the noon hour.

He left Blaze at the livery and on the footpath leading to the Salsburg location teamed up with Rush Biggers. The Salsburg location, one row of low houses built at the foot of a stone-studded hill.

The road was littered with slab wood which had fallen from a delivery wagon. Rush pointed out Mrs. Augustson's house, the one with a wash tub set on a half log bench in the front yard. The walk to the location had not taken as long as he had anticipated. He dropped to the roofless porch on Mrs. Augustson's abode, resting his arms on his knees. He visualized Petra inside, aglow in her wedding dress and Mrs. Augustson walking around her in circles tending to fine details.

In the distance the church bell peeled out the noon hour.

He closed his eyes to rest them, opened them to see Petra smiling down at him, her comely face guarded from the sun by a floppy hat. She put her hands to his shoulders, bent down and kissed him soundly. Her moves, still unpredictable. Sentimental moments, the two alone, and thought of a tender kiss often would not come to her mind.

"Oh Jed! It's lovely! And it fits just perfectly. Mrs. Augustson said she's never worked on such beautiful material. Only three more rows of ruffles to sew on and the flowers and buttons... Jed.. I'm so happy."

He got to his feet and closed her mouth with a kiss.

In front of the general store Petra chose to walk slower, she slipped an arm onto Jed's. The wedding ring, she thought. Jed hadn't given mention to the ring and this was a day for tending to important business.

"Maybe it's time we should go in," she said, "to be measured for the ring?"

"We'll tend to that later." With those words he nudged her along. Directly in front of the dance hall they stopped, where Jed read aloud the big print on the colored poster. Arm in arm they strolled to the town hall, their heads high. The door of the town hall was wide open and they entered. A client standing at the counter of business was being served by the male clerk. There was seating space on a deacon's bench beside a ruddy faced man clad in bibbed overalls. They sat down to await their turn.

The face of the woman standing before the clerk was not visible, but judging from her huge shape and guttural voice they knew it could only be Lil, who kept her daylight appearances at a minimum. Standing straight and unabashed, she fired retorts to the clerk's questions in unwomanly language. Argued about the $100 fine for operation of a house of ill fame and sarcastically threatening to take the alternate of ten days in the lockup. Finally resigning to defeat she flung her purse to the countertop, opened it and reached in for a fistful of money and paid up.

The man sitting beside them accurately aimed his chew into the brass spittoon at his feet. At the counter he dickered a while with the clerk about releasing two heifers from the pound. Emphasizing it would be better if the damn Swede women busybodies kept their noses to their knitting. The clerk felt his talk made good sense and the man was exempt of a fine.

The clerk looked in the directioin of the young hand-holding couple, each of whom as individuals he well knew. "You're next."

Petra and Jed took their stand at the counter, Jed standing astride, his shoulders back. He hooked his thumbs in his wide leather belt ready to utter the request which would begin to solidify their life together, but the clerk's quick tongue peppered the air.

"Hear tell all that machinery that come in on rail yesterday is consigned to the Holyoke "

Jed confirmed that it was. The clerk eyed Petra. "Haven't seen your father around for well over a month. He's well, I hope."

"Up and at it every day," smiled Petra, choosing to abbreviate any unnecessary conversation, as had Jed, knowing from the many stops here with her father, to collect bounty money, how endlessly the clerk could rabble on.

The clerk slapped his hands on the countertop. "So. What's your business?"

"We're here to apply for a marriage license." Jed's voice was clear and steady.

From underneath the counter the clerk retrieved a fireproof cash box which contained only legal forms, no cash. He opened it, moistened his thumb and flipped out the uppermost parchment. Methodically he closed the cover and set the box back where it belonged. He asked some questions, neatly filling in the blank spaces on the printed paper as they individually responded. He slid the completed certificate before them and shoved forward an ink pot and goose quill. "Now if you'll jest affix your signatures to this license of marriage, I'll affix the official seal. And two dollars will cover the fee."

Petra's eager hand reached out first for touch of the license. She picked it up and held it at reading distance. With reserved poise her eyes moved over the short lines of print. She set the parchment back on the counter, dipped the quill in the ink pot and signed her name. Her glowing face looked up to Jed's shocked countenance.

"You must sign your name below mine..."

Jed frowned, his eyes were glued on her face... you must sign... Now his jaw dropped slowly as if he were going to speak, but no words came.

246

Her eyes were yet searching for response.

The clerk shrugged his shoulders. "What gives?"

"...uh... it's nothing at all, sir." His eyes held on Petra, but his mind could frame no words. With unprecedented gentleness he took her in his arms and kissed her long and thorough. He put his cheek to hers and whispered words that only she could hear.

He signed his name on the certificate with the goose quill pen, and together they smilingly blew on the ink to dry it.

Reverend Culbertson lived in Tangletown. A location just east of Partridge Creek. Comprised of an amassment of houses identical in one construction design or another, scattered along unnamed roads. Tangletown was noted for housing the real trouble-makers in town. Petra and Jed inquired of an urchin rolling a hoop as to which house was Reverend Culbertson's.

Petra rapped lightly on his door and they were greeted by the good Reverend himself who admitted them to his front parlor. An elaborate setting for a preacher of bachelor status! A china cupboard, hanging brass lamps. Even a piano!

The Reverend had made his mark on the townsfolk since his arrival approximately one year ago. Upon horseback he had drifted into town, an itinerant preacher, quickly detecting that a fair portion of the inhabitants had no religion. In no time at all he picked up a following who staunchly adhered to his preachings, who converted themselves to understanding that Sunday was a day of thanksgiving and praise and not a day for getting full and foolish.

The Reverend was a thickset man in his middle years. He had a mop of black curly hair, beautiful eyes by women's standards, a serious countenance which spontaneously could erupt into boisterous laughter. He always wore a vest with a heavy gold chain looping

247

across the front.

A fiery preacher he was, one who usually delivered his sermons with outstretched open hands. He preached positively and without gloves. Expelling weighty words about the ills that the flesh is heir to, about the fires of hell, then easing off with joyous words of salvation. After listening to Reverend Culbertson's sermons most everybody was much perturbed about his possible positioin in the world to come.

A delightful visit it turned out to be, blended with consumption of late afternoon tea and cookies. Yes, the Reverend responded to the purpose of their call. He would be most happy to perform the bonding rites of matrimony. Privileged indeed, he expressed himself, to be asked.

The day had worn itself out. Petra and Jed climbed into their rented rig and with horse sense Blaze headed toward the homestead. The ominous bluff on the edge of town cut off half of the setting sun, and shadows were settling over the row of log houses which nestled near the shores of the bewitched lake. Bullfrogs in wet lowlands were making heard their croaky voices. Jed slipped an arm around Petra and drew her close.

It had been a good day.

    *   *   *   *   *

A reminding notice of the forthcoming monthly meeting had been received at the mine though Captain Sommers needed no reminder, the date being marked on his calendar. Turbulent thoughts captivated his mind as he sat in meditation in the shanty office, his head downcast, elbows resting on his knees.

It was a while before he picked up a pencil to begin writing the report to the stockholders. Again his thoughts wavered. He reached over for the log books and made a recheck of figures, conscious that it was a weak stall of committing to writing known facts.

It was but a few scanty lines that came from the blunt end of his pencil.

'Seven weeks have passed since the re-opening of the Holyoke Mine. Blasting, mucking and tramming have deepened the tunnel to a depth of 385'.'

He dropped the pencil in the binding of the open report book and got up from his nail keg seat. Five paces took him to the cobwebbed window overlooking the workings. Hands in hip pockets, feet astride, he watched a loaded car being dumped on the stockpile. For weeks, it had been difficult to detect much glitter in the broken rocks. He went back to the task awaiting him.

'During the first three weeks not a day passed that ore was not mined, evidenced by the increased height of the stockpile, now on level with the adit and spilling to a width of approximately 75'.'

He raised his pencil to pore over the few lines written, then finished writing his extremely brief report.

'Progress was favorable in both tunnel and shaft with tonnage produced at a satisfactory rate until Monday of the past week. On which day as on each subsequent day coarse grained rock rebounds the hammers and picks unlike contact with veined quartz. There is silent uneasiness among the men.'

The report would go hard with the stockholders, though Hank Manson had been kept informed.

*   *   *   *   *

The diggers awaiting Pete's return with the sledge hammers packed fresh chews into their cheeks and began scraping up the loose rock laying around and shoveling it into a tram. Their limited conversation, void of any emotion, was gapped with intervals of silence.

"Rock, rock and more rock. Shoveling nothing but pure rock..."

"Same as what we been doing for three straight weeks."

"Ole Cap been damn quiet for the last couple of days."

"Wonder how long the stockholders are gonna swallow this."

Pete returned quicker than expected with three sledges all fixed up with new handles and accompanied by Captain Sommers. Sommers minced no words but issued new work orders, a spur of the moment decision. Three shifts would go on, round the clock, to drill an eight foot test hole on a down trend into the face and to proceed from that point.

The hole was drilled and filled with black powder. The fuse was weighted down with a chunk of scrap iron and a candle flame sputtered the wick.

In the thinning out smoke eyes searched all around. Only rock was in evidence, in the face, in the newly broken pieces. A few chunks revealed yellow flecks.

"It's gold, sure as hell," muttered John, "but our bloody mill will never separate it from the rock."

That night beside the keg in the cookhouse it was decided to sink a small shaft in the tunnel, to go down a level and drift out from there.

The passing of the next two weeks saw the deepening of the shaft which at the seventeen foot mark struck solid rock.

"Drill a test hole." ordered Captain Sommers.

The test hole was started, the drill grinding in under alternating blows from the sledges. Another vibrating blow, and the drill rod snapped off in the rock. The diggers exited the tunnel their souls drained of hope. Captain Sommers resigned.

The officers of the Holyoke spent uncounted hours at the mine the week following, revealing little of their thoughts but retreating to the shanty office from time to time for closed discussions. Alex and John were instructed to load explosives and attack trenched areas to the southwest. Pete, to direct burning of vegetation at a designated area southeast to expose more bedrock.

Ed Morley's frequent treks to the property provided him but little news due to the reticence of the officers, other than he was told, to set up ads offering Holyoke stock for sale. This he eked from the diggers themselves, that the latest blasts held gold, but it didn't hold a few feet below surface.

Hank Manson held successive meetings in the company office in town, and at each meeting the eyes of the stockholders told that each knew the truth.

CHAPTER 16
The Wedding

None more perfect weather could have broke for the day of the wedding. The sky gifted a ceiling of blue with white cloud gatherings drifting far to the north. The air was dry and warm. From late morning on right to the hour of the mid-afternoon wedding, carriages, rigs and wagons churned the dust of the roads in the north country, most turning into Kelso's roadgate. All conveying friends from town, and neighbors, dressed in their very best, with the menfolk assisting the women down from the vehicles. Also helping them carry wrapped presents into the house and tote in dishes of food. Most everybody mingled outdoors exchanging greetings with one another, their conversation light, free of daily cares.

For the Kelso family it was the day of days. Pa Kelso, clad in a new suit of store clothes, previously unworn, mixed freely with all guests, his head proud and high. Eric strutted around dressed in newly sewn clothing, Timo wearing his brother's outgrown suit emulated the mannerism of his father.

Pa had seen to it that all general needs were taken care of, but now Florence was summoning him from the kitchen doorway, to bring in the boiler in which coffee was to be made.

Two tables formed by planks laid on sawhorses had

been set outdoors, positioned to fall in the shade of the
large double birch to break the heat of the afternoon sun.
Benches paralleled the tables. Now Florence was all
smiles as she moved back and forth along the tables,
setting down Kelso's unmatched dishes, borrowed dishes
and tinware. She made treks to the roothouse to be
double sure of victuals being in readiness.

Pa's sit-down session last night with Eric and Timo
about behavior and good manners seemed to be taking
effect. Deep down the boys were tingling up their spines
because Jed was to be a part of their family. Since
Christmas time they had been calling him "Muscles".

Dust was again clouding the roadway alongside the
split rail fence, the vehicle turned in. It was Reverend
Culbertson at the reins of the buckboard accompanied
by Sam the barber and Mrs. Anderson. They alit from
the wagon and brushed off the dust which had collected
on their clothing. Reverend Culbertson reached on the
seat for his tailed coat, and in what he hoped to be an
inconspicuous move, ridded himself of a chew of tobacco.
He offered a helping hand to Sam, who was lightly
struggling with a portable organ.

The good Reverend mingled with the guests, making
small talk, pumping the hands of those whom he hadn't
seen for some time. The eyes of most of the men kept an
off and on hold on Effie Dolan, outstandingly charming
in a lacy gingham dress with matching bonnet, on her
low cut neckline, wasp waist, and during Reverend
Culbertson's discourse with Effie a housefly sunning on
her bosom caused some distraction.

"A lovely outfit you're wearing, Mrs. Dolan."

Effie was flattered. Such ear pleasing words were
reward enough for the many long nights she had spent
hand sewing it by lamplight. "So nice of you to take
notice, Reverend."

Stig walked up and the parson laid a hand on his
shoulder. "Stig Nilsson himself! Where have you been

253

hiding out this past winter?" There was more hand pumping.

Mrs. Holmstrom intruded. "Loovely day for a vedding, ain't it so Reverend."

"They make such a sweet couple."

"Wonder which one will be the boss."

"Jed over there looks slightly nervous to me."

"I'll just wager that Miss Neeley and Stig will be the next to get married."

So the pratter continued, until Reverend Culbertson noted the time on his gold pocketwatch and beckoned everybody inside. The humdrum of voices abated and simultaneously everybody was gripped with the sobriety of the hour at hand.

Jed Carter spat on the ground for good luck. He waited until all the guests had entered the house, lastly he and Ikey went in.

For a good part of yesterday Florence and Petra had bustled about beautifying the living room and rearranging the furniture to make it distinctively becoming for a wedding. Now as the wedding guests entered the living room they were open-eyed to ground pine adorning the doorway and window frames, the stand supporting the family Bible, and to clusters of wild roses set on the mantle of the fireplace and vases of wild flowers decorating the window sills. From one corner of the room soft music emanated from the portable organ, produced by Mrs. Anderson with no reference at all to the sheet music before her. Everybody found seating on borrowed benches and undertones of conversation gradually ceased. The music faded away and an air of absolute quiet prevailed.

Eric read his cue from Reverend Culbertson. He rose from the three legged milk stool set in a corner by the fireplace, rigidly paced seven even steps to the face of the fireplace and reached up to light two tallow candles on the mantle, concealing the discomfort of a stiff collar cutting into his neck and new shoes unwelcome to his feet. The candles burning freely, Eric sat down. Now Reverend Culbertson clad in his long tailed coat got up. He moved beside the stand which supported the family Bible, opened wide, scanned the seated guests and then looked to the doorway. Simultaneously the trained fingers of Mrs. Anderson touched the organ keys.

Ruggedly handsome in a new suit of clothes, Jed Carter entered the room, his head held high by a white collar buttoned tight at the neck. Closely followed by Ikey, immaculate in his Sunday best. They took a place by the glowing candles.

Light, tiptoeing footsteps could be heard descending the stairway off the kitchen, there was the rustling of skirts, and all heads twisted to the doorway. The smile of Petra, standing there, attired in full skirted white organdy, reflected nothing but happiness. She clutched a bouquet of wild roses to her bosom. Her eyes met Jed's, and their smiles deepened.

Now the wedding music was being played very softly. In an unrehearsed move Petra turned but slightly to ease her billowing skirt through the doorway. With slow, unfaltering steps, and followed by Florence attired in pink organdy, she walked almost precisely in the steps taken moments earlier by Jed. By the fireplace Petra found her place beside Jed, Florence beside Ikey. They turned to face the assembled witnesses to the ceremony.

It was a short ritual. Reverend Culbertson put on his reading glasses and turned to face the couple. A prayer was given. In his high-pitched voice he read some passages from the family Bible. Another prayer was offered. He opened a black leather bound book and his voice liltingly expelled the lines of the traditional wedding ceremony.

'Dearly beloved. We are 'ga'thered here today, to unite this man and this woman in holy matrimony......'

His eyes raised, to scan the faces of the guests sitting in raptured silence, he uttered, that if there were any objections to this marriage to speak up or forever hold silence, and he interpreted the complacent faces before him as unanimous response of approval. The ring was slipped on Petra's finger. There was a closing prayer, and with the Amen the ceremony was over. Reverend Culbertson snapped shut the black book, removed his glasses and hardily shook the hands of the newlyweds. Only then did Jed release his secret, that both the wedding ring and engagement ring were made from Holyoke gold.

The wedding gifts were numerous, reflecting the good wishes of family and friends. There was a very large kitchen stove, a gift of Pa Kelso, which had already been set up, and a shiny base burner, regards of the entire Holyoke crew which stood in Blumstrom's store ready for delivery. Stig's best wishes tied in very nicely - a generous supply of cut wood. There were wrapped gifts of various shapes and sizes.

"Jed! Just what we talked about buying! A cast iron frying pan!" Petra opened an attached card showing two doves of peace and read aloud... "con--con--gratulations on your wedding day. From Effie and Sam Dolan." She looked to the Dolans, her eyes and mouth smiling. "Thanks so much, Sam and Effie. So thoughtful of you."

The next package produced a cast iron frying pan. Petra read aloud the note attached, "...from the Holmstroms."

"Two is none too many," quipped Jed.

The next wedding gift was a clock with a large alarm bell on the top. "Can't stay in bed too long," chuckled Jed, as did several of the guests. The next package to be opened revealed a coffee mill. Jed was touched when Timo and Eric walked in proudly bearing their personal gift, an iron with a detachable handle.

The next gift was a galvanized wash boiler and two

galvanized water pails. Gifts included a cow bell, bread pans, an enameled coffee pot, a rocking chair. A note read aloud by Petra stated that she and Jed were now the owners of one milch cow, a gift of Hank Manson.

Everybody shared in the joy of the day. Jed took the privilege of kissing his bride, plenty often. Petra was hugged by the guests, kissed, and wished the best of everything, with everybody standing open-mouthed when told that her rings were made from Holyoke gold!

Jed's hand was pumped, his shoulders patted, all actions accompanied with congratulatory words.

Everybody filed outdoors, where good food on plank tables was ready to be devoured. Jed and Petra yet lingered a while inside while Reverend Culbertson wrote their Christian names and wedding date on the inside cover of the family Bible.

The newlyweds, with the parson behind them, stepped outside into the sunlight. At the porch entrance the deliriously happy couple paused, to drink with their eyes the festive setting before them.

Then the racket began! Such a confusion of noises had never vibrated the eardrums. Wooden spoons being pounded on dishpans, wooden clubs thumping on tin pails, tin cans containing loose rocks being rattled, a hammer clinking sharply on a bell. "Chivaree! Chivaree!" Pandemonium created by local youngsters, excluding none, and including a few in tattered bib overalls, barefoot, who did not witness the wedding ceremony. The advancement of the newlyweds was blocked off and the racket became more intense. The continued shouting of "Chivaree" grew in magnitude.

To the hilarity of everyone present the mock serenade had just begun. The racket seemed to grow still louder. The banging, rattling, pounding, clanking, clinking, bonging vibrated the air along with the repetitious shouts of "Chivaree"!

Ikey read the look of perplexity on Jed's face and he scaled the porch railing to stand beside him. In undertone, from the side of his mouth, Jed addressed Ikey. "What do I do?"

"Ya gotta pay 'em off," whispered Ikey. "Toss out some coins."

Jed felt deep in a pocket, the vacant look on his face indicated a vacant pocket. Ready Ikey slipped him a fistful of pennies. "Toss 'em all at once."

The coins scattered through the air and there was mad scrambling for the money by the noisemakers as it fell to the ground. With that the serenaders were silenced.

In the shade of the birches all feasted, the well-dressed and the tattered. The tattered shoveling food into their mouths as though they hadn't eaten for a long time, and everybody else following a much similar pattern. Jorn and Sarah sat together, holding hands beneath the table. Florence and Stig were inseparable. Which was confirmation enough to all gathered that they surely would wed.

Never was there a gathering at the homestead that the challenge of the steel ball was overlooked and this wedding day was no exception. Resting on the ground by the side of the shed, the ponderous weight of the sphere continued to captivate the attention of the menfolk and there were repeated attempts at lifting it. Some of the women drifting over to observe their efforts but gently repelled from the area by essences emanating from manure fertilized ground.

The daylight hours so quickly became spent and darkness of evening began dimming the countryside. Pa Kelso went into the house and reappeared, with his fiddle tucked in the crook of his arm. He summoned all to the barn.

Helping hands lent assistance in lighting lanterns and suspending them from pole beams, while Pa Kelso settled himself upon a sack of oats and concentrated on tuning his fiddle. Unharmonizing notes riddled the air, then miraculously blended to withdraw a tapping rhythm from Pa's foot. All at once hopping music filled the barn.

Rhythmic hand clapping of some of the neighbors and Holyoke men skirting the edge of the lighted circle grew louder when Petra and Jed appeared and moved to the center of the circle. Jorn and Sarah who were in quiet waiting in the loft above, dropped a shower of hay upon them, a token of good luck. Now to the lively tune of Pa's fiddle they danced. Alone, at first, then joined by Florence and Stig, Sarah and Jorn. Shortly the entire circle was swarming with hopping, jumping, swinging guests, exploiting the country music in exhilarating fashion, kicking up the dust and inhaling much of the same. Sam the barber took over Pa's fiddle to show what he could do with it, whereas Pa linked his arm onto Petra's to steal the dance from Jed. At the same time showing off with self-concocted nimble steps never executed before.

There were crocks of apple cider for dry throats and more stored in the roothouse, yet throughout the night of festivity some of the men stealthily paced to the wagons for nips of hooch. Some noticed by Stig and Florence who stood outside in the shadows where he held her quietly in his arms. Only when the pink glow of a new dawn began to show did the wedding shindig come to an end. Weary, footsore merrymakers settled themselves in their vehicles and horse sense relied upon to bring them home.

CHAPTER 17
The Demise of the Holyoke

The officers of the Holyoke, mentally burdened with facts and figures from Captain Sommers' reports, now being issued weekly at their request, and in possession of financial statements drawn up from the account books, reacted with no surprise when a written request for a special meeting was received, signed by a great number of stockholders. Stating, it was their preference that the meeting be held on the mine property, and specifying that the subject of the meeting would be the fate of the Holyoke. Handwritten signatures of sixty percent of the owners of capital stock were legibly written at the bottom of the request, sharply contrasting the request of the last special meeting in mid-winter which bore no more names than the twenty-five percent minimum requirement. Hank Manson, faithfully enacting the duties of his position steadfastly adhered to the written Articles of the Company, and took care that notification of the special meeting was regularly published in the POST. All the while unwavering to supplications and pressure being put on him for faster action by investors invading his warehouse office in Iron Bay and those successfully tracking him down at various locales in the district.

The waiting period of four weeks required to hold a special meeting came to pass. Four uneasy weeks during which time much Holyoke stock was being shaken.

A dazzling red sunrise initiated the red-letter meeting day. Stockholders began arriving at the Holyoke within half-hour intervals and by mid-morning a good majority were on the premises, many probing the stockpile. Then scattering, singly and in small groups to other areas of possible mental appeasement. They roved in the deep tunnel, stumbling over the slippery rail sills with many venturing to the full depth. Several of the physically fit unhesitatingly descended the wooden ladder in the North Beaver shaft to check out the bottom.

Reappearing into the sunlight from both dark excavations, every man was more disheartened, in lower spirits than before.

Sun of high noon sparkled the blue ripples of the Yellow Dog, a neutral divide between laughing, prattering school children of the district along with their teacher picnicking on the last day of school, and financially crushed men standing on the brink of decision.

High noon. The designated hour of the meeting. Twenty-two grave faced men crowded into the mine office, some choosing to sit on empty powder boxes and plank benches specially provided for the meeting, others too tense to sit for any length of time preferred to maintain a standing position. The work force of the Holyoke, what was left of it, hovered outside not far from the office shack, smoking and chewing to help pass the uneasy hours. Reduced in number by John and Curt who had quit to seek other employment, convinced that the mine would not pay. Minus Jallu, and the expert from out-of-state who superintended the mill work who a month back had sneaked off the property in the middle of the night, taking with him all his personal belongings.

Hank Manson scanned the bleak faces before him, his precise words were spoken in an unwavering voice. "It is not news to any of you, I'm sure... to know that the

261

situation of the Holyoke is indeed perilous. The day has come when a serious decision must be made. It is well that a majority of owners of capital stock are present... any and all decisions made at this meeting shall be considered valid."

Alex and Pete, their huge frames now blocking the open doorway alist on one leather hinge, shifted their stance to let enter an old man, a stranger. Dignified appearing he was, with intelligent features. Manson's delivery of speech was fast gaining momentum and the newcomer was noticed by only a few.

"I must regrettably inform you... that the result of recent tests of Holyoke ore in three Eastern laboratories were not gratifying. All reports that have come back in the past four weeks point out one fact. The property has changed from pay quartz to near barren. The stamp rock is no longer rich enough for profitable mining."
Manson proceeded to read a report of the financial condition of the company, and rendered an account, in detail, of the situation of the property. Progress had been downhill since the arrival of the mill expert. At which time pay quartz had been abundant but was not properly selected. When selected, the amalgamation had been entrusted to a man who proved to know nothing of the business and the gold was lost.

The drop of a pin could be heard when Hank Manson finished, asking for a motion, with every stockholder present hesitant on making a motion acknowledging the failure of their gold mine. It was Thor Blumstrom who finally rose, who found the strength to speak in an unquavering voice. Blumstrom, who secretly had half-worried himself to death, having allowed the Holyoke Company ridiculously high credit contrary to good common sense.

Thor took his pipe out of his mouth. "In view of hearin' the facts direct, hearin' all this bad news, I move we raise hands on a vote -- to close down the mine and put the machinery up for sale. Salvage what we kin outa our investments." He put his pipe back in his mouth and sat down.

Talk became rabid upon hearing the motion and words between some men became heated. Only then, more of the group became aware of the stranger among them, there were a few arched eyebrow looks.

With tempers assuaged and pent feelings released, Hank Manson restored to the meeting a semblance of order. "The motion of Thor Blumstrom stands to be put to official vote. The vote shall be by stock, each share shall be entitled to one vote."

The voting took not long. The unanimous decision to close the mine proved the finish.

In the heat of the afternoon sun the blank-faced stockholders untethered their horses and in small groups began leaving the property, with the skeleton crew witnessing their somber actions, each digger beginning to sift thoughts as to what direction life's lot would cast him.

Ears pricked, when from across the stream voices of the school children raised in song...

...America, America, God shed his grace on thee And crown thy good, with brotherhood........"

Pete worked the toe end of his worn boot into the ground and a sure smile grew on his lips. "So maybe we didn't come out with bags of riches for old age. But defeat! Hell no! It damned well showed man's strength." Walking straight, shoulders back, he went into the office shack, near empty, save for Dan, and Jed, whose hands were gripped tight on the shoulders of the stranger. "...we tried hard, Gramp, awful hard. Gave it everything we had...."

The old man's watery eyes were becoming sparkled with life. "Jed. My heart's been up here for a long, long time. Just had to come up to see your mine... to see this countryside once more..."

Pete held out for Gramp's taking an age yellowed map which had blown from Gramp's rig seat to the ground, pronounced with but one coded marking.

"Something you probably left accidentally on the seat, with all the excitement of your getting here."

Gramp eyed the map, he groped in his coat pockets, half expecting to touch the very map where he figured he had last put it, only then did he reach out for it.

"It's the marking of a mineral lode half mile down stream that sort of raised my dander when I came upon it. Took it along with the notion you might want to expand operations." His outstretched arm held the map for anybody's taking. "Never any harm tapping in a claim stake."

Dan reached out for the map and eyed Pete and Jed. "Tomorrow we're gonna see what that site does to our dander."

They would pull themselves up by their bootstrings.

And smiles crept over their faces.